The
Clan

Johnathan W. Stoller

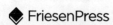 FriesenPress

Suite 300 - 990 Fort St
Victoria, BC, V8V 3K2
Canada

www.friesenpress.com

Copyright © 2017 by Johnathan W. Stoller
First Edition — 2017

ISBN
978-1-5255-0898-1 (Hardcover)
978-1-5255-0899-8 (Paperback)
978-1-5255-0900-1 (eBook)

1. FICTION, MYSTERY & DETECTIVE, POLICE PROCEDURAL

Distributed to the trade by The Ingram Book Company

Dedicated to my friends and family who helped me through this project. Thank you all very much, and remember, this is a twenty-year-old idea, so the characters resemble the people—they don't replicate the people. To everyone else, I hope you enjoy the read.

The
Clan

Prologue

As the sun rose between two mountain peaks and rolled over the horizon of an overgrown clear-cut, a shadow resembling a long set of prison bars slowly crept towards the thick line of trees. The warmth of the sun's rays started to burn the mist away from the air as two hikers dressed in fairly new camping gear stopped in their tracks deciding what to do about the obstacle in their way.

"Just smile and nod—the piss and moan section is already full," Jimmy said as he awkwardly wedged himself through the narrow rungs of a tall and weathered fence.

With an unimpressed look on his face, Nate replied back, "Hardy-har-har, Jimmy. The sign says, 'No trespassing.'"

"I know Nate, I can read too, but we want to get from here, which is nowhere, to the town of Edwardson, which is way the hell not here, this is going to be a huge shortcut."

"Shortcut or not, I heard that a shitload of people have gone missing in these camping grounds," Nate said. "I heard that's why this place was closed down, and why we're not supposed to be trespassing."

Jimmy popped through the fence and dusted himself off. As he stood up and waved his hands for his friend to toss over his backpack, he said, "You hear too much sometimes... but people go missing all the time travelling around the world, and yet, you still go across the equator every year for *senoritas* and Bananarama drinks!"

Nate stood there for a second, and then shrugged his shoulders. "Good point." He tossed their backpacks over the fence then pushed himself through making sure he didn't tear his jacket or get it too dirty.

Both men stare into the darkened forest where the sun failed to break through yet. It didn't look very welcoming and didn't make Nate feel any better about the idea but the two slowly hiked into the trees when Jimmy looked at Nate and said, "And really, what are the odds that something bad is going to happen to us?"

Nate sighed and slowly rolled his eyes. That unimpressed look crept over his face once more.

Chapter I

The aroma of bacon and eggs wafted through the bedroom door, signalling the start of a crisp September morning. The mouth-watering smell prompted the red-haired man beneath the sheets to roll out of bed, yawn, and stretch, just as he heard his sweet wife call out, "Wake up and get your ass out of bed!"

He looked at the alarm clock: 4:58 a.m. He sighed sleepily, gave one more stretch to the morning, and then got off the bed and padded toward the bathroom. As he got to the door, the alarm clock went off—*beep, beep, beep.* The man felt groggy. He turned, dragging his feet, and walked over to the alarm clock, sliding it to the end of the nightstand until it fell off and hit the carpet. The cord followed it and pulled out of the wall, and silence commenced once more.

The man headed back toward the bathroom, and then stopped at the bedroom window. He cracked it opened, took a deep breath of fresh air, and looked outside at the morning light that was trying to break through the abundant amount of trees in his backyard. The man thought to himself, *I should cut some of them down to get more light into the house.* Right then, a ray of sunshine cut through and shot straight into his eyes. The man cringed. *Maybe not.* He rubbed his eyes, continued to the bathroom, and stepped into the shower.

5:25 a.m. rolled around, a refreshed and rejuvenated man dressed in camo pants and a red, long-sleeved undershirt slowly shuffled down the hallway. He stopped and quickly peeked into the bedroom where both his son and daughter were sound asleep. He headed down the stairs to see a thin, short woman standing by the stove. He slowly crept into the kitchen and flipped up his wife's robe then smacked her ass. Startled, she jumped and playfully smacked him on the arm. He laughed, and she smiled back.

"Morning, Lorne," she said. "About time you got up."

"Morning, Joan," Lorne replied, then sat at the table. "Breakfast smells great." His wife put a plate of bacon and eggs in front of him.

"You're in a chipper mood this morning," she said. "Is it because you're heading out with the boys for your long weekend, or because you won't have to see me for three whole days?"

Lorne shoved a piece of bacon into his mouth. With a smirk, he asked, "Do I have to pick?" Joan grabbed a dishtowel from the counter and used it to hit Lorne over the head. Lorne blocked the flurry of towel whips with his arm. He quickly answered, "The first choice." Getting off his chair, Lorne kissed his wife. "You know I love you, Joan, but let me finish my breakfast, please. The guys are going to be here at 6:00 a.m. sharp."

Joan rolled her eyes and scoffed. "I know your friends. They're never anywhere on time. They won't be here until 6:30, or even 7:00, so you have plenty of time to eat breakfast and get razzed by me."

Lorne sat down and ate the rest of his breakfast, watching his back for more towel thrashings. When he finished eating, Lorne got up and put his dish into the sink where Joan was washing the others. He rubbed her shoulders. "Thanks for breakfast, dear. I'm going to see if I packed everything I need."

"You should have done that last night."

"Yeah, yeah. Nag, nag, nag."

"And go and kiss your kids goodbye, also," said Joan.

"That advice I will take!" Lorne smacked Joan on the ass again, then darted upstairs to finish packing.

* * * * *

The Clan

The hands on the kitchen clock had hit 6:45 a.m. when the sounds of AC/DC's "Hell's Bells" and the roaring engine could be heard as a blue, early-90s F-250 came fishtailing up the driveway. The horn and over-revving of a 400 big-block engine brought Joan out the door still in her robe. There were three men in the truck. The driver honked faster.

A tall, thick man stuck his head out of the passenger side front window. "Whoo-hoo, sexy lady! Where's that waste of a husband of yours?"

Joan tightened her robe against the cold breeze and leering eyes. "Morning, Lee," she said. "Just because you guys are out of bed this early for the first time in your lazy lives, doesn't mean my neighbours have to be. By the way, you're late. What happened this time?"

The short, stocky, and heavily built driver stuck his head out the window and shouted, "Waiting on Lee!"

Lee puffed up proudly and said, "I gots to look good for the ladies!"

Dan, the driver, looked at Lee and replied, "We're going into the bush. No ladies are going to be there."

"But there might be some on the way," Lee reasoned, "and you've got to be prepared for anything."

In the back, a slim man was slouched in his seat with his cowboy hat over his face. He asked Lee, "Aren't you in a relationship?"

Lee smiled. "Big grey area, Walter." Dan and Walter shook their heads.

Joan rolled her eyes and said, "Lorne will be out in a minute. You guys keep it down a bit—I still have some neighbours who like me."

Dan rapped his hands on the side of the door. "Whatever you say, good-lookin.'" Joan smiled, shook her head, and then went back into the house.

The three men pulled their heads back into the truck. Lee turned down the music, looked at Walter in the backseat, and asked, "Why is it, Walter, when I say, 'Hey sexy,' she does nothing, but when Dan says 'good-looking,' she smiles?"

Walter adjusted his cowboy hat over his eyes and slouched back into his seat. "Because when Dan says it, it sounds like a compliment. When you say it, your man-whore comes out, and you sound creepy." Dan looked at Lee in agreement.

Lee hung his head and pretended to pout, but then he smiled naughtily. "She did look pretty yummy in that robe," he said.

"I'd take a round out of her if she were my wife." Dan replied.

Walter frowned and looked at both of them. "If I had a girlfriend or wife, would you talk about her like that behind my back?"

Dan and Lee replied at the same time, "Hell yeah!"

"Good. I'd be offended if you didn't."

Lorne came out of the house right then with Joan and his gear. She gave him a kiss. Walter looked up, then jumped out of the backseat and walked over to grab Lorne's pack and sleeping bag. Walter tipped his cowboy hat towards Joan. "You have a good weekend, Joan." He turned to Lorne and said, "I've got your shit, so finish makin' out with your wife and get your ass in the truck."

"The magic words, hon, I gotta go!" Lorne replied.

"Okay," said Joan. "Be careful. And that means all of you!" Joan yelled toward the truck.

The three men replied in unison, "Yes, dear!" Amidst chuckles, Lorne kissed his wife one more time while Walter threw the gear into the back of the truck. Both men climbed in the backseat. Dan pulled out of the driveway and onto the road. Arms waved at Joan through the open windows.

"Love you!" Lorne shouted to her. "See you when we get back!"

Dan, Lee, and Walter yelled twice as loudly, "Love you! See you!" Dan squealed the tires all the way down the block with his hand on the horn. Joan shook her head and looked around, worrying about the neighbours. She didn't see anyone, and quickly scurried into the house with a smile on her face.

Dan steered the truck and peeled around toward town. Lorne put his head back and sighed. "You know I'm in shit when I get back home, right?" he said. "You realize that, don't you?"

"We all are," Walter replied, then gestured with his thumb toward Dan. "This guy picked us all up the same way."

"Yeah," said Lorne, "but you don't have a wife or girlfriend to bitch at you."

Walter nodded. "That's correct. But I do have neighbours."

Dan turned up the music and said, "That's the price for making me drive, so suck it!"

Walter changed the subject and asked, "Speaking of driving, not sucking, where'd this beast come from?"

"The boss said I could use the work truck for the long weekend while mine was in the shop," said Dan. "And none of you pussies have anything big enough to fit all our asses in."

Walter smirked. "Not our fault you bought a Chevy and it blew up on you."

Dan pointed his middle finger at Walter. "It blew up because it had too much power."

"All I know, is your truck was a Chevy, and it's not here. And this great-running Ford is."

"You know what 'FORD' stands for?" Dan asked. "'Found On Road Dead.'"

Walter removed his smile. "You know why there isn't any acronym for 'CHEVY?'" he asked. "Because people have better things to think about."

Snickering, Lee piped up to stop the bickering these two were prone to having. "Okay, girls, it's too early to start this conversation, so shut up and suck this instead." Walter, Dan, and Lorne looked over at Lee, who pointed down at his crotch—then, thankfully, produced two beers that were on his lap. The men chuckled. Lee passed a beer to Dan then reached over the backseat and gave Walter one, as well.

Dan took a sip and put the beer in his cup holder. "So," he said, "it's too early to argue, but not too early for beer?"

Lee looked at Dan in mock astonishment. "Uh, *yeah!*" he replied. Lee cracked two more bottles open. He passed one to Lorne and kept one for himself. "This trip is for hunting, fishing, drinking, swearing, farting, spitting, and whatever else women don't want to hear or see us do," said Lee. "What time is it, by the way?"

Lorne looked at his watch and said, "7:10 a.m."

The men raised their beers to clink them together. "Cheers to 7:10 a.m.!" they said.

Dan pulled into the local gas station. The men jumped out, placing their bottles on the truck's floor. Grabbing the gas nozzle, Dan said, "As soon as I top the four-wheeler in the back and this thing up, we're outta here, so if you want something or you forgot something, get it now, 'cause I'm not stopping until we get to the cabin. Piss breaks are the exception, of course."

Dan fuelled up while the others went into the store. After ten minutes, all three came out with a couple bags of groceries. Lorne suddenly yelled, "Shotgun!"

Walter and Lee realized they'd been beaten, so they sighed and both said, "Damn it!" They put the grocery bags in the back of the truck.

Dan asked, "Do you have everything?"

Lorne answered back, "Yeah, we got everything—well, only the necessities."

Dan quickly glanced into the bags. "The whiskey also?"

"I said 'the necessities,' didn't I?"

Dan smiled and then started the truck. "Then pitter-patter, let's get at 'er." As he started to drive away, all three quickly ran to their doors and hopped in awkwardly as Dan slowly kept going.

"Thanks for keeping it under thirty for us," Lorne said mockingly. They all laughed as they put their seatbelts on and looked for their open beers, which they couldn't find.

Lee asked Dan, "Where did all the beer go?"

"Your first beers went to a better place, and I don't need another one—you guys took too fucking long." As soon as Walter heard that, he reached into the back of the truck through the sliding window, grabbed two more, and passed them to Lorne and Lee.

Lorne asked him, "Only two? Where's yours?"

Walter smiled, put his hat back on his face, and slouched back into his position. "Wake me up when we get there." He was out before AC/DC's "Thunder Struck" had finished playing.

* * * * *

After two hours, a couple more beers, and many loud tunes, Dan steered the truck off the main highway and onto a dirt road without slowing down. No one batted an eye; this had been done so many times before. Dan looked in his rear-view mirror at Walter, who was still sleeping.

"So, bets start now," Dan said. "How long before Walter wakes up?"

Lorne stretched and took off his seatbelt. "How long was it last year?"

Lee also took his seatbelt off. "An hour and ten minutes," he answered. "I won betting on that time last year. This year I'll bet it again."

"I'll take forty-five minutes," Lorne said. "How about you, Dan?"

"It's about three more hours to the cabin, so I'll say two hours and fifteen minutes."

Lee set the timer on his watch. "All right, the bets are in. What's the wager this year?"

Lorne spoke up first, "Losers get the firewood."

Lee put in his two cents, "And Walter unloads the truck."

Dan eagerly agreed and replied, "Done!" The three men smiled and nodded as Dan careened up the road, spitting dirt and gravel around corners and spinning the tires up the hills.

Lee watched the time of forty-five minutes go by with no signs of life from Walter. With a smirk he said to the others, "Well, Lorne's time is down. Two to go."

Lorne looked back, watching Walter's head bob up and down. "How does he do that?" he asked. "This has got to be *over* our twelfth trip up this road. I don't think he's ever seen the whole road yet."

"That boy could sleep through an earthquake if he wanted to," Dan answered back. Lorne and Lee nodded.

More trees and gravel whipped past as 10:50 a.m. rolled by. Walter was still dead to the world. Dan honked the horn three times in a row without Walter moving a muscle. "Well, that's that," he said. "I get to drink beer while you guys work."

Lee said, "I'll bet he sleeps all the way this time."

Dan raised his eyebrows. "Double or nothing? I'll bet he'll be up at my time, give or take thirty seconds. Loser cooks dinner."

Lee rubbed the bottom of his chin. "And does the dishes," he added. "You want in on this, Lorne?"

"No way! I'm done losing for the day."

Lee shrugged and then reached over to shake Dan's hand, confirming the bet. Lee started the timer on his watch. Dan slowed down a bit—but not as much as he should have, due to the overgrowth that consumed more and more of the dirt road each year. He pushed the truck through, knowing the overgrown trail would only last about another ten kilometres. There were enough bumps and turns to keep the bet interesting. As the final seconds on Lee's timer started to run out, both Lee and Lorne chanted down the count. "Ten, nine, eight...!"

Dan kept his eyes on the road and said, "Wait for it..." He swerved the crew-cab into the shrubbery on the side of the road. Twigs, leaves, and branches whipped the passenger side of the truck. The tires rode the drainage ditch along the side for about twenty feet then hopped back onto the road. The guys bounced all over the cab. Lee hit his head on the roof. Lorne grabbed the "holy shit" handle and rode it out like an eight-second bull-rider.

Then there was Walter. He bounced around like a rag doll in the backseat. Dan straightened the truck out. Walter finally opened his eyes, put himself back into a seated position, stretched out his arms, and cracked his neck.

Lee also sat properly back into his seat and said, "You bastard. You just about spilled my beer, damn it."

Walter looked out his window and asked sluggishly, "We there yet?"

Lee glared at Dan from the backseat and replied to Walter, "No!"

Walter yawned, rubbed his eyes, and asked. "Who won the bet?"

"Was there any doubt?" Dan boasted.

"Asshole," Lee muttered, looking out his window. The three men chuckled.

Lorne asked Dan, "Was that worth scratching the shit out of the side of the truck?"

"Uhh, yeah, for one. Plus it's all baby scratches—that shit will buff out." They all smiled as Dan stopped the truck. They had arrived at a locked gate blocking the road that had a bright red and yellow closed sign strapped to the front of it. Lorne and Walter got out of the truck and walked to the gate. Walter dug out two keys from his pocket while Lorne lit a cigarette.

"So, you think the cops and the forestry service changed the locks this year?" Lorne asked. "This will be year four if they haven't."

Walter replied, "Let's try the first one." Walter heard a click. "One for one. Now, let's see if the narcs have been around."

Lorne frowned and said, "The James Gang wouldn't come out here." Then he made his voice high-pitched and whiny-sounding. "It's too much money and time wasted to come out here," he mocked. "And my nose is too far up the mayor's ass to get this place opened up to everyone again."

"Hey, man, cool down," said Walter. "You know James is just doing his job."

"Yeah," said Lorne. "I know, but he shouldn't be so good at it. Let some shit slide, sometimes."

Walter sighed and shoved Lorne. "Look at it this way," Walter said. "If this place was opened to everyone, we might have to be more responsible while we're out here."

"Point taken. We all know we don't want that to happen, so try that lock and let's get this show on the road."

Walter put the key into the second lock and gave it a turn. Both guys heard a *snap* as Walter looked down at a broken half of a key in his fingers.

"Hmmm. Well, the key worked, but I don't think it will open the lock anymore."

Walter showed Lorne the other half of the key. Lorne rolled his eyes and said, "Way to go, Jerkules. I believe I can fix that, though." Lorne ran to the truck and jumped into the back. He rummaged through a packsack, and then ran back over to Walter with a pair of bolt cutters.

Walter saw the fairly new cutters in Lorne's hands. "Where'd you get those from?" he asked.

"About six months ago I was at a pawn shop when I saw these bad boys. Soon as I laid my eyes on them I thought, 'We need these for some reason.' *When* and *where* didn't pop into my head until last night."

"Nice snatch!"

"Thank you," Lorne said, and then smiled. "Now, let's see if they work as well as they look. Grab that lock."

While Walter and Lorne were outside fumbling with the locks, Dan watched out the window, wondering why it was taking them so long while Lee jumped from the backseat over into the front.

Lee quickly asked Dan, "What's taking them so long?"

"Who knows? Lorne grabbed something from the back, but I missed what it was. Good thing he didn't see you switch seats."

"Not my fault he left it. I didn't hear 'spot save, seat save.'"

"Well, while you're up here, look in Walter's tape collection and change the tunes."

Lee looked at the cassette tapes, and then back at Dan. "He does realize that CDs were invented, and that it's not 1986 anymore—right?"

"Not exactly sure on that, but he has the portable stereo and keeps remembering to bring it."

Lee smiled and replied, "Well then, do you want '80s rock or '80s country?"

"More *AC/DC* will be fine."

Back outside, Walter pulled the lock out as far from the fence as he could. Lorne grabbed it with the cutters. They heard a snap.

"Just like cutting butter with a hot knife," said Lorne.

The lock fell to the ground in two pieces. Lorne and Walter pulled the chain loose and opened the gate wide enough for Dan to drive through. Lorne and Walter shut the gate and dummy-locked it. Walter jumped back into his seat as Lorne jiggled the handle on the passenger-side door, and then he noticed Lee was in his spot. Lorne quickly spun and hopped into the back seat.

Lorne said to Lee, "Well, that didn't take long."

Lee took a sip of beer, passed Lorne his, and quickly changed the subject. "I see the keys worked again this year," he said.

Lorne shrugged his shoulders. "More or less, but we're going to need another one for next year."

Dan scowled. "I call bullshit!"

Lorne looked at Dan. "Calm down, man. Those locks only cost about ten bucks."

"Not that," said Dan. "This whole situation is bullshit. We've been coming up here since we were kids—way before a bunch of dumb-ass tourists went missing. Shit happens, but because one of the missing schmucks is the son of some rich bastard, the town closes the best hunting, fishing, and camping spot—and not to mention, one of the best-built log cabins we've ever seen. I call fucking bullshit!"

Lee nodded in agreement. "You have a point, but it's not just tourists who have disappeared around here."

"I know," Dan answered, "but when you compare how many times we've been out here and how many others have been to this place and use it, there is no way this place should be shut down. If a thousand people swim in a pool and one person drowns, does that mean the pool should close down? Or should that person have learned how to swim?"

"We all know that the group of granola-crunching tourists had no wilderness training or experience whatsoever," replied Walter. "But when you have a rich daddy threatening to shut down the town and who has the money to back it up, closing this place seemed like the easiest and best solution."

Lorne took a drink from his beer bottle. "Fuck it," he said. "We're here once again for the umpteenth time and no one's noticed, and like Walter said outside, we don't have to fight for a spot, and no one's going to complain about how obnoxious and loud we're going to be except for nature. I'm done complaining about it."

Dan shifted gears and sighed. "You're right. If no one's bitched about us being here and we haven't been caught trespassing yet, then what the hell, right?"

"Here, here!" they shouted as Dan proceeded towards the cabin.

* * * * *

About an hour went by as Lorne switched the *AC/DC* cassette over again. Then Dan turned the corner and headed up the hill. A couple kilometres later, the brush-covered road widened and a field of green surrounded by huge fir trees appeared. Dan drove over a fern-covered driveway and parked the truck at the end. Right in front of the grill stood a beautiful, rustic, hand-built, two-storey log cabin. Dan turned off the engine and looked through the window at their home away from home. "We're finally here, boys!" he said.

Walter smiled and said, "It feels like we never left." They all jumped out of the truck and stretched out the kinks in their bodies as they gazed at the cabin basking in the sun.

Lee looked directly at Walter. "The sooner you unload the truck, the sooner we can load ourselves with beer."

"That was the wager this year?" said Walter.

"Yup," Dan replied. "Also, losers get the firewood, and Lee has to cook me dinner. It's going to be an awesome trip for me this year."

"Wow! Big wager this year," said Walter. "What happened to you, Lorne?"

"I quit while I was already behind."

Dan smiled. "Never bet the driver on the exact time a person is going to wake up. You'll lose every time."

"Not if you play fair," Lee piped up.

Lorne looked incredulously at Lee. "Are you new here? Do you remember who you hang out with?"

Lee shook his head. "Duly noted!"

They all began to laugh then suddenly stopped, and just as they had done when they were in elementary school, they started pushing and shoving each other to get to the front door first.

There were six beds in the cabin. Two were actually comfortable; the other four were only a notch nicer than sleeping on the floor. The first-come, first-serve rule came into play here. Whoever touched the front door first got to pick which bed they wanted. Lee was slightly ahead, so Lorne grabbed the back of Lee's pants and used them to pull himself closer. Dan dove and snagged both of Lorne's legs. The three of them crashed to the ground like dominos. Walter came shooting up and jumped over the three like a football player going for the touchdown, when suddenly an arm reached out from the pile of bodies and snagged his ankle. Walter dropped like a sack of potatoes into the pile. Arms, legs, and clothes flailed in a big, dusty mess. For several minutes there were flying elbows, headlocks, and figure-four locks until Walter squirmed out; he was the first to break free. As soon as he was loose, everyone followed suit. Walter scrambled up the cabin's stairs and smacked the door a half-second before Dan. Lorne and Lee stopped running all together, knowing there was no need to rush now. The four were still breathing hard, checking for scrapes and bruises while Walter dug out the cabin's door key from his pocket. When it was unlocked, Dan pushed open the handcrafted, three-inch-thick wooden door. The breeze swirled a year's worth of dust away from the door.

Dan took a deep breath of stale air and declared, "Home sweet home!"

Walter nudged Dan. "Top or bottom?"

"Bottom,"

Walter quickly replied, "Done. I'll start unloading the truck." Lee looked back at Lorne. "Which one do you want?"

Lorne cocked his eye. "Does it really matter?"

Lee shrugged his shoulders and replied, "Not really."

Lorne looked behind him at the tree line. "Well, let's get a start on that firewood."

Dan jumped onto his bed. "I'll just try out this bed and see if it works."

"Can you get the power started first?" asked Walter. "The sooner we get that freezer working, the better."

"Yeah, good call," Dan said. He went back to the truck and grabbed a jerry can of gas, then walked about twenty feet from the cabin to a rickety old shack. He tried opening the door; it wasn't locked, but the door had swelled with water and age, making it difficult to open. He slammed his body into the door. It flew open and hit the wall behind it. Dan tenderly held his shoulder for a moment, then grabbed the gas can and started fuelling up the generator. He checked the oil and pulled the cord three times before it started up. He heard a cheer from somewhere around the cabin.

When he went back inside, he said, "Wake me up when the chores are done and the drinking starts."

Walter unloaded the gear and the four-wheeler as the other two helped with the firewood.

Around 2:00 p.m., the boys had just finished cooking lunch when Dan woke up, rejuvenated and ready to get at 'er. The sun was shining brightly, and *Guns n' Roses* were playing loudly in the background. The men were enjoying hotdogs and beer. The day couldn't have been any better.

After they'd all had their fill of food, they shared the tidying up and then settled into lawn chairs to relax. Time, sun, and beer won the battle and soon the guys fell asleep—even the freshly napped Dan.

* * * * *

A few hours passed mostly in silence—except for the farting and snores expelled here and there—until everyone was rudely awakened by Dan yelling, "Get out of here, you fucking coon!"

Lorne jumped up and yelled back, "Don't be racist asshole, Dan."

Dan looked back and called, "Raccoon! We just got here, and the vermin are trying to steal our shit."

Lee rubbed his eyes and looked around, saying, "Well, it's gone now, and we're all awake. Wow, look at the time. It's already 6:30 p.m. We've been passed out for four hours."

Walter looked up at the sky, and then at his stomach. "Anybody hungry? Should we get dinner going?"

Dan shook his head. "Nope, it's happy hour now, no time to eat."

Lee sat down and relaxed in his chair once again, and then said to Dan, "That means I don't have to cook your dinner then."

Dan told Lee, "You mix my drinks for me tonight, and we'll call 'er even."

"I can do that."

"I have to piss anyhow, so I'll get the necessities," Lorne said as he got up and went into the cabin. Moments later, he came back and passed bottles of rye and Coke straight to Lee.

Lee got out of his chair to make Dan a drink when he leaned over to Walter and whispered into his ear, "The stronger I make his drinks, the faster he'll pass out, and the fewer drinks I have to make." Walter smiled and nodded at Lee, but in his mind he had doubts that that was going to work.

Lorne stopped before sitting in his chair, looked around, and thought for a bit. "Let's hold a little on the food and get our gear ready so we can get up in the morning and leave. We all know none of us are going to be coordinated enough to do it later."

Walter popped out of his chair and agreed, "Sounds like a plan, Stan."

Lorne and Walter started to arrange gear into the crew-cab. Lee quickly mixed Dan a double and gave him his drink. Dan sat there somewhat uncomfortably, watching everyone do something, but he quickly got over it and happily settled in his lawn chair.

* * * * *

The day turned into late evening. Walter cooked up some dinner while Lee and Lorne started a fire. Lee grabbed all the lawn chairs and put them around the fire pit. Lorne grabbed the portable stereo and put it onto the picnic table. Dan staggered slightly closer to the campfire. Walter dished out some pork n' beans, a potato, and some ground beef onto all four plates. Dan was three sheets to the wind, but he was still functioning fairly well considering the five strong drinks in him now. While Dan was feeling ten-feet tall and bulletproof he stood up, staggered to the table, grabbed his plate of food, and then staggered back to his seat. Everyone watched in disbelief, wondering how he was even moving in his condition. They shrugged their shoulders and grabbed plates of food, cracked open beers, and had a seat at the fire pit.

The night sky was filled with bright white stars, and a hint of dampness was brewing in the air. On the ground was a slightly oversized campfire with four overfilled fellows sitting around it—or as close as they could get to it without melting their clothes or themselves. Ryes, beers, and bullshit were flying like hotcakes around the fire. Ozzy Osborne serenaded them in the background.

Lee got up from his chair to take a piss. "I gotta break the seal. Who needs a beverage on my way back?" All three raised their half-empty drinks into the air and shook their glasses. "Sorry I asked." Lee staggered towards the cabin in the darkness.

"No More Tears" finished playing in the background as side B of a cassette tape clicked off on their portable stereo. Silence fell over the fire pit.

Walter looked over at the stereo, and then at who was closest to it. "Hey, Dan, change the tape? Maybe some country for a bit?"

Dan looked straight at Walter and said in a fake English voice, "Fuck you."

"Thanks, dick," Walter replied while Dan laughed. If there was something one person liked that was different from the other guys, they would be sure to mock it as much and as long as possible. Dan made sure Walter saw him tossing the country tapes underneath the picnic table. While Walter and Dan were giving each other dirty looks, Lorne broke the silence with a joke.

"So, a man walks into his bedroom and sees his wife fucking the mailman. He yells out, 'What's going on here!' The wife looks at the mailman and says, 'I told you he was stupid!'"

They all laughed as more jokes went around. Walter said the first joke that came into his head. "Why did the chicken cross the road? Because the chicken was a slut."

The Clan

Dan made the shameful trumpet sound. "Wah, wah, wah—lame. What do you call a dead blonde in a closet? The winner of last year's hide-and-seek contest."

Walter chuckled and then said, "Funny, but I got a better one. What's the difference between an oral thermometer and a rectal thermometer? The taste."

Lorne spit a bit of his drink out of his mouth. "That's gross, but I think we have a winner."

"Thank you, I knew those *Maxim* magazines would come in handy one day."

Dan, also laughing, looked at Walter and asked, "Besides just for jerking off?"

Walter nodded back. "Yes, that too."

Lorne looked into the darkness and towards the cabin. "Speaking of jerk-offs, where is Lee? I'm just about finished my beer."

Dan also looked into the darkness. "Good question. He should have been back by now. I might have to get up. That worries me. Even worse, I might have to make my own drink."

Walter waved his hands at Dan. "Whoa there, pilgrim. Don't get hasty. Maybe a bear just got him, and he's fighting him off."

Lorne replied, "Or maybe a sasquatch could have gotten him. It's their mating season right now."

Walter said, "I thought that was early spring."

"No," Dan replied, "it's right now, but they fuck like monkeys, so they can hump you at anytime."

Lorne waved the smoke from his face and took another sip of his drink. "I was listening to one of those shows on the radio, and they had what they called a 'scientist' on it. His theory was that if a sasquatch were ever real, it could be as smart as a human."

Walter stopped laughing, and a serious look instantly came across face. "That's wrong. They'd be smarter."

"Why do you say that?" Lorne asked.

21

Walter cracked a smile once more. "Well, for starters, they don't have to pay taxes, they don't have to buy property, and they get to run around all over the place naked all the time."

"They have fur, though," said Lorne.

"Yeah, but their junk still gets to whip in the wind."

Lorne started to chuckle.

Dan cocked his eyebrow and looked at Walter. "You're messed in the head," he said.

They were all laughing, when suddenly the silhouette of a large beast came charging out of the shadows. Before the three could make a move, the beast's charge quickly turned into staggering and then into stumbling, and then finally it finished with a barrel roll into the fire's glow. They watched as Lee scrambled to his hands and knees and then crawled to his lawn chair and sat down.

Dan looked at Lee, who was covered in dirt. "Way to go Twinkle-toes," Dan chuckled.

Lee wiped his face and said, "You guys would be pissing your pants and crying like babies if I didn't trip."

Lorne sighed. "Whatever. Where's the alcohol?"

"Hey, I'm fine, by the way, thanks for asking."

Lorne sighed once more. "Sorry, hope you're okay. Where's the beer?"

Lee wiped more dirt off his face. "I couldn't scare you guys *and* bring back alcohol."

Dan chimed in, "Seems like you couldn't do either."

Lorne sighed for the third time and put his hands in the air. "Now one of us has to go get it," he said.

Everyone yelled, "Not it!" as fast as possible. Walter and Lorne tied for last.

Walter looked at Lorne and put out his fist. "Final Answer?"

"Final Answer" had been this group's decision-maker, argument-stopper, and problem-solver ever since they could remember. Some call it "Rock–paper–scissors"; others call it avoiding the situation.

The Clan

They used "Final Answer" when wrestling wasn't socially acceptable. After four rounds of Final Answer, Lorne wiped his brow; Walter had lost.

Walter slowly got up from his chair. "I'm going, and I'm bringing the other cooler out with me."

As Walter walked away, Dan replied, "Good thinking. Better late than never." He then resumed picking through the cassette tapes once more.

Lee looked over at Dan and asked, "How about some country for a little while?"

Dan saw Walter disappear into the shadows, then looked back at Lee and shrugged, "Yeah, why not. I could listen to some *Nitty Gritty* right now. It should be under there."

Lee saw all the tapes underneath the picnic table. "Screwin' with Walter again?" he asked.

"Yup!" Dan replied. All three laughed.

Lorne asked Lee, "Hey, you were gone awhile. What happened? Were you becoming some Bigfoot's love slave?"

Lee shook his head. "Naw, they're never shaven. Although I'd rather be Bigfoot's love slave any day than be some alien's butt bitch. At least the sasquatch is local. You have no idea where those aliens have been."

"We could say the same thing about you, Lee," said Dan.

Lorne leaned toward Lee and spoke in a quiet voice. "He's pretty witty for being hammered. I thought you were making his drinks a double."

Lee replied with a shocked look. "I was making them triples, man. He should have been out by now."

"Resilient little bastard."

Dan noticed Lee and Lorne talking to each other, but couldn't hear what they were saying. "Hey, stop talking about me, or talk louder. I can't hear shit over the music."

Lee changed the subject and started talking about the camping trip. "So, anyhow, where do we want to start tomorrow?"

Lorne answered, but as the alcohol was kicking in he also started to talk with his hands. "Well, if we drive to Meadow Creek and park there, we can split up into two teams of two and we should be able to spot something on the ridge." Lee was dodging Lorne's hands as Lorne kept talking. "Hopefully we can flank something down towards Turtle Hill where we can drag it to the truck easily if we kill it."

Dan got a chill down his spine. "I always get a bad feeling around there. That's where those loggers went missing a long time ago."

"That's also where Walter shot that five-point elk four years ago, and where I shot that grizzly two years ago," Lorne replied, "so that sounds like a good place to start. Besides, it's the closest spot and easiest."

Lee looked down and shook the rest of the dirt off his pants. "Good, 'cause we're not going to be very fast in the morning or afternoon."

Lorne and Dan agreed.

Walter came back to the fire dragging the overfilled cooler. He parked it in front of his chair and looked over toward the stereo, realizing he was whistling along to "Fishing in the Dark." A smile brightened his face. Then he reached into the cooler and passed everyone a beer. They cheered to 10:30 p.m. Walter eased back and put his feet up on the cooler. "So, where are we on topics?"

Lorne took a big sip from his cold beer. "Aaahh! Well, we just talked about Bigfoot and briefly mentioned aliens and missing people. We still have to talk about ghosts, water monsters, freaks of nature, creepy hillbillies in the bushes—"

Dan cut Lorne short, "That's us."

"No, we're redneck with a dash of smart-ass. Oh I almost forgot, we also have to mention old Indian tales about ancient spirits before we can call it a night," Lorne finished.

Walter sighed. "Remember when we were kids?"

Dan put his beer can on his face to cool down his face from the heat of the fire and said, "Who can forget? I loved coming up here with our dads, James, and James' grandfather, watching them get all hammered-up listening to Chief Gramps tell his stories. They were awesome."

Lee nodded. "I loved the fact that he let us call him 'Chief Gramps' instead of his real name." He snickered. "I think he let us call him 'Chief Gramps' because whenever we tried saying his real name, it always sounded like we were swearing."

Dan agreed. "I still can't say 'Chief Foocadonke' without saying 'Chief Fuck-a-Donkey.'" They started to laugh.

Walter tapped Lee's can with his. "You're right on that one. The best story I remember Chief Gramps telling us was the one about this cabin, and why they built it here."

Dan remembered the story and cut in. "Oh, yeah. And every ten years the spirit of White Squirrel, the murdered Indian boy, appears."

"Whenever people talk about this place, they don't mention that guy," Lorne replied.

"Because no one has any proof that Flying Squirrel ever existed," Lee commented back.

"White Squirrel," Walter corrected.

"White Squirrel, Flying Squirrel, Butt Squirrel, it doesn't matter," Lee said flippantly. "The only proof they had was the stories of an old man who drank more then he should've until he died three years ago."

Walter looked around at everyone. "We all drink more then we should. They were wicked stories, though."

Dan agreed. "Chief Gramps always liked this place. Maybe his spirit is here right now, keeping us and White Squirrel company." He raised his beer into the air and the others followed. "Here's to the best non-related Grampa we ever had. He taught us some cool shit on the way, and freaked our asses out every chance he could. Love ya, Chief Gramps!"

Just then, the stereo clicked off and everything went silent. All four men looked at each other without a word, then started to laugh.

"Holy shit!" said Lorne. "That was creepy. I think I peed a little bit there."

Dan laughed. "Even Chief Gramps doesn't like country."

Walter rolled his eyes. "Funny fucker, aren't ya?" Walter walked over to the stereo and opened it to find the cassette tape all bound up in the machine. He carefully took it out, fixed the cassette, and then pressed "play."

"Ha! Can't get rid of us that easy," Walter said triumphantly. He looked over and noticed Lee was staring into the woods. He poked Dan and both of them leaned over and nudged Lorne. The three watched Lee watch the dark woods for several seconds.

"How're your shorts, Lee?" asked Dan. "Do you need a changing?" Walter and Lorne chuckled. Lee didn't move or make a sound. He just kept looking toward the trees.

Lorne sighed. "The moment's over, dude. We aren't scared anymore."

Lee answered, but kept looking into the woods. "I thought I heard something over by that stump there."

Walter looked in the same direction as Lee. "Probably a squirrel or packrat. Or an imagination."

"I wouldn't be sitting here looking at one spot this long if it was my imagination, puss-nut. I should be keeping at least one eye on you bastards."

Lorne rolled his eyes and said, "Here, I'll fix it." He leaned over his chair and picked a cookie-sized rock off the ground, stood up, and gave it a toss into the bushes. The rock hit the ground near the stump—which moved and jumped further into the shadows.

"Fuck me!" Lorne shouted.

Walter jumped back and also shouted. "That's not a squirrel!"

"No shit, Sherlock," Lorne said as he stared into the shadows. "Are those *eyes* shining near that tree?"

Dan replied as he sat up straighter in his chair. "I'm not sure, but where are the guns?"

Walter pointed back towards the cabin. "Packed up and tucked into the truck, ready for tomorrow," he replied.

Dan looked into the bushes, and then back at the other guys. "Shit."

The Clan

*****

A dusty police Bronco drove along a dirt road. A husky man with short black hair and a beautiful, short, full-figured woman with long black hair sat inside. A call came through the radio.

"Chief James, Chief James, are you out there? Over."

"I'm always out there. What's up McCrae? Over."

"Your Auntie called again. She says your cousin Walter hasn't called her yet after his trip. Over."

James Haul rolled his eyes. "No shit. He's a thirty-year-old man camping with a bunch of buddies, and he didn't call his mommy? Hmm, I wonder why? Over."

A slight snicker came across the radio. "Well, she said he should have been home yesterday. Over."

"He's with three other friends. Tell her to cut the cord already. Over."

"Really Chief? Over."

James looked over at his co-pilot, Officer Twin. She didn't say a word. James sighed once more. "No. I'll stop in and talk to her later. Do me a favour and call up Joan Mackenzie and see if Lorne is back, then call me back. Over."

"All right, I'll call you as soon as I find something out. Over and out." James hung the CB back on the dash and then looked back at Officer Twin. He smiled slightly. "I guess I should explain some of that to you, Gail, with you being fairly new here. You will find we are a pretty small and easygoing town. So when we get a call from my aunt or my mom—who're twins, by the way—about their children, we usually let the calls go three to five times before we check it out. Ninety-nine percent of the time they call back and realize it wasn't a big deal. They have a tendency to worry too much. They have good hearts and mean well, but they just don't stop and think."

Gail raised her eyebrows and cautiously suggested, "Not to be out of place, but why don't you talk to them about it?"

James let out a laugh and said, "That's cute! It does sound logical when you say it, but my cousins and I have had many discussions with them over the years. It never helps. First, there's an argument, then crying, then a prolonged guilt trip with a brief moment of silence. Finally, they convince themselves 'we' were just having a bad day. We all just gave up. They're like a broken fire alarm in your house. You would rather take the battery out and pretend it works and watch your house burn down instead of hearing the same annoying noise constantly beeping the same thing over and over into your ear."

Gail smiled and nodded. She thought there was more to that issue, but she let it be.

"Who is Joan Mackenzie?" she asked, changing the subject.

"Joan is Lorne's wife, and Lorne is one of the buddies Walter went camping with. So if Lorne isn't back and Joan hasn't heard from him yet and is worried, then there is some concern. Joan is probably the strongest woman I know, so when she says something is wrong, you usually jump on that right away. Some towns have Crime Stoppers and some have Neighbourhood watches. We have Joan."

Just then, a call came across the radio once more. "Chief James. Over." James grabbed the CB.

"Give 'er. Over."

"Joan said they were due home yesterday, but said you know how they get sometimes. She said Lorne has to work tomorrow, so he should be back tonight by 7:00 p.m. Over."

"Thanks, Dean. Tell her and my aunt I'll give them a reminder, please. Also, tell my wife I'm going to be late coming home. Over."

"Got 'er. Say 'Hi' to Gail for me. Over and out."

"Over and out." James looked over at Gail. "Dean says 'Hi.' Has he asked you out yet?"

Gail sighed. "Not yet, but I have a feeling it's coming soon."

"How many is that now? The seventh or eighth guy who is hopelessly, madly in love with you?"

Gail blushed and chuckled, "Crazy isn't it? I've only been here for six months, and I already have guys asking me to just about marry them."

"Well, the guy-to-girl ratio around this town is about three to one, and I have to admit, you're pretty easy on the eyes. Even my wife agrees."

Gail sighed and said, "Thanks, Chief, but right now I just want to do my job—dating is not in my plans."

"Just stick to your guns, you'll be fine. They're guys, they'll find something else that's shiny and new in a week or two and try jumping on that, instead."

Gail laughed. "Thanks, Chief, I hope you're right."

"Always." James looked out the window. The glare of the sun shone back.

"So, Miss Twin," he asked, "want to go for a longer and more boring drive to nowhere and hand out some 'no trespassing' tickets?"

Officer Twin shrugged. "You're the boss, boss. Whatever you want."

"Thanks for the opinion. And I'm not the boss, I'm the Chief! Big difference—'Chief' is way cooler."

Gail smiled. James stepped on the gas and the Bronco sped up, heading further down the road. As they tore down the highway they passed a sign on the road that read, "Pinkston Peak, 2 km," with "CLOSED" stamped across it. James slowed down a tad and then turned and continued up the dirt road.

Gail straightened up in her seat. Her eyes got brighter as they passed the sign. "Are we going into the park? I've always wanted to see that place."

"I figured as much. It's been a while for me. Even my kids haven't seen this place, but I'm sure it's as good as the day they closed it."

As they pulled up to the locked gate, Officer Twin noticed evidence that a vehicle had been up there. She looked over at James. "Why do you think these guys will be up here?" she asked.

"Because I grew up with these guys," James answered. "I know they're all stubborn as mules. They try sneaking up here every year."

James stopped the truck and got out. He walked up to the gate and rattled the chain. Gail saw the chain drop to the ground. She jumped out and helped James open the gate.

"Like I said, stubborn as mules," he repeated.

Gail ran around to the driver's seat then proceeded to drive through the gate entrance. James closed the gate and dummy-locked it the same way the guys had. He got in the passenger side and let Gail proceed driving as he pointed and told her which road to go on next. He started telling her about the mountain and why it had closed down, sounding like a tour guide.

He saw fresh tire tracks heading up the road, and saw Gail notice them, as well. He started to question the rookie. "So, what do you think? Which way do those tire tracks go?"

"Well, the road is pretty dry, but judging by the way the dirt is and the tread-mark pattern, it looks like they were going pretty fast and heading north."

"Knowing these guys, I can guarantee they were driving faster than they should have been," James replied.

They drove up and took a few switchbacks when James' attitude changed from casual to slightly concern. "Slow down a little," he said. "I want to see those tire tracks a bit better."

James stuck his head out the window and stared at the tracks on the road. They appeared extra reckless in the dirt, and one track was making more of a mess than the other. About two kilometres later, James asked Gail to pull over.

Officer Twin noticed James' demeanour changed once more and was deep in thought. "Got something, Chief?"

"Not sure. Get out with me and take a look at these tracks." Together, they looked closer. "What does that look like to you, Gail?" he asked.

She knelt and felt the dirt with her fingers, then smelled them. "It smells like they're leaking coolant, but it also looks like their truck had a flat tire. They were still driving on it, Chief."

"I believe you're right. So, why wouldn't they stop and change it?"

"Maybe they didn't have a spare."

"Good point, but why are they not slowing down? These guys are hauling ass on a dirt road with a flat tire. What does that sound like to you?"

Gail looked at him and answered cautiously, knowing these guys were the Chief's friends. "Either the driver was drunk, or they couldn't stop."

"Once in a while, these boys have the tendency to have a beer or two while driving, but judging by the speed of these tracks as they went around this corner with a flat tire, I don't think the driver was drunk, so now I'm wondering why they couldn't stop."

Gail thought for a moment. "No brakes?" she suggested. "Gas throttle stuck?"

James rubbed his chin and stared at the road. "If there was a problem with the truck, they could've just turned it off and coasted until they stopped."

"Could they be chasing something?"

James nodded and added, "Or something was chasing them."

They looked at each other, and Gail felt a chill go down her spine. Gail asked James, "What would make your friends run away in a truck?"

"I don't know. I've seen these guys stand their ground and kick a 300-pound black bear in the ass because it came into camp and stole the food cooler. Let's get back into the truck and keep going. Stay alert."

* * * * *

They continued driving for another ten minutes until a cabin came into view. Gail drove up slowly and gazed at the beautiful-looking cabin. James told her to stop the truck. He reached behind the seat and grabbed the vests out of the back.

"Put this on, Officer Twin. And be ready. Something is not right." Gail noted how he had called her 'Officer' in a serious voice. She felt another chill and quickly put on her tactical vest. They both pulled out their Smith & Wesson revolvers. An eerie silence filled the air until James used the walkie-talkie on his vest.

"Chief Haul and Officer Twin are out at the Pinkston cabin checking out a disturbance. Might need assistance. Stand by. Over."

"Bullshit, Chief. Over."

James looked at his radio and frowned. He repeated himself.

Officer Dean McCrea quickly corrected himself. "Sorry, Chief. Over."

James saw what appeared to be the cabin door, but it was now on the road about twenty feet ahead of him. He and Officer Twin walked up to it slowly. They both noticed claw marks and blood on the door. They looked at each other, and then back towards the cabin. As they walked, the smell of blood and death became more evident. Holding his gun ready, James took the lead and strategically crept to the cabin entrance. He saw a body hunched over in the corner. There was no mistaking that the man was dead. James and Officer Twin continued on.

They searched the cabin and found the other rooms were clear. James headed up the stairs to the loft with Twin right behind. He popped his head up the stairs and with his pistol pointing forward and peeked into the open loft. "Don't come up any further," he said. "It's, uh ... clear."

"Are you all right, Chief?" Twin asked.

James swallowed hard and waved her off. "Yes. It's clear, but you don't need to see what's up here. Let's check outside the cabin. You take the left, and I'll take the right."

They both went back downstairs and headed outside. James went around the deck. He noticed the generator shack had collapsed. He slowly scoured the area and noticed more blood and chaos everywhere and continued around. Then he heard Twin call him to the other side of the cabin.

James ran around to find her staring at a rust-stained standing freezer. He pointed his gun around the area and asked, "Are you okay? What did you see?"

Officer Twin pointed over to the stand-up freezer where there was a pool of red liquid forming around it. James cautiously walked up to the freezer with his gun pointed in front of him. He opened the freezer door. The door popped opened, and warm blood and meat rushed at him and poured onto the floor. James quickly jumped back as large, skinned chunks of meat rolled out; they looked like parts of a human bathing in a pool of blood that was pouring over the deck. Officer Twin instantly leaned over the side of the railing and threw up. James walked over and patted her on the back. He called back on his radio.

"Chief Haul here. All is clear, but you better gather a crew and get them out here as soon as possible. We have a crime scene up here."

Chapter II

The sun rose over the uncut forest on a crisp fall morning. There wasn't a cloud in the sky to block the sunlight as it hit the mountain peaks. A helicopter broke the silence as it flew overhead, scanning the forest for a safe place to land. It hovered for a few minutes until the pilot saw an officer waving them in with orange flags. The helicopter circled over a cabin surrounded by about six hundred square feet of yellow ribbon and three police cars. It landed on a temporary pad and shut down. The door opened and a mountain of a man stepped out, hunching over and making sure to avoid the spinning blades. Officer James Haul walked over to meet the big man, who stood to shake his hand. The two men walked away from the piercing sound of the helicopter and toward a travel trailer that was parked near the edge of the police tape.

"Professor William Robson, good to meet you. Wow, people say *I'm* a big guy. Looks like they make 'em big up in Colorado, too. I'm Officer James Haul, no relation to Hall or Oats. You can call me James—never was a fan of that formal crap. Makes people get all uptight and awkward, then that makes me nervous and uncomfortable, then the conversations goes to shit after that. Know what I mean?" James looked at the man who stared back at him with an overwhelmed look. James realized he'd just rattled a rapid-fire of questions at the man. "Sorry about that. I've had too much coffee already, and I'm a bit on edge."

"Good to meet you, too," said William. "They make everything bigger in America. And no problem, I am also not a fan of formality. I know what you mean. You can call me Will if you like."

James smiled, took a relaxing breath, and then calmly said, "Thanks for coming on such short notice."

"Well," said Will, "the call I got from you made me drop two seminars and a book-signing to jump on a helicopter as soon as I could and check this out. And I hate flying!"

"When we saw what we saw, we knew we needed the best bear expert to help us out. Everyone we talked to recommended you."

James and William walked over to a foldout table beside the utility trailer and both had a seat. James asked Will, "Want a coffee? I can assure you, it's good, my wife made it." Will nodded, and James poured two cups. Will sensed James had been on his feet awhile. James took a sip from his cup, and then continued, "I've seen your picture before, and I'm saying this as a compliment. You don't look like a professor."

Will smiled and said, "Thank you. I actually just liked bears and decided to film and study them, then realized I knew more about bears than a lot of 'experts' did, so I continued to pursue the topic and become a certified 'expert,' as well. If you don't mind me saying—also as a compliment—you do not talk like any RCMP officer I have ever met before"

"Welcome to the 'Forgotten Borders,'" James replied. "Here in the middle of the forest, we're so close to the American and Canadian border that both sides shied away on claiming what side we're on. Over the years, we've had a marshal, a Mountie, a constable, and even a Texas Ranger, if you can believe that. I was deputized once on a manhunt near here about ten years ago, and I always wanted to become an officer, so I hung out with the officer who was working here at the time. I went to a class two nights a week for two years and became an auxiliary cop. The officer was called back home, and we've been waiting for a replacement ever since. That was over five years ago.

They're just happy someone is here keeping the peace and quiet. I'm an auxiliary cop and a deputy . . . a double whammy."

"I didn't know there were such places like this," Will said.

James chuckled. "No one wants anyone to know about these rare spots. If they did, imagine how many terrorists or refugees would think they could just walk through. It's kind of cool—I obey the laws, keep the peace, and run around without a stick up my ass."

"Sounds like you have the best of both worlds."

James sighed, and then replied, "Pretty much, until something like this comes along. I like to shoot straight from the hip. Hiding things around this town is just too time-consuming and usually doesn't last long, anyhow. I'm telling you straight-up, this case is personal. To everyone here, it's personal. We already have a small search party looking for two guys. We're all here until this is solved. I'm probably going to get fired before this thing is over, but I don't care. We knew these guys since they were boys. I hung out with all of them, and one's my own cousin, for god's sake!"

Will sat back in his chair, appreciating the intensity in James' voice. He really did shoot straight from the hip. James continued, "Nothing pisses me off more than watching all these hyped-up TV shows with different bureaus like the FBI or CIA charging in and taking over while withholding information. It's a lot of bullshit. We've never had someone come in and take care of our problems before, and I don't want it to start. I want to figure this out as soon as possible and be involved every step of the way."

"Well, you tell me what you know so far. We will start from there and see if we can keep the acronym'd people out of this, shall we?"

James nodded, finished his coffee, and then poured himself and Will another cup. He took a deep breath and then told Will what he knew. "First of all, this is a town of 5,000 people. Just about everyone knows everyone, so unless we go to another town and grab a whole new police force, there is no way this case won't be personal. We got a call about two days ago that four guys went on a hunting trip and haven't come back yet. I grew up with these guys, and if I weren't a cop, I would have been up here with them. Lorne Mackenzie, Daniel Cartier, Lee Macpherson, and Walter Frisby were the four hunters. Lorne is a smart-ass with a heart of gold. He's married to Joan with two kids and drives a truck for a small logging company. Dan is a short, stocky guy. Quiet but quite the life of the party when he drinks. He's been with his girlfriend named Marie Turtle for some time now. He's a faller for the same logging company. Lee is a heavy-duty mechanic for the city and a ladies' man, and he knows it. He has an on-again, off-again girlfriend named Dianna Revel."

Will had removed a notepad and pen from his breast pocket and was jotting down words as fast as James was talking in order to record all the info he could get on the case. James wrapped his hands around his mug as he continued. "Walter is a shy, short, wiry bastard with a quick-witted sense of humour. He's the only single guy left of the group and he kept the tradition of coming out here every year with the guys. He is also my cousin, so when his mom—my aunt—phoned in to say they weren't back yet, I shrugged it off. Walter's mom and my mom are twins, and they have the exact same amount of caring, good-hearted, annoying, crazy bitch in them. The guys stayed out past their return time before, so I figured it was just another weekend extension. Walter, Lee, Dan, and Lorne used to my best friends when we were younger, but we all drifted apart after that bigwig, Frank Gilmore, tore our town apart ten years ago."

Will sat back and asked, "You mean the multibillionaire, Frank Gilmore?"

"The one and only! His son and a couple of his friends decided to become famous ghost hunters and catch the legendary spirits that supposedly haunted this place on camera. They ended up disappearing."

Will looked at James with a hint of surprise. "I remember hearing about that, but I did not realize it was *here*."

"I know, a lot of strange things happen around here. We had about 10-20,000 people a year visit our town because of that story. It's not as bad as it sounds when you compare the number of people who've come up here to visit the area to the number who've gone missing. Anyway, Frank's son, Hans Gilmore, wanted to be a filmmaker with his friends, but none of them were ever seen again. We searched for three weeks and nothing—not even their equipment or vehicle. To tell you the truth, we're not even sure if they made it up here. Frank Gilmore paid a rescue crew to search for another week, but got the same results. He went to plan B and told us to close down this whole area or he would sue and close down our town by himself. To prove he wasn't bluffing, he bought one of our local mills and then fired all the employees. A hundred and fifty-eight people lost their jobs that day. So when our mill and tourist attraction were shut down, the town took a major financial hit. We're still recovering from that."

Will sat dumfounded, and then said, "That's terrible. For everyone."

James undid three buttons on his uniform and stretched out his collar around his neck. "I understand and feel bad the man's son went missing," he said, "but damn, it wasn't the community's fault. Anyhow, budgets were cut, as well. We couldn't afford to maintain the other parks and keep people from sneaking into this place, so that's how these four guys came in." James stood up from his chair, looked around, and then waved another officer over. The young man came running up and stopped in front of James.

"Yes, sir?"

James frowned when he heard the word "sir." "Call me Chief, rookie, not 'sir.' Any muffins or donuts still kickin' around?"

"Sorry, sir—I mean, Chief, there might be half a box at the other table."

"What are the odds of getting them over here?"

"I'll bring them right over for you, sir—I mean, Chief."

The young officer's face turned red in embarrassment. He took off at a quick pace toward the cabin. James smiled, topped up his coffee again, and then sat back down. "Got to ride the rookie a little," he chuckled. "Besides, he's not ready to see the scene yet. He can stay outside and be innocent for a little while longer."

Will took a sip of his coffee and wondered what he was getting into. He also wanted James to carry on with the story. "So, what about the four guys?" Will asked.

James took a gulp of coffee and continued. "We got a bunch of local help to maintain and look after the other parks, but these guys . . . we got them to help without them knowing it. Walter, Dan, Lorne, Lee, and I had been going on annual hunting trips up here for several years before it was closed down. We were all pissed off and tried to fight, but it was no use. I had to enforce the law and make sure no one trespassed. These four decided to go anyways, and I had to arrest them. That put me into their bad books, and we started to hang out less and less."

As James was talking, Will saw the rookie hustle over with a box of muffins; suddenly, he stumbled and dropped the muffins onto the ground. From the corner of his eye, Will watched as the rookie looked around to see if anyone had noticed; then the young man picked them up and quickly put them back while James continued to speak. "Walter stayed in touch, though, so we ended up making a deal under the table. Walter would come up here twice a month to maintain and generally look after this place. In return, I would make sure the other officers were busy doing something else. But if they got caught up here it would be at their own risk, and Walter agreed. To keep the other three thinking they were still sticking it to the man, Walter would replace the locks every three or four years. It's the biggest park we have, and we couldn't afford to pay anyone to maintain it. Because of the closure, we couldn't let anyone volunteer to help out, either. This seemed like the best option I could come up with. It saved the city money and grief."

"Until now," Will replied.

James bowed his head. "Yeah, until now."

"So that's why you believe you'll be fired?"

James looked at Will. "Wouldn't you fire my ass?" he asked. "It's my fault no matter how you cut it. If I hired a maintenance person and they went missing, then I should've found someone more qualified or hired more than one. If it was a volunteer, then why didn't I have a guard watching them? If I paid another company to come in, I'd be accused of wasting city money and giving jobs away. The last option is to do nothing and let it overgrow into a free garbage or body-drop site. These guys knew more about this country and area than anyone, so I had no doubt in my mind they would be okay. Until now, as you mentioned."

Will was silent for a moment as the rookie came up to the table with the donuts. James quickly opened the box and grabbed a muffin from the top. "Thanks, Rook. What would you like, Will?"

Will looked at the young man and gave a small smile. "I'll take any one from the bottom, thanks . . . They stay fresher." The rookie's face went from pale white to bright red. As Will took his muffin from the rookie, the young man quickly put the box on the table and said to James just as fast, "If you need me, I'll be over by the car, helping the others."

With a mouthful, James nodded in agreement.

In three bites, Will polished off his muffin, took a big gulp out of his cup, and then slapped the table. "Well, let us try to get some answers before you get kicked off this case. I just have to make a quick call to my agent."

"No one told you? There is no cell service here."

Will paused, and then said sarcastically, "No cell service, no power up here, and no certified policing—have you guys discovered fire yet?"

James laughed. "We have, and we also have power in town—we just have to wake the hamsters up to start running on their wheels to generate it. On a serious note, if you need to make a call, you can use the CB radio and one of the officers could relay it to someone."

"Well, my call is not that important, so let us move on. First thing is first: Who is missing and who is dead?"

James replied, "I can only tell you there are two missing and two dead. Until we get the blood samples analyzed, we can only recognize one of the bodies as Dan Cartier. Off the record, I believe the other one is Lee Macpherson. I recognize the clothes and his body type, but I could be wrong."

Will took a sip of coffee to help ease down the lump in his throat. "Well, let us get started then."

James heard the doubt, and asked Will, "How's your stomach?"

Will thought about it, and then looked at the box of muffins. "It is probably better if I eat another one later, just in case." He followed James toward the cabin's entrance.

"We've been here since yesterday evening, taping things off," said James. "We took all the pictures we could last night and this morning, so do whatever you need to. Myself or anyone else here'll be more than happy to be at your beck and call."

Will nodded thanks and flipped to a new page on his notepad. James ducked under the yellow tape and held it up for Will, who took the ribbon from James' hand and lifted it about six inches higher before ducking underneath. James walked a few paces and then came to a halt. Will looked up, wondering why they'd stopped so far from the cabin, and then back at James in astonishment. "You've got to be kidding me," Will said. "Was that on the cabin?"

On the ground lay the front door, with its hinges dangling and four long gouges carved into the front of it. Will inspected the door and found the gouges were claw marks about a foot long, an inch deep, and another inch wide, evenly spaced at about four inches. Will grabbed the camera hanging from his neck and snapped some pictures of the door.

"That's got to be the biggest bear claw I have ever seen!"

James sighed with relief. "That's a bit of good news."

"Why is that?" Will asked.

"We thought it looked like a bear claw, but we also have never seen one that big before, so of course rumours started to fly, and myths and legends came out. Plus, I don't have to listen to my uncle telling more Indian tales about the spirit beast that haunts this place. It gets a little tiring hearing about it over and over, but it's always the same story, so I can translate it quite well to the white man."

Will stared at James for a long second. "My apologies, but I did not see the 'Native' in your looks."

"I'm one-eighth Sinixt Indian. My German side took over the rest of me, but my grandfather was half-Sinixt and was Chief of the Sinixt band that still lives here. When he died, my uncle took over."

Will rubbed his chin. "So your uncle has a theory about this place?"

James rolled his eyes. "My uncle and his tribe have many theories about this place, but he's going senile and smokes too much peace pipe, so his ramblings come and go."

Will chuckled, "Sorry to hear that."

"It happens. Can't change it, so we just deal with it. Just want to keep the monster stories down a bit."

"Well, the stories may not be that far off. It is a bear claw mark for sure, but it is also a monster. If I had to guess, I would think it would be a grizzly, but I have never seen or heard of any type of bear being this big before."

"Well then, I'm glad we got the best bear expert to come down and see this."

A self-conscious smile spread across Will's face. "Me too. Let us carry on." When Will realized he was smiling, he stopped and said, "Sorry about that James, now is not the time for smiling."

James shook his head and assured Will it wasn't a problem. "I get it, this is new territory for you. You should be excited. Might as well have some good come out of this."

Will continued to investigate the door a little longer, and then wrote something down. He and James walked to the entrance of the cabin and looked inside. Will noticed a large blood trail leading from the entrance of the cabin that wrapped around the deck toward the back. He looked at James and said, "That is a lot of blood."

James took off his jacket and pointed toward the woods. "That's where the blood trail came from. We'll go that way after you check this scene first."

"How many crime scenes are there?"

"To tell you the truth, we're not sure. We only found two, but we think there's at least one more. This one gets a little confusing, and it's also the closest."

Will looked back at the front door thrown down the path. "This bear ripped that door off while it was locked, so these guys knew they were being run down. What pissed this beast off enough to rip a locked door off the hinges and toss it thirty feet away?"

"I know these guys can be annoying sometimes, but this seems a bit much. Could it be because it was hungry?"

"If it was hunger, you would not have found two bodies."

James choked. "Actually, it was only a body and a half."

Will cocked up one of his eyebrows. "Beg your pardon?"

"That's why we can't identify the one guy."

Will dropped his pen. He quickly picked it up, hoping James hadn't seen. Both continued into the cabin, and Will noticed another blood trail. He wrote again in his book. They followed the blood trail to the body covered by a sheet. James pulled it off to reveal Dan Cartier sitting in a pool of dried blood that had soaked into the floorboards. He had a rifle in his hand and an eight-inch-wide gash where his stomach should have been.

James noticed the colour change in Will's face. "Are you going to be all right? We can go back outside."

Will quickly wiped his face with the sleeve of his shirt. "I have seen a lot of bloody carcasses studying all types of bear encounters, but never anything this gruesome. I will be fine." He scanned the main floor and wrote down what he saw, and then deliberately kept his eyes on the staircase as he walked past Dan's body and headed upstairs. James followed behind. At the top, Will noticed another sheet that was half the size of the last one, but it had more blood around it. His face changed from pale green to bright white, and he said, "Maybe not!" He quickly turned and ran down the stairs to throw up outside.

James steadied himself as Will rushed past, and then he walked down to check on the bear expert. James found him sitting at the table with his head in his hands. Will wiped his mouth with his sleeve and looked up at James.

"Sorry about that," said Will. "Probably not the most professional thing to do, was it?"

"There's no such thing as 'professional' around here, so don't worry about it. Thanks for not running me over in your travels, by the way. You're a scary bastard when running forward."

"Sorry about that, also."

"Don't be, I just thought I was going through the railing."

Will smiled sheepishly. James grabbed the muffins and coffee and put them next to Will. "Relax. We'll go back in when you're ready."

Will nodded and put his head back between his hands. James went to check on how his officers were doing.

Will sat at the table for about twenty minutes with only drinking one cup of coffee and leaving the muffins untouched. Food still didn't agree with Will's stomach. James came back to see how Will was feeling.

Will had collected himself enough to carry on with the investigation so they headed back to the cabin. He wrote notes on what he'd seen, and then walked upstairs once more. James slowly peeled back the sheet for Will to see a pair of amputated legs lying on the floor. Will quickly swallowed as he watched the blood trail head out the window. Looking out, he noticed another blood trail heading off into the forest. Will continued staring out the window as he gestured toward the legs behind him. "I am guessing that is the way the other half of him went."

"That's what we thought," said James. "Let's go check that out next. Are you done up here?"

Will glanced at the blood-soaked floor and the set of legs, and then looked up. "You said you took a lot of pictures—that means I don't have to. Definitely, I am done."

The two men walked outside to the back where the blood trail continued. Will took a deep breath and then started to cough.

"Is that cough because of fresh air," asked James, "or did you get that whiff of death that keeps wafting by?"

"Actually, it was the fresh air. If it were the smell of blood, I would be throwing up again. Despite the circumstances, this place is beautiful. It is a shame they closed it down."

"You're telling me. This place had everything, and it was also free to stay here. It was first-come, first-serve, and people understood that. A big waste of a cabin, I tell ya."

"Well, from what I have seen and from things that have happened here over the years, you might want to consider trying to move it to another place."

James looked at the cabin and sighed. "Unless this cabin is the curse itself. Although I don't think anyone would want to stay in this place anymore. Getting blood out of the wood's going to be impossible." James remembered something and snapped his fingers. "FYI, don't look in the freezer on the side of the deck, or you'll lose your breakfast once again."

"What was in the freezer?"

"Just a huge pile of spoiling deer meat," James replied. "But earlier it was half on the floor, and it looked like it could have been the remains of the missing two guys. The deer was quartered and wrapped up, but the generator shack collapsed and shut the freezer down. Luckily, it didn't catch on fire. When one of my officers, Gail Twin, opened the freezer, she thought someone had been cut up and thrown in there. Scared the shit out of her. I decided she should stay in town and deal with other matters."

"I will be sure to avoid that," Will said.

Both men followed the blood trail that led from the top of the second floor into the woods and stopped about ten feet later. Will searched the ground, and then looked up.

"What the hell?" asked Will.

James understood Will's bewilderment.

"Yup . . . I said the same thing when we checked this spot. I told you it was going to get even more weird."

The blood trail they were following had completely vanished— there was no pool of blood or body parts, and not a single thing was disturbed from that spot on.

Will held his hand over his eyes to block the sun and scanned the area. "How far of a perimeter search did your crew do around here?"

"About fifty feet."

Will looked back, even more bewildered. "And still no sign of anything?"

"We had six guys searching and got nothing."

Will replied in disbelief, "Where could this blood trail have gone? A bear with this sort of claw dimensions might possibly be able to jump out of that second storey window from the cabin with a half of a body and crash onto the generator shack. That is only about a fifteen-foot drop; it would be astonishing but doable for a bear that size. But there is no way it could jump fifty feet carrying that same weight—or even by itself, for that matter."

"You're more than welcome to do a search of your own if you like."

"It just seems—"

James cut Will off mid-sentence. "Ridiculous, stupid, confusing, nonsensical?"

"Well, yes," Will replied.

James scratched his head and told Will, "I thought the same thing for hours while waiting for you to get here. I was hoping you would be the man to tell me why."

Will rubbed his face and looked at his notepad. "Let us think about this rationally. A bear with that size of paw would only be able to jump twenty feet maximum while carrying that amount of weight. Empty-clawed, it could do thirty feet, so if you searched a perimeter of fifty feet that should have been large enough." Will paused and thought for a minute. "I am not saying you and your crew missed anything, but I will not be able to sleep until I have checked it out myself."

"I figured as much, and I understand completely. If you need any help whatsoever, my officers and I will be working over by the tables."

Will nodded, and then looked closely at the blood trail for any signs of direction. There were none. He sighed and kept on with his search.

* * * * *

Two hours went by. The sun slowly hit the treetops. Will walked back to James sitting on the steps of the cabin. James saw the look on Will's face, and knew it all too well; he had had a similar expression that morning. James tossed a bottle of water to Will, who cracked it open and drank half of it in one go.

Will was about to tell James he was right when James spoke up first, "Total mindfuck, ain't it?"

Will paused in mid-step, and then nodded in agreement. James tapped him on the arm.

"So, do you want to take a break and get some food, or check out the second site and become more confused?"

Will blinked. "More confusing than what I have just seen? Or not seen? Never mind. Let us check out the next spot. Maybe it will help."

James looked at Will. "Don't get your hopes up." Then he got up from the stairs of the cabin. "We'll start from the side of the cabin and work our way down," he said. "We'll snag a water or two, because this blood trail goes for about a kilometer and a half. By the looks of it, Dan met up with the bear before the attack on the cabin. Kind of like it followed them here."

Will's eyes followed the blood trail into the bushes. "It is amazing he was alive long enough to get here."

James agreed with a sad look on his face; it was his friend's blood. He put that into the back of his mind and said, "I remember bow-hunting one time. We shot a deer with an arrow, and it took us on a three-kilometer hike to find it. Are you ready to go?" he asked.

Will took another breath of fresh air. "Actually, besides being confused, I am actually a little excited by these circumstances. I have been studying bears for seventeen years, and I have never seen anything like this before. This is making me feel like my first day in the field again."

"Well, like I said before, hopefully some good can come out of this whole scenario and you can at least get another book out of it."

Will got a guilty look on his face. "Does that seem selfish?"

"Not at all—it's your job, isn't it?"

"Well, let us hope we can both get some answers," said Will.

They each grabbed a water bottle and followed the blood trail into the woods, documenting everything that might be useful. Will took pictures of his own along the way.

They walked for about an hour, starting and stopping to give Will time to think, see, and take notes until they came to the end of their travels, moving through the bush and into a small clearing. Here they saw two more officers searching a blue, freshly damaged, early-90s F-250 crew-cab. Will thought the scene looked like a post-war battlefield. His mouth dropped and his eyes widened. He stood in silence, looking around.

James looked over at Will. "That's pretty much the same look we all had when we first saw this place."

"That truck is missing a door!"

"Hmm, you noticed that, did you? The officers are just finishing up, so you can have at 'er whenever you want."

Will scanned the scene for a while, and then said, "If you don't mind, I would like to go through this scene alone also and come up with my conclusions. Then we will compare notes afterwards."

James shrugged. "Sounds good. If you need anything, just ask. Call me when you're done."

* * * * *

It was about 2:00 p.m., and the shade of the trees was not stopping the heat. James was talking to one of the officers when Will walked up, wiping sweat off his brow. The officer James was talking to grabbed a water bottle from the trunk of the police car they were standing next to and handed it to Will. Will nodded thank you and downed the one-litre bottle without taking a break. As soon as he finished, he stretched out his back, looked up at the sun, and let out a burp.

"Wow! Excuse me," Will said with a smile. "I thought it was always supposed to be cold up here."

James smiled. "Yankee. We have all four seasons here, you know. Not just winter." James took the empty bottle from Will and tossed him another full one. "You gotta love Indian summers. Actually, this is one of those odd falls we have about every seven or eight years. Cold in the morning, stinkin' hot in the afternoon."

"I noticed."

"So, what did you come up with?"

Will cracked the new bottle open and took a sip. "I would like to know your thoughts first. You seem to have a keen eye, and I am still a little parched."

"All right then," James said. "We gathered it was a bear attack, and with the size of tracks and claw marks, we believed it was a huge grizzly, but there are a lot of bullet casings all over the place. So either the boys were awful shots and this was a fast and furious bear, or there was more than one. The thing is, I was to believe grizzlies don't travel in packs, and I know these boys ain't shitty shots. The truck in that condition is also a mystery, because it was in pretty good condition when they left, and now it looks like it was thrown off a cliff. They definitely drove it here from a southerly direction, which means there is another scene somewhere else. We lost the tracks on the dirt road a kilometer back, though. Realistically, we're not sure what the hell happened."

Will tried to erase some of the doubt from James' mind. "Well, I will tell you right now to stop thinking rationally. I once found a pack of grizzlies; it was a long time ago, and it's extremely rare. They were fighting for dominance. A bear this big should never have to fight for dominance unless there was one just as big—"

James cut Will off. "So you also think there was more than one bear?"

"I think there were three, actually, and all about the same size."

James sighed in relief because he had been right, but then he shivered, realizing there were more than one of these beasts around.

Will continued, "I also think they are all related."

James looked at Will with a surprised look. "How the hell did you figure that out?"

"Because tracks don't lie. I also believe one of them is wounded. Let us go through it together."

James was becoming as intrigued as Will. He jumped up from leaning against the police car. "I'll grab a recorder and we'll get started. Plus, I'd like to get this all cleaned up before we have to start fighting off the wildlife."

Will stopped. "About that—how long have the men been missing?"

"About two days, but Dan's body looked to be dead about three."

Will looked around at the trees and ground, and then mentioned his observation. "So that's at least two days of flesh and the smell of blood in the woods, yet there are no other animal tracks around. The other thing is that there are no other sounds."

Both men stopped to listen into the woods. Besides the sounds of human movement and the leaves rustling in the wind, there was absolute silence; no birds, squirrels or even crickets could be heard.

"You're right," James realized. "I didn't even notice, but living here in these parts I kind of take those sounds for granted. Now that you've mentioned it, it's slightly eerie when you stop and listen."

"That is a bit of an understatement. I noticed it when we were walking here through the woods, but like you, my mind was on other things, so it did not seem important at the time. Whatever happened here scared all the wildlife away. That alone is quite astonishing."

They walked over to look at the damaged truck. Will continued with his analysis. "Seems they came in here pretty fast, judging by that rear flat tire." Will walked up to the front of the truck and said, "There is blood and a chunk of animal fur on the corner of the front-end. With that much damage, they had to have clipped a very large animal pretty hard. If I had to take a guess, I am pretty sure it is grizzly bear fur. The driver hit his head pretty good also on the steering wheel, because there is blood on that. Human tracks drop out from all four doors, but there are four different shoe prints, so I believe all four were alive and accounted for at this spot, as well." While Will was explaining the scene, James followed him with the tape recorder like a dog on a leash.

James told Will, "We sent samples of the blood and the animal hair to get analyzed this morning. It's going to take a while to get the results—that's technology we don't have in town. Continue on, though."

"Well, as I mentioned before, I noticed there was a door missing off the side of the truck, but I do not see it around. One of the men jumped into the box of the truck and started shooting from there in one direction while two of the others ran the opposite way and were shooting in another direction. This is why I think there were at least three different bears. The bear tracks are similar, but definitely different. It seems like these bears attacked like a pack of wolves and ambushed your friends."

Will walked over to the tree line and pointed at bear tracks that ran towards the truck. He followed them, and then looked back at James. "This grizzly charged out of this side of the bush and attacked the man in the box of the truck from behind. With the amount of blood in the box of the truck, I believe this was your friend Dan. You can tell this is where the other man picked him up and ran to the cabin. That would have been quite the human feat, carrying a person that long and that far. The odds of Dan living after having lost that much blood in that distance would be slim. These guys were way out of their league dealing with *one* grizzly bear this large, let alone three."

James let this information sink in before asking, "Why would they ever have thought there would be more than one of these beasts running around?"

Will agreed. He wiped his face and continued to give his analysis.

"These two guys who are missing—they both ran this direction, but they ran straight into one grizzly in this bush, where it attacked and threw one of the guys against that tree over there. You can tell the other guy ran toward the tossed man, but that is it. This is also where all the bear tracks lead and disappear into the woods, just like those ones at the cabin. I am sad to say it seems like the bears took the other two men with them. In my studies, I have never seen a bear of any type take living food back to their den on purpose. I am afraid they probably took the men's bodies to feed on later. Until you get all the samples back and find out who and how many types of blood you have, this is the best I can do."

James rubbed his temples and stayed silent for a moment. Then he asked Will, "So you believe the men are dead?"

"Do you want me blow smoke up your ass, or do you want me to shoot straight from the hip, like you?"

James looked at Will and sighed. "That pretty much answered my question right there, but I still have to believe they're alive and just missing. Thanks for your opinion, no matter how good or bad."

Will felt sympathy for James. "I agree with you, never give up hope," he said. "This is just what the evidence is showing me. Within a fifty-foot radius, everything disappeared—bear tracks, footprints, bodies of people, and animals. We couldn't find anything, but this is a big forest and evidence could have been missed. We are only human." James smiled slightly, but he didn't take too much comfort in Will's words.

Will then asked James, "You also mentioned this truck was in good condition before they left?"

"Dan's boss bought it used that same week, but it was in great condition. Why?"

"Just that the damage on this vehicle is quite sufficient. It definitely did not all happen here, so until we find where this crime scene actually started, this is where I have to stop. This is absolutely amazing to me, but I am at a loss."

"We have a couple guys still looking," James answered, "but with all these back roads, it's like a needle in a haystack. I'll keep someone on it as long as I can. It's going to take at least a week for all the blood samples to be returned, so it's up to you; we could get you back home, or would you like to hang around our town for a little while?"

Will stretched and arched his back. His stomach started to growl. "Well, I am here now, and I would not mind seeing your town and get some pictures downloaded. I also would not mind getting some food. If I stay for a couple days, your officers might find the other scene, and hopefully you will find your missing friends in-between."

"That would be great. You can stay as long as you want. We'll get you a room at the Revel Motel. It's the nicest one we've got. We should get you some food sooner than later, also. A guy your size must be starving." Will smiled and agreed eagerly.

They got into a police car and rode back to the helicopter at the cabin. As soon as the men got out of the car, Will jumped into the helicopter as the pilot started it up. James grabbed one of the boxes of muffins and a few waters off a table and then also jumped in. The pilot flew the men to the town's small airport. James scanned the forest from his higher vantage point, hoping to spot anything to help find his friends.

* * * * *

After landing about half an hour later, James and Will were met by Gail Twin in James' personal single-cab Ford Ranger. As the door shut and crammed the three in like a can of sardines, James said, "Will, this is Officer Gail Twin, Gail, this is Professor William Robson."

Gail and Will reached awkwardly over James (who took a deep breath and sucked in his gut) and shook hands. James adjusted the rear-view mirror back to its original position.

"Sorry about this, but my truck is the only other vehicle we can use. Officer Twin's shift is almost over, and she lives only twenty minutes from here. Town is about twenty minutes after that. We can drop her off, and when we get to town, Officer Dean McCrae can show you around."

Will looked past James and at Officer Twin. Will stared at Gail for a moment without saying a word, then instantly came back to his senses and said, "No trouble at all." In his mind he thought, *If I had known this beautiful creature was riding with us, I would have gotten in the truck first.*

James looked over at Gail and asked her, "Didn't you tell me once you'd read all of Professor Robson's books?" Officer Twin's face turned red. She smiled shyly, and then quickly looked forward out the windshield and started driving. She jammed her elbow into James' side, but being as cramped as they were, it didn't really hurt as much as she wanted it to.

Will smiled and tried flirting with her a little. "I always like to hear I have pretty fans," he said. Still blushing slightly, Officer Twin smiled again and relaxed a bit.

As all of them started to talk more on the road, James was fading out of the conversation, and soon just the two were chatting. James' head slowly dropped down and bobbed back and forth as he fell into an uncomfortable slumber.

Will asked Gail, "Did you know the group of men?"

"Not really. I was transferred to this station just six months ago, so I only know *of* them. A little wild, but the Chief always spoke well of them. He kept saying he was going to introduce me to his cousin Walter, but the timing was never there, and I'm not really into the dating thing right now."

Will's face showed a little disappointment when he heard her say that.

"That is a shame—" Will began, then quickly rephrased, "that you did not get to meet Walter—not that you do not want to date." Will's face slightly went red with embarrassment. Gail smiled and looked at Will. Both laughed awkwardly as Will changed the subject. "So, where do you recommend to go for something to eat while being in Edwardson?"

Gail replied, "Do you want high-quality food at a high-quality price, or a lot of good food at a decent price?"

Will looked at himself and then said, "With the size I am, usually a lot of all-right food at a cheap price, otherwise I would be bankrupt. I would not mind having a nice meal this time around."

Gail smiled and replied, "I believe I might know a place."

As they continued to small talk, James slept between them. Sometime later, he woke with a start. "Ahh, shit! Sorry, people."

Will smiled. "Not a problem, we were having a lovely conversation, and you are a very quiet sleeper. Barely any snoring."

James gave his head an embarrassing shake and then rolled it around for a stretch. They drove by a sign that read, "Welcome to Edwardson."

Surprised, James asked Gail, "Weren't you supposed to drop yourself off at your house?"

Gail smiled. "I figured I'd drive all the way and let you rest for a while. I don't mind at all."

James looked at her, and then at Will. "I'll bet," he said as he snickered. He then asked, "How do you plan to get back?"

"We made a plan. I'll show William around town after lunch instead of Officer McCrea."

Will asked James, "You do not mind that I have invited Gail to eat with us, do you?"

James rolled his eyes and then smiled. "How about you two just go? I still have to break a lot of bad news to a couple of good people."

Officer Twin had a sad and slightly guilty look on her face. "Did you want any help with that?"

"No thanks, you take care of our friend here and get him settled in. I'd rather tell them in person, anyhow. Just don't say anything to anyone. If you get questioned, just say we're still working out there."

They pulled up to the police station and got out, stretching.

"All right then," Gail said, looking at Will. "I have some civilian clothes in my locker, so I'll be only a minute."

Will waved a hand and said, "Take your time. I will wait here until you get back."

Gail quickly ran into the station. Will watched her go. He turned back to see James leaning against the station wall, looking at him with a cheeky grin. "You don't piss around do you?" James said.

Will answered with a smile. "She is one opportunity I could not pass up. Wouldn't you, if you could?"

James lifted his hand up, spun his wedding ring on his finger, and then looked up and down both sides of the street. "I'm going to say 'No' just to be on the safe side."

"You are a very smart man. Are you sure you do not want to eat with us? You must be starving also?"

"I'll snag something on my way out. Speaking of which, I should be off."

"Okay then, I will get settled and maybe come by the station later to see how you are doing."

James shook Will's hand. "Sounds good. I'll be here all night organizing another fresh search party for tomorrow. Tell Gail that I told you to go to the Homefront Restaurant, and charge the lunch on the officers' card. Have a good 'date'—I mean, lunch. Stay out of trouble, eh?" Just then, Officer Twin came out of the station looking well . . . very well.

James quickly waved at the two, and as he jumped into his truck he told Gail, "You two go on without me." Then without hesitation, he drove off before there was any discussion.

As he drove away, Gail smiled and then looked at Will. "Shall we?"

Will's mouth had dropped a little bit in awe, but he replaced it with a debonair grin. "We shall." He took her arm and they walked down the sidewalk. Then he asked, "Would the place you were thinking of taking me for lunch happen to be called the Homefront Restaurant?" Gail, a little shocked, wondered how he knew that. "Because that is where James told us to go," Will added.

Gail replied, "That James is a good man."

The Clan

* * * * *

At 10:30 p.m., James heard a knock on the station door. He got up from his chair and welcomed Will into his office. James sat back down in his chair and gestured for Will to sit on the sofa. Will put a to-go container on the desk and sat down.

"Have you eaten yet?" Will asked.

James smelled the aroma of food seeping out of the Styrofoam. His stomach rumbled. "Only a bunch of cookies and coffee from Walter's sister—she's a tough gal."

"Gail got you this chicken and spaghetti—she figured you probably had not eaten yet. It is cool, but it is good. I had the same thing."

"Oh yeah? You and Gail go for dinner also?" James turned the container, opened it up, grabbed a fork from his desk, and then dug in. With his mouth full and spaghetti sauce on his chin, James looked from the container to Will. "How did your 'date' go?" he asked.

"Extremely well, thank you. Gail is as smart as she is enchanting."

James replied with another mouthful of spaghetti, "Fucking hot, too."

Will cocked an eyebrow, slightly shocked, and then nodded in agreement. "That too, but I thought you did not think that way."

"Are you nuts! She's probably one of the hottest girls around here, and also one of the strongest. She takes no shit from anyone. A little intimidating to the single guys around here."

"It must be difficult for a married man to work around a woman like that."

James let out a small burp and sat back in his chair. "On the record: not really. You do your job, adapt, overcome, and get over the fact that she's a beautiful woman. Off the record: occasionally you hope she drops a pencil and has to bend down to pick it up."

Will chuckled. James went back to the container of food and shoved more mouthfuls of chicken and spaghetti into his mouth.

"I noticed she has a mighty protective wall up," Will mentioned. "So I do believe I will not try to break it down, for I am here only a little while. That is why I am the only one bringing you your food."

"You're a good man. Kind of stupid, but a good man."

"As are you," said Will. Then he asked sombrely, "How did the ladies of the men take the news?"

James sighed and sat back. He put his fork down, as he had just lost his appetite. "As well as can be expected, I suppose. I don't know what's worse: telling Dan's fiancée Marie that Dan is dead, or telling the others that one is dead and one is missing. Or the fact that we have half of a body that they have to come down to identify."

"Yikes," was the only thing Will could say.

James agreed, "That's what I thought. It's a shitty deal either way." James paused and then asked, "Would you rather find out the truth and know your loved one is dead and move on, or do you pray and hope that your loved one will be found one day no matter how long it takes?"

Will thought about it, and then replied, "That is a question I never want to have to answer, James. I am sorry you have to."

James nodded. He had hoped Will would have had a better answer, but sadly he said, "Me too Will. Me too."

James stretched out in his chair, rubbed his stomach, and glanced at the clock. "Man, this has been a long day. I'm going to have to kick you out now, Will. I've got to get up early tomorrow and start that search party."

Will stood up quickly from the sofa. "Not a problem, I just came in to see how you were doing, and to make sure you had something in your belly."

"Greatly appreciated, sir. It definitely hit the spot." They shook hands.

"Have a good night, and I will talk to you later," said Will. He left to head to his motel. James closed his office door, grabbed a blanket from the top of his filing cabinet, turned off all the lights, and made a bed on the sofa. He set an alarm clock for 4:30 a.m. He made a quick call, talked to his wife and kids, and then within minutes he'd fallen asleep. There was still spaghetti sauce on his face.

* * * * *

Three more days went by without a trace of the two missing men. Will, still in town, dropped by the busy police station to find that James had just gotten into his office. Will walked by the hustle and bustle of police and volunteers with minimal acknowledgement and knocked before opening James' office door. James waved him in while untucking his shirt and crashing facedown into his sofa.

Will walked in and sat in James' chair at his desk. "How is the battle, James?"

With his face full of pleather, James replied in a muffled voice, "Fucking useless!" He turned his head and looked up at Will. "It's another long, useless, wasted day with fuck-all to show for it."

Will looked with concern at James' exhausted face. "When was the last time you slept?"

James sighed. "I don't know—what time, day, or week is it?"

Will looked at his watch and then told James, "It's time to get some sleep."

"You came in here to tell me that?" asked James sarcastically.

"Actually, I came here to tell you I'm leaving."

James put out his lip, pouting dramatically. "You're leaving me! Is it me, or are you sick of our town already?"

"Neither, actually, it is that I just got a call from my agent in Alaska. A game warden shot a polar bear that was apparently charging him. Said he had to put a whole clip into him to take him down."

"American ten clip or Canadian five clip?" James asked.

"Your Canadian five clip," Will replied.

"Either way, that's either a big bear, or a bad shot," said James.

"I believe it is option number one," said Will. "It sounds like this polar bear had similar dimensions to your group of grizzly bears, so I am going to go up there and check it out. Maybe it will shed some light on what is happening here."

James rubbed his face. "Anything at this point will be better than what we've got now. It's going to be at least another three days before the blood results come in, and we haven't found shit yet."

"Well, give me a call when you get some answers. I will call as soon as I check out Alaska, but it might take a bit because we have to go by dog sled—and there is no cell service there either, I am told."

"Hamster-powered also?"

"Could be; it is a way into nowhere."

"Well, good luck over there, and thanks for your help down here. It was a pleasure meeting you, and I hope to hear from you sooner than later."

Will gave James a sympathetic smile. "Not a problem, I wish I could have done more. I truly hope you find your missing friends."

James smiled back and replied, "Me too. Thanks again and take care, eh?"

Will got up from the chair and walked over to where James lay on the sofa. James was about to get up, but Will waved him off. "Don't worry about getting up, just get some rest, and we will talk again soon."

James fell back into the sofa and reached out awkwardly to shake Will's hand. "Can you do me one more favour?" asked James.

"Name it," Will said without hesitation.

"Tell one of the officers outside to wake me up in a couple of hours, if you don't mind."

Will nodded. "That I can do. I will tell Gail on my way out."

"Good pick!" James gave Will a thumbs-up and then put his face back into the sofa. Will shut the door and walked through the station over to Officer Twin. He whispered in her ear, and then leaned back and grabbed her hand to kiss it. Half of the crowd in the station stopped what they were doing and stared for few seconds, and then carried on. Gail and Will smiled at each other; then Will walked out of the station. Officer Twin watched the door for a few seconds, wondering if he would come back in again, but she returned to work once she realized he'd gone.

*****

Three weeks had gone by with no news of the missing men. James was at home one day tying his boots as his wife was making toast and feeding his kids when he got a call from a new familiar voice.

"Afternoon, James. How is the weather down there?"

James smiled over the phone with a mouthful of toast. "Tropical compared to yours, Will. We thought our town had cursed you and you went missing, too. One of your agents called our office and said you were indisposed for a while. They didn't explain what that meant, and they didn't wait to be asked any questions."

"They did not know much themselves," Will replied. "I had only enough time to tell my agent Alex that I was fine, and that the group and I were stuck in a freak snowstorm."

"Sounds like fun. How was that?"

"Not the trip I was expecting. We landed in an even smaller town than your town, and of course, it was your weird Canadian -50 Celsius without the wind chill. As soon as my cameraman and I got off the plane, our gear was packed onto some sleds. We took a fourteen-hour dog sled journey to a secluded supply cabin in the middle of nowhere. When we left, the weather report mentioned that a 'small storm front' was coming in. That was an understatement. We had twelve smelly dogs and five smelly men trapped in a cabin about twenty feet by forty feet for five days without communication until there was a brief break in the storm. We used the satellite phone to relay we were fine, and that we had enough food for a while. Three more days passed before it was clear enough to go outside. As soon as we went outside, we all helped shovel snow off the sleds and towers and the shed where the dead polar bear was being kept. All that shovelling took three days because of the darkness. Six days and seven nights in a cabin is not my favourite way to spend my time."

"Damn!" James said. "It's dark all the time there right now, isn't it?"

"Not quite, but close," Will replied. "We had light for about four hours a day. It was also dark when the warden in question shot that polar bear."

"Holy shit!" James replied.

Will started to laugh. "That is what the warden said, also. I checked that bear out, and I just about shit my pants. And it was already dead! This bear was ten feet, two inches tall. It weighed nineteen hundred and forty-five pounds, and it had about the same-sized paws as your grizzlies did up at the cabin. So there is definitely evidence of bears that size kicking around."

"Did anyone see more than just the one polar bear?" James asked.

"No, but I am not disclosing that info yet," Will said. "There might be."

"The main thing is you and the others made it out okay."

"I am glad we all made it out, too," Will sighed. "I have to tell you, between this event in Alaska and yours in Edwardson, a lot more questions and great opportunities have opened up for me. I am booked solid for three straight months."

"Well," said James around a mouthful of toast, "at least some good news will come out of this clusterfuck. I'm happy for you."

"Thank you. How are things going on your side?"

"A lot of false bear and missing fella sightings. We discovered that two hikers trespassed through the park in late September. They were a little sheepish about it, but as soon as they figured we were investigating the missing person case, they opened up and said they had no problems when they walked through there, just an eerie feeling. Otherwise I haven't been in the office for a while though."

Will paused before answering. "I phoned your office first, and knew something was wrong when I talked to a secretary who put me on hold for a Detective Copeland. He told me you were let go, and said this case was closed to the public. I did not tell him who I was."

"I was suspended without pay until further notice, I was told I was taking the case too personal by a CIA agent. Of course I told them 'No, shit, Sherlock!' and that didn't go over too well either. Detective Copeland, the one that's in charge right now seems pretty good. He was understanding to my situation, but he never lost his game face. I could have farted in his mouth, and his nose probably wouldn't even have twitched."

"Interesting mental picture, James, thanks."

The former officer laughed and finished his toast. "No problem. I'm going to guess you will be getting a call from them anytime. This group took every piece of evidence we had and wanted every detail we had. They also called off the search and barricaded the campground to all volunteers and public. Something doesn't feel right. They say they're CIA, but I just don't like it." James hesitated for a moment then decided to continue. "We're told to keep quiet about what we know and not to talk about the case, but you were my first pick on this case, and I trust you—they also haven't spoken to you yet, so they don't know what you know already. So, we found some blue paint and a couple of scraped trees on one of the roads, but we lost the trail again once the road branched out, so there went our best lead."

"Thanks, James. How about the blood samples? Can you tell me anything about them yet?" Will inquired.

James snickered once, and then grumbled, "That's the best part about this whole thing. We sent the samples out to professionals to do it right. Then a few days after you left, a parade of black Suburbans filled with meatheads in suits pulled up and took over everything— our station, our jobs, and our case. Some high-strung pencil dick with little-man syndrome named Inspector Johnson started ordering me around. Said we screwed up the blood samples and mixed them up. All of them came back inconclusive. He called me incompetent and made all my officers his fucking lackeys. I could have crushed the little shit with my fingers."

"You didn't though, did you?"

"No, I'm on thin enough ice, and there's still a slight chance I can get my job back. He was only around for a week, then Detective Copeland came in and straightened things out. Moved Inspector Gadget somewhere out of town and also gave my officers a better part in this case again."

"Well, that's some good news, then."

"I was happy they didn't get punished for my decisions. Oh yeah, we did find out that the two missing men are for sure Walter Frisby and Lorne Mackenzie, and the half of the other was Lee Macpherson. We could snag another blood sample from the legs, but we had no extra from the bears, and like I said before, we are now restricted to talking to anyone about this case. That was the rule. They could be on the case, but everything was confidential. It's been a week since I've heard anything new, and now I'm out of the loop."

Will sighed over the phone. "Wow, sorry to hear that, James—others taking over, you losing your job, and then not getting more information on your friends."

"Yeah well, shit happens, I guess," James replied. "As long as they get results, then it doesn't matter who works on it. I also have the wife and kids' support, still so that's good, too."

"That is very true." At the other end of the phone, Will waved in his secretary, signed a cheque, and then nodded as she left. "So, what are you going to do now?" he asked James.

"Well, I'm not giving up, and neither are a lot of people. I am now the head advisor for a volunteer search party. We all keep searching where we are allowed to until we can't anymore . . . there's always hope, and it's a big forest."

"You sound like you have some very big shoes to fill right now. I am glad I am not in them."

"I wish I wasn't in them, either. I'm on my way out with a search group pretty soon, so I'm going to have to let you go, but thanks for the call. I'm glad you're doing all right. Don't be a stranger, Yankee-boy."

"Thanks. Take care, you damn Canuck. I may stop in again when these months slow down and see how things are going. Come see you and Gail on happier circumstances. How is Gail doing, anyways?"

"Oh, about the same . . . Focused. Staying the course, working hard, beating the guys off with a stick. She's still single, just in case you were wondering."

A silence came across the line, and then Will spoke once more, "Maybe I will pop down sooner than later."

"Wise man."

"Before I go, what is your address? I want to mail you something. It won't be much, but it will help keep you afloat. It is the least I can do—you probably helped me get another number-one seller."

"That's not necessary, but I'm afraid I can't turn such generosity down right now." James recited his address.

CHAPTER III

It was pitch black. The trickle of running water echoed somewhere in the background. A man opened up his eyes and tried quickly to adjust his eyesight to see something—anything—but he couldn't. He lied still and used his other senses to find out where he was. While still looking into the darkness, he felt a cool dampness in the air on his face. With his fingers he touched what felt to be a pile of branches underneath him; he sniffed cedar branches, to be precise. He also caught a musty odour reminiscent of his grandparents' basement.

The man assumed he was in a cave. He decided to sit up, but he was stopped abruptly by pain. The man let out a groan and cringed. He couldn't detect a spot on his body that didn't hurt. He dropped back onto the cedar branches like a brick and lay still and scared. His groans were loud enough to echo through the cave. He wondered if something was there with him—if it would hear him and come for him. The man could feel his heart quicken.

He calmed himself slightly, thinking maybe he was there alone. His breathing slowed, but then came back just as fast as it left. About ten feet to his left he heard rustling and animal-like grunts, and then a slight hiss. The man blinked toward the sounds but took care not to move. He heard more rustling and grunting. The sounds seemed to be getting closer. He tried to move out of its way, but couldn't. He was broken and in too much pain to go anywhere.

He was about to yell when a flicker of light came from the same area as the sounds. Something inside him told him not to scream quite yet. The rustling kept on, each time ending with the same faint spark of light. Whatever it was, it was about three feet away when it stopped coming at him. The man was about to gather all the gumption he had to defend himself when he heard a hiss again. This time it sounded more like someone shushing him to be quiet. The man tried to focus into the dark to see what it was. Then he heard a raspy but somewhat recognizable whisper.

"Shhh! Lorne, keep it down, you crazy bastard, you'll wake the dead."

Dumbfounded, Lorne whispered back, "Walter? What the fuck? You scared the shit out of me."

Walter grunted and continued to slide his body towards Lorne. He tried flicking his lighter a couple more times to light up the cave, but it still didn't work.

"Sorry, but this is about as loud as I can talk," said Walter. "I think my vocal chords are blown. I also think both my legs are broken. I can't feel them right now. Do you still have your lighter in your pocket?"

Lorne started to feel panic rising again. Walter's legs were broken? What was going on?

"I don't know, I can't move around to feel if it's still there," said Lorne.

Walter dragged himself to Lorne and dug into his friend's pocket. "Don't get any ideas, and don't make this anymore awkward than it needs to be, queer," said Walter.

Their laughter quickly turned into coughing and hacking. Walter found Lorne's lighter and flicked it. The small glow gave the two men a warm, comfortable feeling. It also allowed them to look at each other. Lorne noticed the familiar figure in front of him, but couldn't focus; Walter was just a blurry mess.

Lorne freaked out a little. "I can't see, man. You look all blurry, like you're underwater."

"Calm down and stay quiet, kemosabe." Walter grabbed Lorne's hand and slowly put it on his face.

"Feel, I'm here, and you're here, and we're breathing, so let's call that good for now."

Lorne noticed Walter had what felt like a damp rag wrapped around his neck. "Jesus Christ, man. You feel like shit."

"Yeah?" Walter replied. "You look like you had a fight with a truck and lost."

Lorne sighed and put his hand back down by his side. He sank into his bed of cedar. "I feel that way, too. Where the hell are we? Why is it so dark? What the fuck happened?"

"Holy twenty questions, Batman," Walter chuckled. "First thing's first: calm down. Secondly, my throat says I can only talk a little longer, so choose your questions wisely."

Lorne took a deep breath and then asked, "What the hell happened?"

"Next question. I'm not exactly sure, still pretty hazy on that one, but we're safe for now."

"Okay then. Have you seen Dan and Lee?"

"Nope, I thought I was alone, and I was being as quiet as I could until I heard you shuffling around."

"Why are we being quiet? Is there something here with us?"

"Right now we are by ourselves, but they can't be too far away, so the quieter the better."

"Who are 'they?'" Lorne asked. "What is it we are being quiet for?"

Walter looked at him, not knowing exactly what to say. "We're not in danger at the moment, and we're too mangled to do anything anyhow, so just relax. All I know is they don't like loud noises. If we become trouble, they'll have no problem disposing of us."

Lorne started to get worked up again. "Is it some kind of creature? Or some inbred hicks? Or are Gramps's tall tales actually true?"

Walter's eyes quickly widened, and then he sighed a little in relief. "Let's take number three. That's probably a better explanation than I could give. It's around 3:00 a.m., I think. Go back to sleep. In the morning it will be a lot clearer to explain. Good to see you kickin', though."

But Lorne was now alert, and he knew he wasn't going to be able to fall asleep. Walter closed the lighter and their surroundings became black once again. He patted Lorne on the shoulder and closed his eyes.

Lorne took a deep breath and slowly calmed down. He whispered to Walter, "Good to see you, too, buddy."

In a quiet whisper, Walter replied, "Fag!"

They both snickered.

* * * * *

Lorne woke slowly to the sound of chirping birds. He opened his eyes but remembered not to make any big moves. He looked up to see a blurry, damp rock above. He felt around and noticed his cedar bed had some fresh branches underneath. He also noticed Walter wasn't beside him anymore. Lorne quietly moved his head to take a better look around. He felt better now that there was enough light to see some of his surroundings. As quietly as he could, he shimmied up into a half-sitting position.

With a few grunts, he got comfortable and noticed a lump about ten feet away. Lorne tried to focus. He watched it for a few minutes until he noticed a red rag. It was comforting to know the lump was Walter, but disturbing to see that the rag was red because of blood. Walter also lay on a bed of cedar. Lorne thought there was no way Walter would have been able to get back over there by himself without Lorne hearing him. He looked around and saw three or four empty cedar beds in the cave. *What the hell are we dealing with here?* he thought to himself. While pondering this question, a faint ray of sunshine beamed in over the cave walls. Lorne squinted and then felt the warm glow on his face. It was small, but greatly appreciated. He closed his eyes, basking in the limited sun. He heard a familiar voice come from the Walter lump.

"That picture means *'family.'*"

"What means 'family?'" asked Lorne. "What's going on?"

"Oh shit, sorry man, I thought you were looking at the ceiling. I forgot that you can't see very well. If you can, take a good look at the wall closest to you."

Lorne put his hand up slowly and reached until he hit the wall. He held his face a foot away and then took a long, blurry look. He noticed some engravings and felt them with his dirt-and-blood stained fingertips.

"That one you're touching means *'friend,'*" Walter explained. "Chief Gramps used to draw that in the dirt when we were at the fire as kids, remember?"

"Oh yeah," Lorne said. "He used to draw shitloads of these symbols."

"Not sure if I noticed the drawing for 'shitload,'" Walter remarked, "but there were ones for hunting, travelling, and a lot of others. There are also a bunch here that look totally different from Chief Gramps' drawings."

"What do they look like?" asked Lorne.

Walter thought for a moment, and then said, "Think about when we were in social studies in school, then remember Ancient History Week on the *History Channel.*"

Lorne's eyes opened like a kid's at a candy store. History had been Lorne's favourite class in school; he had also been a fan of Egypt. Lorne shouted, "Egyptian hieroglyphics!"

Walter waved his hands at Lorne to settle down, and then smiled. "That's what some of these look like to me."

Lorne stared at the blurry markings again, and his mouth dropped in awe. "Holy shit! I wish I could see them. These markings could be from all over the place. They could be from all types of cultures—East, West, North, Egyptian, Spanish, and other old shit never seen before. Where the hell are we, Walter?"

Walter's smile quickly left his face. He said quietly—and very seriously—to Lorne, "The question should be 'when' are we?"

Lorne looked at Walter, disturbed and slightly scared. "What do you mean?"

Walter started to laugh. "Nothing, I just always wanted to say that. Who the hell knows where we are."

Lorne started to laugh also, but stopped when Walter started hacking. Walter spit out a mouthful of blood and looked down at the frothing puddle. "Ew. That doesn't look good."

Lorne cringed. "Shit, man, we got to get you to a hospital."

"Sounds good, let's both stand up and get going shall we?" Walter picked up one of his legs and then let it flop to the ground. "I hate to burst your bubble," he said, "but there's no chance of me walking out with you. I can't feel my legs at all."

"You're paralyzed?"

"Must be. I hoped I'd start feeling them by now, but I think my back is broke.

"I'm so sorry, bud."

"Hey, at least we're alive still. Not sure I can say the same for Dan and Lee."

Lorne frowned. "Why do you say that?"

"Because you and me are here, and they aren't."

Lorne paused. "Maybe they got away."

"Maybe. Let's hope they did and are looking for us right now, but if I recall, they looked worse than we did."

"Do you remember what happened to us?"

"Nope. Just flashes of things. I do remember waking up in here and watching a couple big, longhaired bastards cleaning and wrapping up your wounds. Then later one of the 'girls' came and dressed mine."

"Big bastards? How big?"

"About eight feet tall."

Lorne's eyes widened. "Bullshit!"

"Bull-*true*."

Lorne sat there looking at Walter in disbelief, and then he thought to himself, *Eight feet? That's impossible. Are they human?* Lorne winced at the stupidity of his question. Of course they were human, but no normal human was that big. But then who the hell were 'they'? Lorne felt terribly disturbed that Walter was losing it mentally. He decided to humour him. What else was there to do?

"So, how many of them are there?" Lorne asked.

"Don't know. At least four of them."

"What do these 'things' remind you of?"

Walter looked at Lorne, knowing he was not believing him. "They're not 'things'. They're huge, fuckin' hairy, and primitive, and they saved our asses."

"All right, settle down. I didn't mean anything by it. It just sounded a little weird, you seeing a bunch of eight-foot-tall humans, let alone one."

"Understandable." Walter calmed down, and then continued, "I'm assuming they all have to be related to all be that tall. They kind of remind me of the tales Chief Gramps' told us. The one with the long squiggly beard sort of looks like Chief gramps, although the girls are pretty hairy also."

Lorne cringed. "A six-pack girl, you say?"

Walter chuckled. "More like a keg kind of girl."

"Yikes! All though, Lee has probably had worse."

Walter chuckled and then said, "I don't think they've ever seen a razor before… you can't be sure which ones are boys and which ones are girls from a distance."

"That could get scary at closing time at the bars."

"They probably haven't even heard of a bar. I'm thinking this might be the long-lost tribe of the Sinixt Chief Gramps kept talking about. I watched one wear a bear hide like a jacket—I thought he was a grizzly bear. If they wore those out in the bush, anyone would swear they saw a sasquatch."

"Maybe that's what a sasquatch really is—just a huge human in a bearskin walkin' around. That would make a little more sense . . . Eases the mind a little bit, thinking that they could be just humans."

"Yeah, I figured the same."

"So, what should we do?" asked Lorne.

Walter shrugged, "Well, hop scotch is definitely out of the question. Also, they don't have sedatives. When they fixed my arm they bonked me on the head to knock me out. When I woke up, they had me patched up pretty good. I don't think they realized I couldn't feel my legs, but nonetheless . . . Looking at you right now, I see your leg needs to be set, so I believe I'm going to watch one of the bushy girls come and do that." Lorne winced as Walter continued, "You'll be fine. She's quite stealthy for a large bitch."

Lorne saw Walter looking past him. He shifted to try and look as well, but saw only a shadowy figure, and then a bright white light.

Walter watched as Lorne sagged down into his cedar bed, out like a light. "That's definitely going to leave a mark. Be gentle with him, will ya? He's fragile."

CHAPTER IV

The morning was damp. Fog rose from the asphalt-paved road while a logging truck driver rubbed his eyes and talked on his CB radio to stay awake. He reached the top of the hill, and at the same time, the sun rose right into his eyes. He squinted and pulled the sun visor down. Just as he got focused again, he glimpsed a shadowy hump on all fours, half on and half off the road. He swerved and jammed on the brakes. The semi veered around the heaped figure and jacked-knifed to a sudden stop. The driver put on his hazard lights and looked in his rear-view mirror to see if he had missed the figure on the road. The mound moved slowly from all four limbs and started walking on two.

The silhouette of a man formed and cast a shadow on the road. He walked away from the truck and headed down the road.

The truck driver quickly said on the CB radio, "Holy shit, mate! I just about hit someone in the middle of Coursier Road. The bastard's walking off. I'll be right back."

"All right, Chris, don't kill him," a voice answered back.

Chris—a tall, thick, redheaded Australian man—jumped out of the truck, irate he'd just about hit a person in the middle of the road, and now it appeared the guy was simply going to walk away. He yelled at the man, whom he'd just noticed was naked.

"Hey, asshole! Are you mental or suicidal?" The figure kept walking away. "Hey! I'm talking to you, mate!"

The man ignored him. Chris started to run after him to make his point more clear. When he got closer, he almost tripped over his own feet trying to slow down. The man was covered in mud, blood, and had a broken arm, which swung independently back and forth while he walked. Chris gagged a little and then swallowed it back. At first, he thought maybe he *had* run the guy over, but he noticed that the mud and blood seemed dry. Chris ripped off his jacket and cautiously walked up to the man, guessing he must be in shock.

"Oh my god, I just about killed you, mate."

The man kept walking and didn't respond.

"Hey mate, can you hear me? Are you all right? What the hell happened?"

Nothing came from the wounded man. Chris wanted to stop him from moving and get his arm secured, but didn't want to tackle him lest he freak the man out or hurt him more. Chris suddenly remembered he'd heard there were two missing guys around these parts. He called out the only name he could remember. "Walter?"

The wounded man stopped. Slowly, he turned around and stared into the driver's eyes. With a disturbingly calm voice, he said, "Walter's dead. They're all dead." The wounded man turned around and walked again.

Chris stood dazed. He waited for the chill to finish rippling down his spine. "Where you going, mate? We have to get you to a hospital." "I'm going home to my wife and kids," the man replied back.

Chris realized this guy had his mind on only one thing, so he told him what he thought he needed to hear. "Well then, let me give you a ride home, and let's get that arm wrapped up, also."

The man looked down at his arm and seemed to notice it for the first time. He tried to lift it to his chest and watched it dangle like a wet noodle. Chris choked back more bile and then attempted to help the man tie the arm using his jacket as a sling. As he was wrapping the man's arm, Chris tried to keep downwind of the man; he realized quickly that the brown mud wasn't the only thing that was covering him.

They both walked toward the passenger side of the truck. Chris opened the door, hopped up, and grabbed a blanket from the back of his seat. He took a deep breath in then draped it over the man, helping him into the cab. He put the man's seatbelt on and opened the door's window. He quickly shut the door and let out his deep breath, followed by coughing and heaving. He ran over to the driver side and got in.

"We'll get you to your house," Chris said. Looking over, he saw the wounded man was out cold. Chris nudged him slightly to make sure he was still alive, and then radioed for help. "This is Roadrunner. You still out there, Gearbox, over?"

A voice filled with static came over the radio. "This is Gearbox. What's happened there? You pummel the dude, over?"

"No, but I need someone closer to town to get hold of a hospital, mate. I'm too far out, over."

"I should be close enough. What's the problem, son, over?"

"I think I found one of those guys who went missing about three months ago, mate. Over."

The radio was silent, and then, "You're shittin' me."

"Not on this one, mate. He's beat to shit and passed out right now, but still breathing. Tell the hospital to be ready for me, because I'm driving like a bat out of hell, over."

"How far away do you think you are from the hospital, son, over?"

Chris looked out the window, then at his speedometer. "Just under two hours at this speed, mate. Over."

"Right on. I'll call it in, over."

"Try to keep it as low-key as possible, if you can. I don't need to be blocked in by a bunch of looky-loos and snoopers, mate. Over."

"I'll do my best, but as you know, there's no private line on these radios. I can't guarantee anything. Over."

"Here's hoping. Over and out."

"Godspeed, son! Over and out."

* * * * *

An hour and a half later, the dirt-covered rig quickly turned off the highway and barrelled down the road towards the town of Inverness, followed by a cloud of dust. Chris pulled up to the hospital's emergency doors, chattering the brakes to a complete stop. The dust-cloud passed by the truck and covered everything in its path. The attendants burst through the doors with a gurney to retrieve the unconscious passenger. When he was strapped down, two attendants quickly rushed him in through the doors while one female stayed out and shook Chris's hand.

"Doctor Patricia Sale. How are you?"

Chris brushed hair off his face and straightened his hat. "Christopher Mackinla. I'm good. Haven't driven that fast in years."

"Where did you find him?" she asked. "All we got was a brief call saying there was a semi-truck bringing in an unconscious man, so be prepared for him."

Christopher wiped his brow. "In the middle of the road on this side of the ferry. He just about became my new hood ornament."

Dr. Sale recalled the missing person's report. "That's somewhat near to where those men went missing. He's on the wrong side of the ferry, though. I wonder if it's one of them?"

"I think so," Chris confirmed. "I called out the name 'Walter' and he acknowledged me before he passed out."

Dr. Sale looked at Chris, intrigued. "So, he was conscious when you found him?"

"Yeah. Dirty and naked as a jaybird. Smells something awful, too. Wrapped him and his arm up with my jacket."

Dr. Sale looked towards the doors where the attendants had taken the man, and in a joking voice, asked, "Are you sure you didn't hit him?"

Chris smiled and nodded his head to confirm.

"Did he say anything to you?" she asked.

"Just that he was going home and that 'they' were all dead. Creeped me out."

Dr. Sale's smile faded. "Oh, my."

As they were talking, Dr. Sale saw the impatience in Chris as he kept glancing at his watch. Chris quickly said, "I'd really like to stay here and find out if he'll be okay, but I really have to get going. My freight is already late, and to make things worse, I passed a circus of TV and news trucks with reporters heading this way. I can't have them blocking me in."

"TV trucks and reporters?" Dr. Sale looked puzzled.

Christopher sighed. "I called for assistance over the CB radio, so who knows who all heard. Words travel through those things like beans on Taco Tuesdays. Those reporters probably heard about it before you did."

Dr. Sale nodded. "You're probably right about that, but it would've been nicer if it were later rather than sooner. Could you leave your name and contact information on a form at the front desk before you go?"

"I might leave my name and number for a dame like you, love, but if I don't get out of here as soon as possible, it's going to be too late. I'll tell you what; get one of your assistants on the phone, and I'll talk to them on my way out."

Dr. Sale saw the Christopher was getting fidgety and restless. She understood. "All right, get going, and thanks for helping as much as you did."

Chris shook Dr. Sale's hand and quickly jumped back into the cab of his truck. He yelled out the window, "Keep the jacket. I'll get a new one."

He left the hospital grounds at about the same speed as he had come in at, and he gave his horn a quick double-pump to say goodbye. Dr. Sale waved into the air more as a reflex than as an acknowledgement, knowing he probably didn't see it as she walked back towards the hospital. As she headed through the doors, she repeated the license plate number of the semi in her head as a precaution. The swinging doors were closing behind her when she heard an extended honk.

Chris had been just about to turn onto the main road leading toward the highway when he saw the paparazzi parade of reporting crews circle into the hospital grounds. He sighed in relief over the fact that he had made it out before the clown show blocked him in. He locked eyes with one of the reporters in the passenger's seat in one of the vans. He knew they'd give their left nut to get an interview from him, so he quickly shifted a couple gears, blasted his horn, and hauled ass onto the highway, trying to get back on schedule.

Dr. Sale headed back into the hospital, knowing the parade was en route. She walked up to two nurses talking quietly to each other and interrupted them.

"Nurse Graham, can you call the police for me and tell them a man was found on Coursier Road, and that he has just been brought into the emergency room, please?"

While Dr. Sale talked to Nurse Graham, Nurse Anderson looked out the doors.

"What do you want me to tell the press, because here they come?"

Dr. Sale looked outside and saw van after van, truck after truck, and crew after crew pull up to the hospital parking lot.

"Damn it! They move fast." Dr. Sale thought for a second, and then said, "Okay, Nurse Graham, you go call the police and get security over to the doors soon as you can. Nurse Anderson, I need you to write down some information for me, please."

Nurse Graham ran off to make her calls as Nurse Anderson got out her pen and paper. Dr. Sale closed her eyes and told her, "Please write down '1976 JS, bright red Peterbilt, Christopher Mackinla, Australian accent, about six-foot-something tall, and about 250 pounds.' Also, get that one new girl with the annoying voice and tell her that her TV career is about to come true. Just tell her to say 'No comment' and 'No details at this time' to whatever the press ask her. Let her annoy the hell out of them for a while."

The nurse chuckled and nodded. Dr. Sale continued on to the emergency room as two security guards ran by and stood guard at the front doors.

* * * * *

Eight hours had passed when Dr. Sale came out of the operating room, drying off her hands. She walked down the hall and cautiously peeked around the corner towards the entrance and was surprised. The waiting room wasn't the circus she had expected, and it was actually fairly quiet. She looked at the front doors and saw they were still guarded to keep the press at bay, but now the guards were police instead of hospital security. She also noticed the only person in the waiting room was a tall, lanky man observing the "Hang in there, kitty" poster. The man, who was wearing a three-piece suit, looked at Dr. Sale while she took off her mask and cap. He walked over to her as she pulled her hair back from her face. As she greeted him, she read his nametag that was sticking out of his breast pocket.

"Hello, Detective Michael Copeland. How are you?"

"Very well, thank you. Dr. Sale, I'm presuming?"

"Yes, it is." While they shook hands she said, "I thought this place was going to be a zoo when I came out."

Detective Copeland raised his eyebrows and looked around. "That was about four hours ago. It took some time to get people to act somewhat civil."

Dr. Sale wiped off her forehead. "I don't even know how long I've been in there for. What time is it?"

"It's 3:11 p.m. Oh, by the way, kudos on sending out the lady with the . . . unique voice, to deal with the press. I think that slimmed down the questions and the herd by half."

Dr. Sale chuckled. "It's a good thing she only works part-time. I think she keeps some of the patients away, also."

"So, how is your patient, anyhow?" Detective Copeland asked.

"He's hanging by a thread, right now," Dr. Sale replied. "With the extent of his wounds and the amount of blood he's lost, it's amazing he's alive. Right now his red hair is the only thing resembling the pictures of the missing man."

"Is he conscious?"

Dr. Sale knew Detective Copeland was there on business. "Not now, but the good news is he's not in a coma. He's on a lot of morphine. I'm not sure when he'll wake up. He looks like he's been through a lot. His body has to recover first."

"Well, I have a woman sitting anxiously in the cafeteria on the verge of bursting through the two officers holding her back." Dr. Sale thought he must have been talking about one of the wives or mothers. "I believe," he continued, "she would bust down the doors to see if this man is her husband or one of the other missing guys. We tried to tell her we weren't sure who this person was, but once she heard a man had been found on the road by the ferry, she drove from Edwardson as fast as she could to see for herself. She is one strong-headed woman."

"Well, he's in the recovery room right now. We can let her take a quick peek to see if she knows him or not, but he can't be disturbed. He's still in critical condition, so we're going to keep a close eye on him for a while."

"That's fine, she'll have to be happy with that. I'll go and get her."

Dr. Sale quickly reached out to touch Detective Copeland's shoulder. "Before you go, the driver of the semi-truck said the patient told him 'They were all dead' before he passed out. I thought you might want to know that."

Copeland thought for a moment, and then nodded and continued down the hall to find Joan. When he got to the cafeteria, he asked the two officers to leave as he talked with the tiny, distraught lady. He sat down beside her while she looked up from her coffee, waiting for any ounce of information.

Detective Copeland put his hand on the woman's shoulder. "Now, Joan, the man is in critical condition, and is under constant watch right now. I was told he was talking and conscious when they found him, but he passed out very quickly afterwards."

Joan Mackenzie—a strong woman who'd been dealing with having a missing husband for as long as she had—kept her emotions in check until the detective finished talking.

"The man is unconscious, but not in a coma. He arrived pretty beat-up though, so he might be hard to recognize. They said you could go take a peek to see if you recognize him, but you can't disturb him."

Joan breathed in deep and asked, "Is that it, or do you have more good news for me?"

Detective Copeland sighed. "I just wanted to prepare you. I don't want to get your hopes up.

"Let's just go up and see if I know this person or not, then we'll go from there, shall we?"

He looked into Joan's eyes, admiring her composure. They got up from the table and headed upstairs to the recovery room, where the man lay unconscious. Copeland quietly opened the door so Joan could look in. Joan saw a doctor in the room standing next to the man, who was lying in the hospital bed with tubes in his mouth and wires connected all over him. Joan stared, wanting it to be Lorne, but she couldn't be quite sure. Joan poked her head in a little more and then saw a tuft of red hair peeking out of the man's bandages. She collapsed to her knees and put her hands in front of her mouth to stop the scream she was about to release. Detective Copeland quickly bent to help Joan back to her feet while Dr. Sale ran over.

Joan, in tears, got back up with help. She wiped her face and whispered, "I'm sorry, I'm sorry, but that's Lorne. He looks like shit, but that's Lorne."

Dr. Sale and Detective Copeland helped put Joan into a chair back out in the hallway. Joan looked up at Dr. Sale. "He looks horrible! Is he in pain?"

"Without the morphine, yes."

"What's all wrong with him?"

Dr. Sale looked at Joan's distraught face. "Do you really want to know right now? Do you think you're up for it?"

Joan wiped her tears away and looked at Dr. Sale. Her face changed suddenly from concern to irritation in a matter of seconds. "I can handle anything you have to say to me."

"I didn't mean anything by it, I just—"

Joan cut the doctor off, and in a calm voice replied, "No problem. I may look small, but I am not fragile, so just shoot it to me straight. I guarantee I can take it."

Dr. Sale was a little taken aback. Detective Copeland put his head down and hoped neither of them saw him smile.

Dr. Sale raised her eyebrows and said, "Detective Copeland said you were a strong woman. All right, first of all, Lorne has lost a lot of blood. We stopped the internal bleeding, and it was a bit of a mess in there. Then his head, nose, and jaw were fractured. His right eye is punctured. Not quite sure if he'll see out of it again. Then there's the dislocation of his shoulder. Those are the most recent injuries."

Joan's eyes widened—as did Detective Copeland's—when she said "recent."

Joan repeated, "Recent?"

Dr. Sale continued, "He had a broken leg, two cracked ribs, and many lacerations. I noticed during surgery that he seemed healed in some areas, and that he had had his leg set at some point. Someone was taking care of him." Dr. Sale watched Joan's reaction, wondering if she was, in fact, handling it.

Joan calmly took a deep breath in and then out. "Is that all that's wrong with him, or is that only the big stuff . . . or the small stuff?"

Dr. Sale realized Joan was a woman of her word. "The recent wounds seemed to be from an attack by a vicious animal. They seem to be less than a day old. His leg, ribs, and other lacerations are over two months old. Surprisingly, most of them are healing quite well." Dr. Sale paused, then said, "I do have to ask you before I go on; did your husband or any of his friends study old medicine or practice Native American healing techniques?"

Joan raised her eyebrows and gave Dr. Sale a strange look. "Besides listening to our friend's native grandfather tell stories, the only thing my husband and his friends studied out in the bush was how to drink, shoot the occasional animal, and party like their fathers and their father's fathers. Why?"

"Well, it's just that your husband has some wounds that . . ." Dr. Sale paused, and was not sure how to put it. Detective Copeland's ears perked up; he wanted to hear. Dr. Sale continued, "Lorne had a gash on his leg that was pretty deep, because his bone was broken and burst through. But it's been set and mended with unorthodox and old but effective medical methods. It was sewn up with a type of long grass, and we found moss, grain, and a plant mixture keeping the wounds from bleeding. This looked to be ancient Indian teachings, or what a medicine man would use to heal people back in the day. If it wasn't your husband or his friends doing it, who was it, and why didn't this person bring in your husband?"

Both Joan and the detective said nothing.

"I have no idea," said Joan as she scratched her head. "Whoever helped him and kept him alive has my sincere gratitude. He's breathing, and that's the only thing I care about right now. Now, what can you tell me about his coma?"

Dr. Sale smiled a little and answered, "That's the good news. He's just unconscious right now and sleeping, no coma. His body needs rest and recover. It will be slow and take a bit of time, but he will wake up."

"That's good," Detective Copeland said, "because we still need answers. That means that Walter Frisby is still out there, even if he's dead." Copeland quickly looked at Joan, as he realized he hadn't told her that part yet.

Dr. Sale saw the surprised look on both Copeland and Joan's faces. "You didn't tell her?"

"Not yet, it wasn't the right time."

Joan rolled her eyes and sighed. "Tell me what, people?"

Detective Copeland looked at her. "As I said before, he was talking, and then he passed out. Supposedly he said that 'everybody was dead,' or something to that effect. He was wounded and also had a major concussion,"

Dr. Sale interrupted and said to Joan, "It seems like Detective Copeland didn't think you could handle it at the time, but you proved us wrong on that already." She gave Joan a small smile and continued, "He's right, though, it's all hearsay right now, so your friend Walter could still be alive."

Joan leaned back in her chair and took a deep breath. "Okay. Thank you both for considering my feelings, and you're right, Walter could be alive, so the sooner Lorne wakes up, the sooner we can all get some answers. Is there any way I can go in and see Lorne?"

Dr. Sale saw the concern and determination in Joan's eyes. She also knew that as well as Joan was taking all of this, she was close to her breaking point. Dr. Sale decided to help her out. "Yes, of course. Just be as quiet as you can."

Joan jumped out of her chair and cautiously walked through the door and over to the bed. She did a double take to make sure it was really her husband. Joan watched Lorne slowly breathe in and out, fighting for his life. She gently touched and stroked his hand. Copeland came over and put a chair beside Lorne's bed. He tapped her on the shoulder to show her the chair. Joan smiled and sat down, and then whispered to Dr. Sale, "Are you sure you have no guesses or predictions on when he'll wake up?"

"All I can say is that he is heavily sedated and will not wake up until at least tomorrow, at the soonest. Otherwise your guess is as good as mine right now—I'm sorry."

"I'm going to apologize in advance, but you're going to have to deal with my stubbornness and bitchiness until he wakes up, because I'm not leaving his side until he does. I'll be quiet, but I will not leave."

Detective Copeland looked at both women. "Well, I'm going to have to leave and tell the press as little as possible, except that we did find one of the men and are still looking for the other. As soon as he wakes up, I need someone to call me—I mean it. Now, I've got to go, so take care." To Joan he said, "I'm glad you have your husband back."

Both Dr. Sale and Joan shook Detective Copeland's hand. He walked out and closed the door behind him.

Joan then shook Dr. Sale's hand. "Thank you for all you've done for him, and sorry for coming off like a bitch. I'm kind of out of my comfort zone—"

Dr. Sale cut Joan off. "Don't apologize. I'm guessing I'd be acting about the same if I were in your shoes. Us independent women have to stick together. There are not enough of us, it seems. I'll have one of the nurses bring some extra blankets and another pillow for you."

Joan smiled and nodded her appreciation, and then sat back in her chair and looked at Lorne.

As the door shut behind the doctor, Joan took Lorne's hand and placed it in between both of hers. She leaned over, kissed Lorne's lips, and whispered into his ear, "Glad to have you back, my love." Then she lowered her head on the side of the bed and cried softly by his side.

* * * * *

After she had left Joan, Dr. Sale noticed that Detective Copeland was still in the hallway.

"What's going on?" she asked him.

"I know you said he won't wake up until tomorrow, but I want to put a guard at this door and make sure that Lorne doesn't wake up and take off. Just in case. There's still a chance you've got a murderer in that room, and I don't need him taking off. I'm just waiting for one of my officers to take my place."

"I understand. What do you want me to do?"

Detective Copeland put his hand on her shoulder. "Just do whatever you have to do. Pretend we're not here. My officer, Dale Klotz, will let Joan go in and out as much as she wants, but that's it—besides your staff, of course. Make sure my officer knows who your staff are. If Joan asks, he's making sure the press doesn't bother them."

"I'll make a list of the staff and give it to him when he arrives."

"Thank you, and let's hope there are no troubles."

Dr. Sale walked away to do her rounds. Detective Copeland continued waiting for his replacement so that he could get on with the rest of his tasks.

In the hospital room, Joan tried to sleep, but she kept waking every fifteen minutes to see if Lorne had awoken yet. As she watched him sleep reasonably soundly—except for a few twitches now and then—she couldn't help but wonder where he had been, and what horrible things had happened to him during his disappearance.

However, Lorne's rest was far from peaceful. As he slept, his mind went back to what had happened during his hunting trip with his friends.

CHAPTER V

"So," asked Lorne, "Rock–paper–scissors for partners? Odd man out?"

"No," remarked Walter. "I think Lee should be allowed to play, also."

"Are you going to be that funny all day?" asked Lee.

"I'm not a fortune teller, but yeah, I'm pretty sure I will be."

"Well then, I want to go with someone else."

"I think you might have contracted 'Bitchitus' or something from your bed in the cabin."

Lorne snickered as the two bickered.

"Shut up, girls," Dan snapped. "It's too damn early to start this shit."

Walter looked at his watch. "It's just about 2:00 p.m. in the afternoon."

"Not the point," replied Dan. "The point *is* you all just lost your decision-making privileges, and we're burning daylight, so Walter, you're coming with me. Lee, you're going with Lorne."

Lorne looked at Dan with mock-hurt. "Why do I lose my decision-making privileges?"

"Casualties of war. You're right, though," said Dan, "you can pick which way you and Lee are going. Don't fuck it up."

"All right then, we'll take the north side, and you two can take the south," said Lorne. "We'll circle around and meet at the bluff and go from there."

"Done. Let's get going, then." Dan said.

"Everyone got their animal tags and walkie-talkies?" asked Walter.

The men double-checked their packs, and then set out.

*****

"So, why'd you pick me instead of Lee?" Walter asked Dan as they set off into the bush.

"Because he was acting like a bitch, and if you piss me off I'll just beat the shit out of you."

"All-righty then!" Walter nodded. "Let's start heading up that ridge, shall we?"

"Let's."

They walked about an hour before seeing any sign of game. Dan knelt to get a better look at a set of deer tracks in the dirt. "These are pretty fresh, man. Get out the deer spray. We'll go into stealth mode from now on."

Walter fished out the bottle and sprayed them both—and then proceeded to throw up.

Dan laughed. "I said be quiet. Are you going to be okay?"

Walter wiped off his mouth. "Yeah, the smell of that spray and the runny eggs didn't mix. I'll be fine. I'll just swallow it back next time."

Dan smirked. "Sounds like a good plan, then."

The two hunters walked quietly, making as little noise as possible while scouring the ground for more tracks. Walter nudged Dan and pointed. Dan looked ahead, then back at Walter and shook his head to show he didn't see anything. Walter signalled "sixty-five" and arched his hand up. Dan looked about sixty-five yards up ahead through the trees and saw the ass-end of a white-tailed deer.

"So, how do you want to do this?" whispered Dan. "Flank or straight through?"

"You have the deer tag, I have a bear tag, so we'll keep each other in sight and I'll circle around. Hopefully he sees me and comes toward you."

They crept toward the deer downwind, flanking it. Walter got about forty-five yards from the animal when he stopped and turned to stare at Dan. He raised his hands up to his head like antlers, and then put up all five fingers. Dan thought Walter looked like Bullwinkle. He gave him the middle finger and mouthed, "Bullshit." Walter shook his head to say, "No bullshit."

Suddenly, the five-point buck brought his head up. The two men froze; Walter still had his hands up like antlers. The buck was now on full alert, trying to figure out what he was sensing. Dan tried to put a shell into his rifle slowly. As soon as he cracked open the chamber, the buck jumped into the air and high-tailed it up over the ridge.

Dan shook his fist. "Aww, for fuck's sake!"

"That bastard was huge!" Walter yelled back at Dan. "We're not letting that sucker get away."

"I can't believe I let him take off like that. Any closer and I could've ridden him."

"Well, the good news is we have some daylight left, and those tracks are deep. We'll get him."

They set off following the tracks again, hoping to spot the beast.

* * * * *

It was 4:30 p.m. by the time the hunters found the tracks had slowed to a walking pace. Walter perked up and said, "Things are looking good, eh? There's still a chance we can find him before it gets dark."

"I don't care if it's midnight and we strap a flashlight on the end of my rifle," replied Dan, "I'm not leaving without that bastard."

"Well, let's hope that doesn't happen. It gets cold out here at night, and I'm not going to spoon with you."

"Pussy."

"I am what I eat," Walter grinned.

"Dickhead," Dan quickly replied.

They were still laughing when Dan noticed some deer droppings, and that the tracks were getting lighter but still visible. They cut through the bush. Dan gave out a sigh of relief. At the top of the hill was Dan's five-point deer standing tall and magnificent about seventy yards away. The sun was setting. A person couldn't paint a better picture.

Dan sighted up the majestic creature with his rifle and scope, slowly easing off the safety. He took a deep breath.

Kapow! A shot rang through the air and dropped the awesome beast to the ground. Dan yelled out in anger.

"No, no, no fucking way!"

"What's wrong?" Walter asked. "That was an awesome shot."

"That wasn't my shot!"

A hundred yards off to the left, Lorne and Lee hollered and jumped up and down. Walter and Dan ran out of the bush while Lorne started shuffling down to meet them. As he got closer, he thought Dan seemed angry, but there was no way Lorne could hide his smile.

"Did you see that shot, or what? Truly amazing! That fucker was a beast."

"Bullshit, bullshit, bullshit," Dan spat. "Me and Walter have been tracking that bastard for over an hour. That was mine, damn it!"

Lorne looked at Dan, and then at Walter. "Sucks to be you guys," he said. "We were up here having a beer thinking about giving up for the day, when Lee just about pissed himself when he saw that mammoth walk up the ridge. I'm just glad I had the deer tag."

Dan stood clenching his rifle, his face turning a deep red. He pointed it to the sky and pulled the trigger. Dan caught the discharged casing right out of the air, not even flinching when the heat hit his hand. He then slung his rifle over his shoulder. "Fuck it. There's always tomorrow. Good luck getting that back to the truck." Dan stomped off by himself.

Lorne hollered, "Aw, come on now, don't be that way. You're not going to stay and help?"

Dan kept walking. Lorne waved him off then turned towards his trophy buck with a smile from ear to ear.

"We didn't even know you guys were down there," Lee told Walter.

"We didn't see you guys, either," Walter replied. "Too busy hunting down this bastard."

"Well, I'd be pissed off too if it happened to me." Lorne stared at the buck. "But it didn't, and I'm still going to need help getting this to the truck. It's huge, in case no one noticed."

Walter and Lee each grabbed a rope out of their packsacks while Lorne took his knife from his belt and sliced the animal up the middle and took the guts out, tossing them to the side. The three men tied the deer and then dragged it like huskies pulling a dog sled towards the tree line.

* * * * *

Some time went by as the group trekked through the bush, trying to find the easiest way through. Keeping the antlers from catching every other tree and branch was time-consuming.

Lorne wiped his forehead and asked Walter, "Couldn't you guys have chased this thing closer to the truck instead of the other way?"

"Dan and me tried to negotiate with it, but you know how stubborn these things can be," replied Walter.

Lee looked up to see where the sun was. "How much longer to the truck? It's getting dark fast."

They stopped. Lorne stretched out his back and took a look around.

A voice came from the bushes. "It's about another hour at your pussies' pace." It was Dan. "Fifteen if we all do it."

Lorne smiled at Dan approaching them. "You decided to join in the festivities after all. Right on."

"Well, I figured I might as well stop bellyaching and come help, otherwise I'd be sitting at the truck by myself for another two hours, and that cuts into my drinking time. I also figured I'd have needed you guys to help if I'd shot the bastard."

Dan reached into his pack and tossed each man a beer. He cracked one for himself. "There's some Popeye-power for you. I have a couple more sitting in the cooler in the truck."

Drinking fast so they could get back at it, Dan, being fully rested, hooked himself up to the ropes and took the lead. As three pulled and on pushed, they soon spotted the silhouette of the crew-cab.

"There it is, Nancies," Dan said. "Pitter-patter, let's get at 'er. Put this cocksucker into the truck."

The four men grunted into high-gear, and they were about ten feet to the truck when one of the buck's antlers caught and dug into the ground. The carcass stopped dead, and all four men fell forward. The three in front piled onto each other.

"I guess the buck stops here, eh?" Walter said. "Is everyone okay?"

Lorne felt his leg. "My shin feels wet, so I'm either bleeding or you pissed on me."

"That better be a rifle digging into my hip," Dan piped, "or someone's going to get hurt."

"You flatter yourself too much," Lorne replied.

Walter looked back towards Lee. "Hey! What happened back there? I thought you were stabilizing this thing."

There was no answer from Lee.

"Hey numbnuts," Lorne yelled next. "You all right back there?"

"I'm fine," Lee answered in a monotone voice. "Let's just get this thing loaded and go back to camp."

"Did you get hurt, or what?" Dan asked.

"I'm fine, let's go."

"All right," Dan grunted. "Get off me, girls, I'm thirsty, god damn it."

They got organized. Lee dug the keys out of his pack and unlocked the truck, putting the headlights on as Dan opened the door, grabbed the cooler, and tossed a beer to Walter and then Lorne while assessing his wounds. He put the cold beer on his shin. Lee jumped in the back of the crew-cab and grabbed some tie-down straps.

Dan was about to toss Lee his beer when he stopped. "Hey Lee, you said you were all right, right?"

"Yeah, why?"

"No reason. I fell on some branches and grass, so I didn't get hurt. What happened to you?

"I fell onto the deer. I had a soft landing."

Dan started to smile. "Did you fall *on* it or *in* it?"

"Shit," Dan replied.

"Literally."

With the truck's lights on, Lee's friends could see he had deer shit all over his face. You definitely didn't want anything weird on your face—let alone deer shit—with this group.

The bantering began, and Walter couldn't let this opportunity slide by. "Hey, Lee, you're supposed to brown-nose to the guy who shot the deer, not the deer itself."

Lorne was next. "We already gutted the deer, we could have told you what his last meal was, you didn't have to look yourself."

"You fuckers," said Lee. "You think this is fucking funny?"

Everyone said at the same time, "Yeah, we do."

"Calm down," Dan said. "Catch this before it gets warm." He tossed the beer to Lee, who caught it while wiping the dung off with the sleeve of his shirt. Lee downed it and tossed the can onto the truck bed, crushing it with his foot.

"Is there another one?" he asked. "I still need one more to wash the taste out of my mouth!"

Dan started round two of the bantering. "You've had worse things in your mouth."

"Your mom doesn't count," Lee retaliated.

Dan squinted his eyes and replied, "That's strike one. You know mom jokes are off-limits, but you do deserve another beer." Dan got the beer and a rag. He threw them both to Lee, who caught the rag with one hand and, without skipping a beat, caught the beer in the other.

As everyone relaxed and stood together looking at their accomplishment, Dan quickly punched Lee in the leg and charley-horsed him. "That was for the mom joke."

Lee nodded and accepted the punishment, knowing Dan usually didn't give three strikes.

Dan then made a suggestion. "So, let's say we load up this cocksucker and get back to camp. I'm hungry and want some whiskey."

Lee nodded happily. "Now, that sounds like a plan to me."

It took about twenty minutes to load the whitetail, tarp it up, and organize their stuff.

"So," Walter asked, "who's drinking and who's driving?"

"Well, I think Lorne technically has dibs on drinking, being as how he's the only one who deserves to celebrate," Lee answered. "I also think I deserve to drink because I've been through a lot."

"And if he doesn't get what he wants," Dan quickly cut in, "he's going to bitch about it all night, so let's make this easy. Walter, drive back to camp."

Walter looked at them. "You all suck," he said while getting into the driver's seat.

They headed back. The moonlit night was quickly disturbed by the high-revving, *AC/DC*-blaring, fuel-guzzling pig on four wheels as it hauled ass down an old dirt road. The four men were singing "Thunder Struck" at the top of their lungs with the windows rolled down. No one would phone the cops for being too loud out here.

The crew-cab caught air on the bumpy road. When they got near the cabin, Lee looked at Walter to see if he was going to slow down, then turned to see Lorne looking just as nervous. Dan, on the other hand, took another sip of beer and calmly grabbed the "holy shit" handle.

Lee asked Walter, "How fast we going?"

"About fifty, fifty-five," Walter replied casually.

"That sounds a little fast," said Lee. "The cabin is just above the hill, you know."

"Yup," acknowledged Walter. "Hmm, you might want to hang onto something."

Lee and Lorne hung on to the back of the front seat. Dan didn't move. Barrelling up the driveway with a dust storm following behind them, Walter first rolled up his window and then slammed on the brakes, cranking the wheel to the left. All four tires started to skid and the truck turned sideways towards the cabin. It came to a stop in a swirl of dust. As the dust settled, Dan opened his door and stepped straight onto the cabin's front deck.

"You bastard," Lee said, smacking the hat off Walter's head and then pretending to choke him. "You scared the shit out of us that time."

"Calm down, Nancy, we're home, we're fine, and if you don't like the way I drive, stop making me drive and let someone else do it."

Walter got out of the truck, his hair dishevelled from the mock-beating, and followed Dan into the cabin. He threw his pack on top of his sleeping bag.

"Cut her a little close that time, eh?" Dan said while sliding his rifle under his bed.

"Maybe a little," Walter agreed. "Throttle stuck. Brakes are good, though." He passed Dan his rifle to also put under the bed.

"Scared yourself a bit, did ya?" Dan asked.

"Might've peed a bit on that one, bud."

Lee walked in, kicked his bed, and then tossed himself onto it.

"Well, I don't know about you guys, but I think we should fuck eating, go to sleep, and get an early start, because I want to rub my kill into Lorne's face when I get something tomorrow."

Lorne quickly replied, "Is that because you rubbed your face into my kill?"

"That's not what I meant, asshole," Lee snapped back.

Dan changed the subject. "Okay, everyone, it's cold enough outside. We can hang up Lorne's buck. In the morning we'll quarter it and fit it in the freezer, and then I'll agree to Lee's plan."

* * * * *

In forty-five minutes, they had the deer skinned and hanging in a tree out back.

"That should be high enough so the animals can't get it," Lee said, "but I have something else to keep the animals away."

While Lee ran to get something from the cabin, the others put the deerskin in a garbage bag and hung it in the tree along the buck. Lee came running back out of the cabin with his packsack. He pulled out some kind of a duct-taped contraption out of his pack.

"What the hell is that?" Lorne asked.

"Just wait. You'll say, 'That's the coolest thing I've ever seen in my entire life,' then I'll say, 'I know, because I made it.'" Lee began hanging a string of cans between two trees just below the deer's legs. Next he stretched a smaller string out about ten feet further to the base of another tree, where he attached a duct-taped box and a nine-volt battery.

"What the hell are you doing?" asked Lorne.

"I figured you'd all want a 'demo'-stration, so I made two. Everyone step back a notch or two. Dan, throw a rock at those cans."

Dan grabbed a round stone the size of a quarter and skipped it off the ground. The rock bounced and ticked one of the cans. The can jiggled and stayed quiet.

Walter waved his hands wildly in the air. "Ooooo, ahhhh! The magic!"

Lee rolled his eyes and told Dan, "It's not a mosquito deterrent, it's a fucking animal deterrent. It's for those pack rats and the raccoons, badgers, grizzlies or woolly mammoths. Fucking move those cans."

Dan picked up a coconut-sized rock and bowled it towards the cans. The rock blew the string of cans everywhere. Dan yelled "*Strike!*" As the cans went flying, the others realized the second string was actually a fuse. The fuse sparked and burned toward the duct-taped box. Seconds later, the box lit up and four roman candles shot up into the air, lighting up the night sky. The mini explosions lasted about ten seconds. A final screech came barrelling out and up into the air. There was a loud *bang* that echoed throughout their surroundings. The four hunters cheered.

"Holy shit," Walter said. "Right on!"

"That was the coolest thing I've ever seen," Lorne agreed.

"I know," Lee replied with a smile on his face. "I built it. Told ya!"

"You are now my new superhero," said Lorne.

"What the heck was that last one?" Dan asked Lee. "It was freaking loud, man."

"Three bear-bangers wired together with a Screecharoo wrapped in the middle. Go big or go home, right?"

"That should scare anything that comes near it," Lorne replied. "Hell, it might even wake up Walter."

"Probably not," Walter answered, "but with that bang, you've probably scared everything off already."

The men looked over at the buck dangling with the moon shining behind it, feeling proud of themselves. Walter, Lee, and Dan patted Lorne on the back for shooting such a great beast, and then they all grabbed a beer and headed to the porch. The beer and bullshit flowed until all four men passed out.

* * * * *

Chapter VI

In the hospital, Lorne was still drugged-up and unconscious in his bed. After playing through the events of the buck hunt, his mind returned to his memories of the cave with Walter.

*****

The sun was up. Lorne wiped at his eyes but felt a stabbing pain. His head was throbbing, but as he tried to touch the top of his head, his neck cracked. He winced in pain and slumped back into his bed of cedar. As he lay there, he could smell the aroma of cooking meat. His eyes adjusted to the light, and he focused on his leg; it was in a homemade splint. There was a ripped shirt used for a bandage around his waist.

With a little more energy, Lorne cautiously sat up in his cedar-branch bed and pulled himself into a half-sitting position. Lorne looked around and discovered he was in a cave. He looked out the cave entrance, but only saw endless blue sky. Lorne noticed two blurry figures crouched near a small fire in the corner of the cave. He tensed up, trying to figure out what was going on, when his memories started to flow back like a tidal wave. The massive headache, the pain in his body, and the smell of cooking meat distracted him from focusing on anything.

Lorne sat there, slowly rubbing his temples with his eyes closed when he heard Walter whisper, "How's the head?"

"About ten pounds too heavy."

"She walloped you pretty good. Not sure what you did to piss her off, but I don't think she hit me that hard when she fixed me up."

"I don't know what I did either, but I think the only thing that's stopping me from crying is the smell of food."

"Great, isn't it? If you can focus, watch those two by the fire." Lorne and Walter watched two of the hairy folk at the fire. One grabbed a strip of meat off the fire, and then it poked a stick through one side and needled it to the other end of the strip. The man proceeded to cook and rotate the meat over the flames.

Lorne whispered under his breath with amazement, "Well I'll be damned."

He heard Walter whisper back, "It's a meat-kabob, or buck-on-a-stick. All the good stuff on a shish kabob, but without the 'shish.'"

Lorne rubbed his eyes once more and replied, "They look so primitive and so much like bears, but then they shock you when their human side shows."

"Do you remember them now?"

"Not really. I remember our little conversation last night."

"That, my friend, was four days ago."

Lorne looked at Walter and repeated louder, "Four days!"

The two longhaired tribesmen turned around to stare, irritated. Walter put his finger to his mouth and shushed Lorne. The first tribesman made a weasel-like squeaking sound twice, then grunted and gestured to the other to get back to their task of slicing strips of meat off the deer carcass with a sharpened stone.

Walter gestured toward the tribesmen and whispered, "I call the one stripping the meat off the deer 'Sparrow,' and the other one 'Badger'— she's the girl that hit you and fixed you up. I think they're stocking up for winter." Lorne stared at Walter speechless while he continued, "That sort of 'bird tweet' you heard was Badger calling the other by name. It's like me calling out 'Lorne.' I heard Sparrow call Badger the similar way, but with a 'squeak' like a weasel a couple days ago." Walter looked at Lorne, who was staring at him with a blank look on his face. Walter paused for a moment, and then asked, "Hey, you awake?"

"Dude, right now I'm having a hard time getting past you *naming* these 'folks,' let alone that fact that we're even *seeing* this 'group.'"

"You've been in and out for a few days, and I've seen a lot more, and I've also remembered more since we last spoke that'll blow your socks off."

Lorne pointed at the couple by the fire. "More than this?"

Walter chuckled and then said, "Did I stutter?"

Lorne smiled and sighed while he lay back down, closing his eyes. "All right, what do you remember?"

"I remember us pulled over to the side of the road, trying to figure out where we were, when you went flying in the air like a rag doll— then all hell breaking loose. These huge, vicious-looking grizzly bears attacked everyone. I ran towards you to see how you were, and then Lee got thrown one way, and Dan was tossed the other way."

"Grizzly bears? How many?"

"Not sure, but more than two. They were huge, fast, and it seemed like they were running on pure rage. I remember Dan hitting the truck then there was lots of blood and a huge howl. The grizzly bears took off as fast as they had come, and then these folk showed up. Two of them walked towards you and me when I saw Lee point his rifle at one of them. He didn't realize they weren't the ones that had attacked us. I quickly jumped in front to stop him from shooting, but I wasn't fast enough to stop the bullet. That shit hurts!"

Lorne quickly opened his eyes and looked at Walter. "Lee shot you?"

"Not on purpose. I think that's why I can't feel my legs. Thinking about it now, it might have not been the best move, but it seemed like a good idea at the time." Walter looked at Sparrow and Badger and then said, "I faded in and out after that before waking up in this cave. I recall us two sailing through the trees with that group smelling like wet dog and ass. We ended up in this cave, sore but mended. I watched them patch you up, and although a little like Neanderthals, they did a good job. As good as any doctor could do back home. I've watched them bring in wildflowers and food for two days now, piling it all by that bunch of bear and wolf furs in the corner. If I had to guess, it would seem they're stocking up for winter."

Lorne stared at Walter, wondering if he could believe all this, but he thought it was likely the sad truth. Walter adjusted the bandage around his neck and coughed. Lorne was about to speak when Sparrow stood up and walked over to both of them. He looked at the two men and sneered, and then tossed two strips of cooked deer meat onto the floor. Badger grunted at Sparrow, who rolled his eyes and sighed as he turned around and headed back to the fire.

Walter frowned. "It does seem like she nags at him a fair bit, but I think if she didn't, he'd be happy to put us six feet under. Don't look at him wrong, he'd probably roast us over the fire along with the deer meat." Walter gritted his teeth in pain while shifting to get more comfortable.

The Clan

Then Lorne noticed that Walter was starting to bleed through the bandage at his waist. "Shit man, you're bleeding again."

Walter looked down casually. "Huh, that probably shouldn't happen, should it?" He unwrapped the bandage and peeled the blood-soaked homemade patch off his side. Badger took notice and started walking over. Lorne leaned over as though to block Badger, but Walter said, "Don't worry, man, this is the nice one. She's the doc out of the bunch."

Lorne gave Badger some room. She sat beside Walter with an old-looking wooden bowl in her hand that was filled with water and clean rags. She removed the blood-soaked rags. Walter helped Badger replace it with a clean wrap and some moss, along with some other substance that did not smell good. Lorne watched in awe. While she was bandaging up Walter, Badger looked over at Lorne. He thought he noticed her eyebrows raise in concern. He wondered why these people would even care if he and Walter lived or died, let alone try to keep them alive. Badger finished up with Walter's wound and then came over to address Lorne, who quickly put his hands up and waved her off.

"I'm fine, thanks! I got it."

Badger backed off and stared at Lorne for a moment, and then turned and headed back to the fire. She stopped mid-walk and sniffed the air, and then changed her direction and headed to the opening of the cave to sit down.

Lorne looked at Walter. "Dude, we have to get you to a hospital as soon as possible. Your wound looks like shit."

"I know it's not good, but I also know I'm not walking out of here anytime soon. There's a slight chance you might be able to carry me out, but that first step outside is a doozy."

"I've carried your weight before. We'll just sneak out when they fall asleep and climb down."

Walter laughed and pointed. "You have no idea how high up we are, do you? Take a good look outside."

Lorne looked toward the opening where Badger sat. He saw nothing but a blurry blue sky, and he thought he heard an eagle. "I guess we must be high up. I don't see any trees—I don't see that eagle, either."

Walter chuckled. "And you will probably never see that 'eagle.'"

Lorne looked back at Walter as the eagle sound got closer to the cave entrance. "You're going to tell me one of these hairy bastards sounds that good?"

"Nope. I don't have to."

Just then, the squawking stopped and a huge hand reached up and grabbed the bottom of the cave entrance. The other hand came up with an old pail. Badger took it away from the hand and carried it to the far end of the cave. The two hands at the opening of the cave brought up the rest of the hairy beast. Lorne's eyes widened as he noticed this one was bigger than either Sparrow or Badger.

"How many of these people are there?" Lorne whispered.

"I've seen four of them so far. Surprise, surprise, I call that one 'Eagle.' She seems to be the biggest one out of the bunch, but not the tallest. She's also not impressed with us here, so don't make eye contact. She got hurt in the chaos when they saved us."

"She must be the one you jumped into the bullet for," said Lorne. "Do you think it was still a good idea?"

Walter scratched his head and shrugged. "We're alive, so I'm about seventy percent sure. The fourth one I call 'Squirrel.' So far, he's the friendliest out of the batch. You've seen Badger and Sparrow. I believe there's one more that sounds like a bear, but I've never seen him or her, so I'm not quite sure."

Lorne rubbed his temples and scratched his head. "Hearing stories from Chief Gramps about the 'old ancient tribes' and thinking they were myths since we were kids—it's kind of blowing my mind to see them right in front of me."

"Just wait until your eyes clear up."

While Walter and Lorne were whispering to each other, Eagle walked over to Sparrow and put her hand on his shoulder. They both walked to the end of the cave where there were furs, a stack of flower petals, and a small pile of dirt. Badger had moved there, and they both sat next to her and the pail Eagle had brought up.

Walter and Lorne were watching the three in the corner wondering what was going on when they heard what sounded like a squirrel chattering up a storm outside. Both Lorne and Walter turned to see a tall, lanky, and more scraggly character jump into the cave from the entrance. The newest longhaired addition squeaked and chattered at an accelerated rate, rapidly waving his arms around like he was telling a story. *This must be Squirrel*, thought Lorne. Eagle looked over and let out a small but serious grunt. Squirrel put down his arms and stopped chattering. He bowed his head. A sad look came across his face, and he slowly walked toward the others. The foursome surrounded the furs and said nothing.

Right then, Walter and Lorne realized the pile of furs was covering two fallen tribe members. The whole tribe and the two men were silent for a few minutes. Badger went further into the back of the cave with her pail while Eagle and Sparrow picked up one of the dead. Squirrel walked to the fire and grabbed a burning stick and then carried it to Badger. He held it above her to light up the corner. Walter noticed more markings painted on the walls and saw a huge crack.

"I can't see," Lorne whispered. "It's too far to see."

"There are more markings and a big crack in the wall," Walter replied. Eagle and Sparrow lay one of the dead members on a mound of flowers and some dirt spread on a bearskin, and then walked back to retrieve the second. Walter and Lorne watched in shock as Badger grabbed the head of the deceased, snapped his neck, and then tucked it down into the front of his chest. Then she proceeded to break every other bone one-by-one, tucking all the limbs toward the chest.

When she had completed the barbaric process, she had made a three-by-three foot cube. She wrapped it up into the bearskin and tied it with a thin vine. Squirrel wedged the homemade torch into a small crevasse in the wall, and then helped Badger pick up the cube and put it to the side. Next, they lay another bearskin down and repeated the ritual with the other body.

Lorne and Walter remained speechless as they watched. When everything was completed, all four members bowed their heads for a moment, and then turned to the entrance of the cave. Together, they stood and raised their hands, then returned to sit down inside the cave—except for Eagle. She stayed at the cave entrance and raised her hands towards the sun, and then she started moaning in vacillating tones. Walter and Lorne looked at each other; it was like they'd heard those moans before. It reminded them of when Chief Gramps had chanted an old Indian prayer when his brother had died. The moans were eerie, but they were also a little comforting.

The sounds echoed through the cave. At the end, Eagle let out a loud and extended howl that put a chill down Lorne's spine. She then walked back to the mourning tribe and helped the others lift the compacted cubes and drop them into the huge crack in the cave wall. Squirrel took the pail and dumped half of the mixture down the crevasse. A kind of perfume fragrance filled the cave. Badger dropped some more dirt down the crack and topped it off with flower petals. Later, all four members of the tribe quietly continued with their regular daily duties.

Walter and Lorne said nothing for about an hour. Walter noticed that Lorne looked upset, but they remained silent until they saw Squirrel grunt at Sparrow while Badger redressed Eagle's wound on her shoulder.

"Holy shit," Lorne whispered to Walter. "Can you believe that just happened?"

"I can't believe these last few days. You look sad, buddy, what's wrong?"

"Listening to them chant and mourning their family just reminded me of how much I miss Joan and the kids."

"Don't worry, bud. You'll see them again, and just imagine how cool it's going to be to tell this story to them."

"You can find a silver lining in a pile of shit, can't you?"

Walter chuckled, "Yup—usually it's the cat's, and it's tinsel from the Christmas tree."

Lorne also laughed, which put him into better spirits. He then asked Walter, "How many of those guys do you think are down there in that crack of the cave?"

"I don't know, but if that's what they do with all their dead, that would explain why no one has ever found the remains of this group." Walter's eyes lit up. He was vibrating with excitement and continued, "If they hang out in caves so high up, that could explain why they aren't noticed all the time. When someone says, 'Look at that deer,' you don't look up, do you? Imagine walking through the woods and having one of them falling from the sky on you."

Lorne shuddered. "Flailing about all naked and hairy—yikes."

Both started to chuckle, but they became silent again just as quick; now wasn't the time to have a smile on their faces. The two men watched Badger put berries and some kind of plants in a small pile as Squirrel and Sparrow piled cedar branches, moss, and other soft materials onto five individual beds. Walter and Lorne had a good feeling there was at least one more in their group running around.

"I'm going to guess that the missing one is the one who you think sounds like a bear," Lorne said to Walter.

"I'm just thinking—these ones we are seeing are pretty big, but they all sound like little animals. So does that mean the one that sounds like a big animal is really small, or bigger than these ones?"

Lorne cringed. "Let's hope it's smaller, because if they need more room in this cave, we'll be the first to go."

* * * * *

The next morning was misty. Lorne woke up with a little more colour in his face. He moved around to get a sense of his wounded body.

Badger was working on Walter again. It looked as though whatever colour Lorne had gained, Walter had lost. His friend looked like a ghost. Lorne knew Walter had to get to a hospital or he was going to die. He wanted to jump up and get Walter and him out of there, but he knew damn well he couldn't. Lorne just watched, helpless. He looked around and saw Badger and Squirrel were the only two tribe members in the cave.

Walter looked at Lorne. "Dude, it looks like you lost your best friend."

Lorne didn't laugh.

"Oh, come on, that was funny," Walter said. "I'm not dead yet."

"You're going to be, if you don't get to a hospital." Walter waved his hands in the air.

"Then let's go. I'll get my coat, and we'll jump out of this cave and run to safety. I figure we might as well try escaping, and if we die at least we died for no good reason."

The Clan

"If you didn't say that so sarcastically, I'd say that was a great idea. Better than dying here, slowly."

Walter sighed. "I know you miss your family and hate waiting here—I do too, but adjust your eyes and take a real good look."

Lorne also sighed, because he knew he couldn't see within ten feet.

"I know your vision blows right now," Walter said, "so I'll tell you what you can't see. Into the shadows of the nooks and crannies of this cave, with the light reflecting around by the sun, you'd notice deeper and darker crevasses around. You then would see a couple drop-offs near where we're lying." Walter saw the frustration in Lorne's eyes, but continued. "There's more fucking levels and deathtraps in here than the Bat Cave. We'd be dead in two steps if we didn't know where to walk. We're not healthy enough to go anywhere. The good news is *you* are getting better, so at least one of us might get out of here alive."

Lorne gave Walter a stern look. "You mean 'we,'" he corrected. "I haven't given up on you, so don't give up on yourself, either."

Walter rolled his eyes. "All right, whatever you say. How're you doing, anyhow?"

"Overall, I can move everything a little better. The arm and my waist are still pretty sore, but definitely better than a few days ago. My leg feels all right, too. How about you?"

Walter shrugged. "Besides feeling tired and sore, it could be worse. The good news is my legs feel great. I can't feel them at all."

"You're an asshole." Lorne shook his head and both chuckled slightly as they heard Squirrel began talking in grunts to Badger, getting louder and louder. The two men stopped chatting and listened, trying to decipher the tribe's language. Squirrel was the easiest to understand, even though he grunted and rambled quickly, because he used his hands to gesture a lot.

Lorne and Walter began taking notes of the grunts and gestures that made sense to them. "*Mat*" meant "meat," "eat," or "food" of some sort. "*Utan*" meant "outside," or "sky" or "sun."

While they listened, Squirrel rambled on and then stopped with a guilty look on his face.

Badger stood up and waved her hand in front of her face, shouting "*Tu Puti!*" Squirrel started to laugh out loud. Walter and Lorne looked at each other, and then started to smell a rancid odour. They, too, started to laugh, gagging a little.

"Uh!" Lorne said. "'*Tu Puti*' must mean, 'You stink or smell like shit.'"

Squirrel stopped laughing. He and Badger stared at Lorne and Walter, who also stopped laughing, and stared back. Squirrel and Badger slowly walked up to the two guys. Walter and Lorne winced.

Squirrel stared directly at Lorne, and then repeated the words again, but as more of a question. "*Tu Puti?*"

Lorne, not quite knowing what to do, repeated, "*Tu Puti.*"

Squirrel started jumping back and forth in front of Badger, repeating the words over and over. Badger tried to settle the seven-foot-ten hairball down as Lorne and Walter sat motionless.

"What did we just say?" Lorne whispered out the side of his mouth. "Were we wrong on the translation?"

"What do you mean 'We,' white man?" Walter whispered back. "*You* said it."

Badger calmed Squirrel down a notch or two, then looked over at the two men and started talking in her language. Lorne and Walter were lost right off the bat. Badger noticed and her words died off.

Walter looked up at Badger. "Sorry, Badger, but we only know some of the words, not all of them." Then Walter looked at Lorne and pointed at a stick on the cave floor. "Hey, Lorne, grab that stick and draw some shit in the dirt on the floor."

"Who do you think I am?" asked Lorne. " Leonardo da Vinci or Mr. Dressup? I can't draw. All my pictures look like a stickman fucking a sawhorse. You're the artist."

"Then give me the stick, and you tell Badger what it is. Hopefully we can figure some shit out."

Lorne handed Walter the stick and was about to draw something, but stopped. "What am I going to draw?"

Badger and Squirrel looked at the two men, waiting.

"Draw a stinky guy, and I will say '*Tu Puti*' again."

"How do I draw a stinky guy and make the odour the point?"

"Fine. Draw outside, and I will say '*Utan*.'"

"How do I draw 'outside' in one picture?"

Lorne threw his hands in the air. "Draw a sun!"

"What if '*Utan*' means cloud or star or air?" Walter asked. "How is that going to help?"

"Look," Lorne snapped, noticing Badger and Squirrel were getting restless. "Draw a bunch of things, and we'll point at them and say '*Utan*' as a question."

"Calm down, Nancy. It's going to be like playing Pictionary with your parents," said Walter.

Badger heard the word '*Utan*' multiple times, so she repeated it and pointed outside the cave. Lorne noticed and shoved Walter's arm. "Start drawing something!"

"All right, all right, keep your panties on."

Walter drew a sun, cloud, stars, and a moon. Lorne looked up at Badger and pointed to the star. "*Utan*?"

Squirrel stood behind Badger hunched over her shoulder. Badger shook her head. Squirrel started to hop up and down and pointed at Walter's sun drawing. Badger took the stick from Walter and pointed at the sun, and then said, "*Sol*."

Walter and Lorne repeated the word, "*Sol*." Badger nodded in agreement.

Lorne pointed at the drawing, and then at himself, saying, "Sun." He pointed at Badger again and said, "*Sol*." Lorne pointed at the drawing three more times to see that Badger understood, but she didn't repeat the word.

Finally, Squirrel shouted, "Sun!" Both Walter and Lorne smiled and started clapping, but it was short-lived. Badger glared at Squirrel and gave him a stern grunt as though she were a mother who'd just heard her son curse for the first time.

Walter was confused. "What just happened there?" he said to Lorne. "I thought we were connecting."

"Me too," said Lorne.

Badger pointed at the moon drawing and said the word, "*Luna*." Lorne and Walter's eyes lit up.

Walter also pointed at the drawing. "We know that one: Luna. Moon!"

Badger pointed one more time and repeated "*Luna*" in a teaching tone.

Lorne and Walter repeated the word again. Badger stood tall and proud with the fact they were doing it her way. Squirrel, on the hand, was again dancing around behind her. Lorne was wondering where the carnival music was.

Walter said, "Well, it looks like we're the ones who are going to learn their language, not vice versa."

"As it should be," said Lorne. "We are on their turf. When in Rome—"

Walter smacked Lorne on the side of his arm, not realizing he had hit him on his sore side. As Lorne winced, Walter said, "You're right! 'Luna' is Roman or Greek, isn't it?"

Right then, the light coming through the cave entrance suddenly became obscured. Lorne and Walter watched as two arms hauled up a massive upper body. The silhouette blocked most of the entrance. The men's mouths dropped open as they registered the dark figure of a man hunched over so as not to bump his head on the roof of the cave. As he moved towards the other two members of the tribe, the cave filled with light again. Walter and Lorne squinted. The mammoth of a man walked over to Squirrel and ruffled his head, then caressed the top of Badger's head. He sat down and gave a couple grunts. Squirrel ran over and helped take off the bearskin the big man was wearing.

As Squirrel helped, he spoke up loudly, pointing outside and then at Walter and Lorne.

"*Sol! Sol! Lor tala Sol!*"

The man looked towards Lorne and Walter, disgusted.

Squirrel continued, "*Lor tala Sol, Mig tala Sun.*"

As Squirrel said the word "sun," the huge beast looked at Squirrel and let out a quick snap-roar. Squirrel cowered and then slunk away into the corner of the cave. The large man calmed as quickly as he'd gotten angry. His face showed some regret for shouting, and he finished taking off his fur coat, sat in his spot, and looked outside.

Walter whispered quietly to Lorne, "I'm going to guess that one doesn't like English, either."

"You think?" replied Lorne. "I'm also going to assume that one is also called 'Bear' or 'Grizzly' or 'Short Fuse.'"

"Let's call him Bear, and let's not talk to him, either."

Lorne quickly nodded.

"What language did that remind you of?" asked Walter.

"Besides Latin? A little like the Egyptian language when watching *The Mummy.*"

"I was talking about Chief Gramps, but now that you mention it, it does sound a little Egyptian-ish."

"I wonder why these guys don't like English?" asked Lorne.

"They likely got tired of the English trying to find and conquer them."

"Sometimes I wonder why people can't leave well enough alone."

"Real estate. Why should others be happy living the way they want if we can't be?"

"Possibly," agreed Lorne. "I wonder if there are more tribes of this sort anywhere else, or if this is one of the last that has accumulated their learning and combined the different languages together to make their own?"

"There are a lot of different languages and cultures kicking around, so you never know," said Walter.

They sat back quietly and watched as Squirrel and Badger took turns filling sacks full of rations and animal traps made from vines, tree bark, and weeds woven together to make rope, snares, baskets, and small nets. For the food rations they used the skin hide of a bear, wolf, or rabbit and wrapped dried fruit, meat, and bark and tied them up with the vine ropes. Those were tossed into the back of the cave to keep cool.

Suddenly, Sparrow popped up into the cave with three dead rabbits and one dead fox. He dropped them by the fire pit. Squirrel and Badger stopped what they were doing and started cleaning the animals while Sparrow made a fire. Each had a task, which they accomplished efficiently. Bear lounged in his bed of cedar, drifting in and out of sleep.

CHAPTER VII

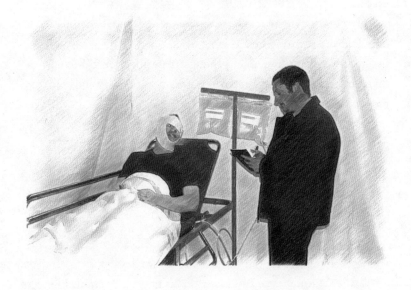

Five days had passed since Lorne had been brought into the hospital. He'd been moved into a private hospital room with two single beds moved together so that Joan could stay overnight. Detective Copeland's agent stood guard outside Lorne's room.

As Joan woke next to Lorne, she stretched her arms and looked over to see Lorne watching her. Joan's eyes widened. She was about to scream when Lorne leaned over and quickly covered her mouth. He winced at the pain of his movement. Joan settled down. Lorne slowly took his hand away from her face and eased his arm back to his side and then moaned, lying on his back once more.

"Oh my god!" Joan whispered. "How long have you been awake?"

Lorne shook his head. "I don't know—about half an hour, maybe?"

Joan scowled and lightly smacked Lorne on the arm, her whispers getting louder by the word. "You've been awake for half an hour and didn't wake me? I haven't seen you in three months and prayed you weren't dead, then some truck driver finds you just about dead in a ditch and in a coma, and then I was wondering when—or *if*—you'd ever wake up."

Lorne quickly interrupted before she got any louder. "Settle down, hon. I woke up, realized I was in a hospital, and then I saw you lying beside me looking so perfect I thought I was dreaming. Seeing you there so peaceful—I just wanted to watch my angel sleep and hold this moment for a while."

Joan sighed and then looked into Lorne's eyes. "That was pretty good. How long did it take you to come up with that hogwash?"

"I meant every word of it. Oh, and by the way—ouch. You shouldn't hit a wounded man like that."

They began to chuckle, but then Lorne stopped abruptly and asked, shocked, "I've been in a coma for three months?"

"No, no. You've only technically been 'asleep' for a few days, but you've been missing for thirteen weeks and two days."

"Really?" Lorne started counting on his fingers. "It seemed longer than that. Damn it! My hunting season is over."

Joan scowled again. "Really? That's what's going on in that mind of yours?"

Lorne shrugged with a grin. "I'm kidding. How are you and the kids?"

"Frightened, excited, and happy you're alive. It seemed longer to us, too," said Joan. "I'm so glad you're awake now." Joan stroked his arm. "So what does, '*Draga anda gott moarte*' mean?" she asked.

Lorne looked at Joan oddly. "I don't know, 'Your dragon named Andy needs milk?'" he chuckled. "Why, what is it?"

"That's what you kept repeating while you were sleeping."

Lorne's face turned from content to sad and his complexion paled. "Sounds like a mouthful of marbles to me." He turned his head away from Joan.

"What's the matter?" She put her hand on his shoulder. "Are you in pain again?"

"Just feeling woozy. I could probably go back to sleep again for a little while."

Joan jumped up suddenly, remembering something. "I'll go get the doctor."

Lorne grabbed her hand. "No. Please just lay here with me for a bit. Please?"

Joan felt worried, but she snuggled up, put her arm gently over Lorne's chest, and hugged him carefully. "Of course," she soothed. "I'm not going anywhere. You just go back to sleep and we'll talk to Dr. Sale later. It'll be okay now."

Lorne lifted his arm, wincing, put it around Joan's shoulders, and then brought her hand to his lips and kissed it. Lorne drifted off to sleep as Joan stared at the ceiling, knowing Lorne was hiding something. She was happy Lorne was conscious, but she feared what might come up now that he was able to answer questions. She waited ten minutes while Lorne slept, and then quietly crept out of bed and retrieved Dr. Sale.

* * * * *

Sometime later, Lorne woke groggy but in considerably less pain. He blinked, trying to focus, and discovered Joan and Dr. Sale standing near him. He flinched and then groaned.

"Morning," Dr. Sale smiled. "I'm glad to see you're awake. Sorry to startle you there."

"No problem. How long have I been out for?"

"You've been in and out of consciousness for about four hours now. Do you know your name?"

Lorne looked at her like she was an idiot. "My name is Lorne Robert Mackenzie. That," he gestured toward Joan, "is my beautiful wife, Joan. I have two great kids who I can't wait to see. Also, two plus two is four and once, in grade five, I cheated on a spelling test."

Dr. Sale cocked an eyebrow and replied, "Is that the morphine kicking in, or are you always this spirited?"

"I was born and raised a smart-ass, Doc. It keeps me alert."

"I'll bet. But for shits and giggles, let's see how your short-term memory is, shall we? What's the last thing you remember before you woke up in the hospital?"

Lorne stopped smiling. His face clouded over with darkness. "I remember one night I wish I could forget." Lorne took Joan's hand. "All the guys are dead, Joan."

Joan nodded, relieved he already knew this fact, and replied, "They found Dan and Lee, but Walter is still missing. Are you sure they're *all* dead?"

"Yes. Walter died in my arms." Lorne bent his head toward his chest with grief while Joan joined in his sadness.

"Do you know where his body is?" Dr. Sale asked Lorne, gently.

Lorne thought about it. "No, I don't remember anything after that. What does that mean, doc?"

"Maybe something, maybe nothing. It does mean we have to do some more tests, but you seem to be recovering well," said Dr. Sale. "You're a very lucky man. You just take it easy, and I'll be back later. Also, I was told to call the police once you were awake."

Lorne nodded his head. "That sounds about right. Do what you got to do, doc. I'm not going anywhere fast."

Dr. Sale smiled, and then left the room. She stopped outside and talked to the officer outside the door. "Joan can come and go as she pleases, but make sure Lorne stays in that room until Detective Copeland or I come back."

* * * * *

Two hours after Dr. Sale called Detective Copeland, he entered through the hospital's front doors to find her.

"Sorry I took so long," he said. "I missed the ferry by two minutes. How's it going, anyway?"

"Good, good. How are things with you?"

"Much better now that 'the' sleepy patient is awake. Hopefully I can get some answers to help close this case."

Dr. Sale replied cautiously, "I hope so, too, but I'm not sure you'll get all the answers you're looking for."

"Why is that?"

"Lorne says he can't remember a lot."

Detective Copeland crossed his arms. "Playing the memory-loss card already?"

Dr. Sale lifted her shoulders. "I still have to run some tests, but I'd like you to ask him some questions anyhow. See if they'll jog his memory."

"That I am happy to do," Detective Copeland smiled. "Let's go see if we can get him remembering again."

They walked to Lorne's room where the officer was sitting in his chair, looking at a crossword puzzle he had been working on for two days now. He saw Dr. Sale and Detective Copeland walking towards him, so he got up from his chair and shook Copeland's hand.

"Hey, Dale," said the detective. "Has anyone come in or out of Mr. Mackenzie's room since I've been called?"

"Just one of the nurses," replied the officer. "She went in and changed his IV about an hour ago. Joan left about half an hour ago, but she came back later with a brown paper bag smelling like a burger and onion rings."

"Thanks, Dale, we can take it from here," said Detective Copeland.

"Great, the smell of that food made me hungry. I'm going to get something to eat." The officer left.

Dr. Sale knocked on the door and walked in with the detective on her heels. They saw Lorne sitting up with a mouthful of cheeseburger and a smile.

Dr. Sale looked at Lorne. "Already sick of our food, Mr. Mackenzie? You just woke up."

"No offence, doc," he answered without swallowing, "but I needed to taste something good, not just feel the food going in."

Detective Copeland looked at Lorne. "I'm glad you're awake, Mr. Mackenzie."

"Me, too. Who are you?"

Joan smiled and did the introduction. "This is Detective Copeland. He has been helping the police find you. He also helped me through the clusterfuck of press and commotion to get to you the other day."

Copeland shook Lorne's hand. "I'm *also* the one who was put in charge of you and Walter Frisby's case. I'd really like to ask some important questions and be able to close it, if you don't mind."

"Where's James?" Lorne asked.

"He's off the case now. I've taken his place."

Lorne lay back in his bed, crossing his arms. He wore a stern look.

"Oh, I see. Well, fill your boots, man. I'll tell you all I can remember, but let me ask a question first."

Detective Copeland saw a change in Lorne's face, but wasn't sure why. "Shoot," he said.

Lorne looked at Dr. Sale. "This one's for the doc. I tried asking my wife earlier, but she became too upset. So, how long was I out for?"

"You came in unconscious and have been out for just about five days."

"And how did I get here? To the hospital, not earth. I figured that one out when I was about eight years old."

Dr. Sale cocked an eyebrow at him, smiling, and then answered, "A logging truck driver found you on this side of the ferry on Coursier Road. He dropped you off here as fast as he could."

"I'll have to thank him, but that's kind of weird, because we were camping on our side of the river."

Detective Copeland jumped in. "As soon as we were told you were found, we put a search team on this side. How do you feel, by the way?"

The Clan

"Like that truck driver ran me over. Looking at me, are you sure he didn't?"

Dr. Sale smiled. "I asked the driver the same thing, but we're sure the one who brought you in didn't hit you. Most of your wounds are now at least ten days old."

Lorne looked at Detective Copeland. "I guess you're up, Dick Copeland. Ask away."

The detective gave Lorne a look, but stayed professional. "You can call me Detective, or Copeland, or even Cope if you like. The first question I have to ask is do you know for sure your friend Walter Frisby is dead?"

Lorne swallowed the rest of the burger around the sudden lump in his throat. "He is definitely dead. He died in my arms."

"In that case, I've got to report that to the search party leaders. I'm truly sorry for your loss. I'll be back as soon as I can, and we can carry on with this conversation."

"Sure thing. I'll count down the minutes, Dick."

Joan lightly elbowed Lorne in the ribs. Lorne gave her a ticked-off look, but he knew she had held back, so he retracted it just as fast. Detective Copeland pretended not to hear the snide comment and proceeded to walk outside and make the phone call.

Joan gave Lorne a dirty look. "Why are you being so rude to him?"

"Oh, am I upsetting you and your boyfriend?" Lorne asked sarcastically.

"Lorne Robert Mackenzie," Joan cried. "Don't be an asshole!"

Dr. Sale turned her head towards the window and tried not to laugh.

Lorne hung his head. "Sorry, Joan, it's just I know what question he wants to ask, and I won't be able to give him the answer he wants because I can't remember it."

Joan looked at him, knowing that wasn't the reason and wasn't sure what the real reason was, but she played along. "I'll be with you all the way," Joan soothed. "Whatever he asks, just be honest. He'll have to take it or leave it. But be nice about it. He's not like all the other stiffs; he's a nice guy."

"That's probably because he wants to get into your panties," Lorne grinned.

Joan raised her arm, pretending to smack him again. "Lorne!"

"All right," he said. "I'll do my best, but I can't guarantee anything."

"That's all I ask. Now, I have to go and phone Mom and see how the kids are doing." Joan kissed him and then left the room.

Dr. Sale said to Lorne, "I didn't say it earlier, but I'm sorry also for your loss, and that you had to see your friend die."

He looked at Dr. Sale. "What's worse is that I'm going to have to tell his sister. She'll be devastated when she finds out. They were more than family—they were each other's best friend, as well. Their parents split up when they were kids, so she ended up taking care of herself and Walter ever since."

"What about Walter's wife?" asked Dr. Sale.

"He never married. He was the last single guy in our group. That's why we went on this trip. It was going to be our last one, because we were all getting busy in our personal lives. Fucking weird how right we were."

"I'm so sorry to hear that, also."

Lorne sighed, "I'm sorry, too. Walter gave the shirt off his back whenever he could and rarely asked for anything in return. I'm going to miss him a lot."

Dr. Sale's phone started to vibrate. "Excuse me for a moment," she said. "This might be about your test results." She started reading her phone, pacing the floor. "Well, I can give you some good news at least. Your heart rate is back to normal, and your brain scan shows normal, as well. You seem to be recovering quite well. You can stay here for a couple more days and we can monitor you being miserable, *or* if you promise to take it easy and can hold down that solid food your wife brought in, you could go home sooner. Only if detective Copeland's allows it, of course."

Lorne's face lit up. "I'll hold the food in and if it comes back up, I'll chew it again and swallow if it means I get to go home"

"That's gross," Dr. Sale said as she made a face. "I'd prefer you didn't have to do that. I'll come back in a couple hours to see how you're doing."

She left Lorne by himself, and as soon as the door closed behind her, he started packing up whatever he could reach around the bed in order to expedite his escape. Detective Copeland came back into the room and saw Lorne attempting to pull the shirt Joan brought for him over his bandages.

"Going somewhere?" he asked.

Lorne looked up. He had one arm in his shirt and mustard on his face.

"Home, just as soon as the doc says I can."

"And as soon as I say, also."

"Of course! Just a little anxious, that's all, Cope—I mean, Copeland."

"Cope is fine. I like it a lot better than 'Dick.'" Detective Copeland smiled slightly, then continued, "Well, until you get the say-so from Dr. Sale, I have some more questions."

"Fire away."

The detective looked around. "Where's Joan?"

"Making a call to the family, why?"

"There are some questions I want to ask that you might not want to answer in front of her."

"Whatever you ask, I'm going to tell her, anyway," Lorne replied with attitude. "But go ahead."

Detective Copeland took out his writing pad, flicked over a couple of pages, and then asked, "What do you know about your other friends?"

"I know they're dead, if that's what you're asking."

"Yes, and do you know how they died?"

"They stopped breathing."

The detective gave Lorne a stern look.

Lorne replied again, "Very brutally, actually."

"So, you remember the attack?"

"Just random visions I wish I could forget."

"How many attacked you?"

Lorne looked at the detective with a disturbed look.

"How many of what?"

"Grizzly bears."

Lorne shook his head as he answered. "No fucking clue! I just remember lots of chaos and my friends screaming and bleeding. Then Walter and me trying to keep alive until one or both of us could move and get help. As you can tell, it didn't quite happen that way."

"Do you remember where you walked or crawled from?"

"Hell no," Lorne snapped.

"Do you remember where you left Walter?"

"In the bush."

Copeland rubbed his face.

"Can you tell me *anything else* from the time you left the cabin until now that could be helpful in any way?"

Lorne looked around, and then pointed. "Looking at the date on that calendar on the wall, I remember missing a dentist's appointment. Does that help you?"

Detective Copeland took a deep breath. "I'm going to disregard the sarcasm and hostility I'm getting and say it's because you're still disoriented and tired. "We'll have time to continue this conversation when I come back in here in a few days, after I've given you a chance to readjust your attitude."

Lorne puffed out a deep breath. "A few days! I'm supposed to go home, like, soon!"

"Only if I give the go-ahead." Copeland paused then continued, "Hospitality is wearing thin on both sides here. James was right when he described you to me. He told me you could be stubborn and difficult."

Lorne sat back and asked him, "I was wondering about that. Did you bastards enjoy waltzing in and taking away my friend's job?"

"Someone tell you what happened?"

"I'm shaken up and can't remember some shit, but I'm not fucking stupid. As soon as you said you took over this case, I figured you big-city cocksuckers came in, flaunted your muscles, and must have fired him. I watch movies all the time."

Copeland shook his head, smirked, and then sighed. "Those cop shows are going to be the death of me. Is that why you've been so polite and hospitable to me?"

Lorne paused, then calmed down and lowered his voice. "Maybe."

"Well, first of all, I didn't fire James; my superiors did that. James has been suspended and can't help with the case, so that's why he isn't here—and also, he's been spending all his time trying to find you guys. That's who I phoned when I left you."

Lorne felt a twinge of guilt for being short with the detective. Lorne was about to apologize when Copeland said, "Go home as soon as the doctor says you can. See your family and friends, get some actual rest, and call me when you remember anything—*anything*—of interest to me."

Lorne nodded and reached out, shaking the detective's hand.

Detective Copeland left, closing the door behind him. He headed down the hall and found Dr. Sale.

"So, did you get any answers?" she asked.

"Not really. Getting a straight answer from that guy is like trying to milk a bull. Wonder how Joan gets answers from him."

A voice came from behind them. "You just gotta be too stubborn to quit milking," Joan said.

Detective Copeland quickly apologized. "Sorry about the comment, Joan. Questioning your husband didn't go as planned. Maybe it's because he's still tired and wounded."

Joan shrugged. "Don't be sorry, he's always been that way when put into an uncomfortable situation. You should've been at our wedding. What a disaster that was. Once he starts acting that way, you're not going to get anything from him no matter what you threaten him with. Even no sex for a week."

"Well, I won't threaten him with that—he's not my type. But do get him to call me when he feels better, all right? I would like to close this case as soon as possible."

"I'll have a talk with him and make sure he calls you sooner than later," Joan promised.

"Thank you, and good to see you again. Take your husband home." He turned to Dr. Sale. "Nice meeting you, Dr. Sale. I should be off. Still a lot of paper work to do." Detective Copeland shook hands with the ladies and then headed out the hospital's front doors.

Joan turned to the doctor. "So, Lorne can go home?"

"I'd prefer he stays longer, but he seems like a man that would just sneak out as soon as our backs were turned. What he needs is rest, and he can do that at home. Let's keep him here for one more night, and you can leave in the morning if you promise he'll rest and take it easy."

"I'll make sure he keeps off his feet."

"I mentioned he might be able to go home early, so he's probably half-dressed by now and waiting by the door for you."

"That sounds like Lorne."

"Do you want to give him the news, or shall I?"

"I'll tell him," Joan smiled. "Thanks for everything—for putting up with me and my husband."

"I'm just happy you have your family back. I'll check in on him in the morning."

Joan hugged Dr. Sale and then hurried off to Lorne's room. She found him with his shirt half-buttoned, his jacket over one shoulder, and his shoes on but untied. She smiled and then coughed to get his attention.

Lorne still had a smear of mustard on his cheek. "Did you talk to the doc yet?" he asked. "Can we go?"

Joan stared at him with a look she would give a puppy who'd just pissed on the floor. "I was told you were being difficult with Detective Copeland."

"Fucking narc."

"Lorne," Joan scolded.

"Sorry, hon, but I didn't like the questions. I didn't want to talk. I don't like this place, I just want to go home."

Joan nodded. "I know, I know. Sale shaved a couple days off and said I can take you home, but you have to stay here one more night. You also have to be good and listen to me all the time."

"God damn it!" said Lorne.

Joan raised her eyebrow. She walked to the bed where Lorne was now sitting, visibly deflated over the fact he wasn't leaving quite yet. She knelt down and took off his shoes for him. Lorne hung his head, disappointed. He took his jacket off, but kept his unbuttoned shirt on.

"Well, at least I get to play with the morphine drip one more time," he said.

"Way to look on the bright side of things. We'll still pack everything up, and as soon as morning hits, we can get the hell out of here."

"Can I stay dressed?"

Joan rolled her eyes.

"Whatever. I'll have to use the phone in the hall and call my mother once more and tell her we're staying one more night."

"Cell phone still broken? You had months to get it fixed."

"I kind of had some more important things fall on my plate."

"Cell phones are a waste of time, anyhow..."

Joan rolled her eyes, as she had had this conversation before with him. Lorne knew the look too well and just said, "Tell her to kiss the kids for me."

"I will. I can't wait for them to see you again."

"I can't wait to see them again."

Joan got up from kneeling and kissed Lorne. She left the room to use the phone.

Lorne sighed in pain and boredom—more boredom. He looked around his room and watched the morphine drip slowly down from the bag. He started flicking the bag, wondering if that would make it drip faster. As the morphine dripped at the same speed, Lorne lay down and drifted back to sleep. Prompted by the questioning Detective Copeland had given him, Lorne's mind returned again to his time with Walter in their temporary home.

* * * * *

Three weeks had gone by since Lorne and Walter had been "guests" in the cave on the mountain—although that was a guess, as they had no real way to tell time.

Lorne's eyes were adjusting; he was starting to see everything a lot more clearly. He was also getting better, enough so that he could walk around a little. With his little walks, Lorne noticed more writings and carvings on the wall.

One day, something caught his eye. At a certain time of day in the right light, Lorne noticed one of the cave's crevasses was actually a step, not just a drop-off. Lorne slowly walked back and sat beside Walter, who now just lay in his bed and wrote into the dirt to communicate, because he couldn't move very much or speak anymore.

Lorne grabbed a rag and dipped it into a bowl of water then wiped Walter's brow.

"How are you feeling, bud?"

Walter drew a dollar sign then put his thumb up.

"A million bucks, eh?" Lorne said. "Well, you look better, so that's good."

Walter rolled his eyes, knowing Lorne was lying.

"So, I've noticed a couple things that might float your boat. First off, there're more writings on the walls further back, and they're looking even weirder than the first batch we've seen, so I think they might be even older. Second, there's a step down the back of the cave. I'm going to take a closer look. It might be a way out."

Walter's eyes showed a little bit of life. He looked around and then wrote, "Be safe" on the floor.

"Yes, I'll be careful." Lorne quickly wiped away Walter's writing as Squirrel approached them. Lorne told Walter to draw a tree. Walter did so. Squirrel popped up, looking over them. Lorne pointed at the picture, then at himself, and said, "Tree."

Squirrel looked around the same way Lorne and Walter did to make sure no one else was around. He repeated it back to Lorne in a gruff but quiet voice, "Tree."

Both Lorne and Walter smiled, and then Walter passed the stick to Squirrel. The long-legged man looked around once more to see if Rabbit was watching, and then sat down, bumping into Lorne with about as much finesse as a Saint Bernard when it thinks it's a lap dog. Lorne spat out some of Squirrel's body hair and started to breathe through his mouth because of the big man's odour. Having only a trickle of water running down the side of the cave's walls as a shower left everyone smelling a little funky.

Squirrel pointed at the tree drawing and then said, "*Copac.*"

"*Copac,*" Lorne repeated. Squirrel started to vibrate with excitement. Lorne put his hand on Squirrel's knee and waved his other hand, tapping the air. "Whoa. Settle down now, Squirrel."

Lorne and Walter noticed these huge people wore emotion on their sleeves—or on their hairy arms, in this case. Squirrel seemed to react the most passionately, but they were all quick to change moods: one minute they'd be joyful, the next upset, then angry, then happy again—all with a flick of a switch.

Squirrel grasped the notion of being told to settle down. He kept his vibrating to a minimum, but he glanced at Lorne with a weird look when he said, "Squirrel."

Squirrel repeated the word. "Sqeeaal?"

Lorne didn't notice he'd said "Squirrel," but when Squirrel tried to say the word, he figured he might as well go with it. Lorne decided to try the whole Tarzan-and-Jane tactic. He pointed at Squirrel and said, "Squirrel," and then pointed at himself and said, "Lorne." Walter rolled his eyes when Lorne pointed at Walter and said his name.

Lorne looked at Walter with a peeved look. "You got a better idea?" he asked. "You knew this was coming as soon as we started communicating."

Walter shrugged in agreement, and sighed. Lorne also sighed. He gave up and put the stick down. Squirrel looked at the stick and then at Lorne, and then grinned. He pointed to himself and said, "Ekorn" twice, then chirped like a squirrel twice and pointed to Lorne.

Lorne looked at Squirrel, then at Walter. "What am I supposed to say?"

Walter took the stick back from Squirrel and wrote down an animal name, and then made the animal's sound.

Lorne sat there for a second, and then figured something out. He took the stick from Walter, looked at Squirrel, and pointed at himself. "Me, Lorne." He then let out a loud elk mating call. As it echoed through the cave, the others looked over, wondering where the sound had come from. As soon as they realized it had come from Lorne, they frowned and continued with their chores.

Squirrel's face expressed shock and awe. He sat for a moment, and then took the stick again. He pointed at Lorne. "Elder Elan." Squirrel then repeated the elk call back to Lorne and said, "Elder Elan," once more.

Walter started to chuckle and coughed. Lorne looked at Walter, knowing what was happening. "All right, all right. This is your house, your rules. I got it." Lorne pointed to Squirrel, then himself, and repeated his name.

Squirrel, now Ekorn, pointed to Badger and made a badger noise, and then said, "Kanin." Lorne repeated the word. Ekorn pointed at Eagle and repeated the process: "Orn."

Ekorn looked at Walter, and then back to Lorne, who said, "Him, Walter," then, "Meeooww."

Walter gave Lorne the finger.

"What?" Lorne laughed, "I thought you liked kitties."

Walter wrote "Asshole" in the dirt. Ekorn looked at both men, confused. He pointed at Walter.

"*Draga Ord*, Meeooww?"

Walter smiled, and Lorne laughed.

"Yup, that's it," Lorne said.

Ekorn jumped up and started his happy dance, and then ran over to Kanin and Orn and started chattering up a storm.

"Well, at least he's happy," said Lorne. "We can't be in danger if we keep him dancing."

Walter raised one eyebrow, and then put his hands on his head.

"I guess . . . if he tramples us, that could still be dangerous," Lorne pointed out. "If he keeps them busy over there, I can go check out that drop-off undetected."

Walter gave Lorne a concerned look.

"I got this," said Lorne. "Don't worry."

Walter rolled his eyes again.

Lorne quietly hobbled into the darkness until he reached the cave's drop-off. He turned to make sure no one was paying attention, and then reached into his pocket and grabbed his lighter. He lay down at the edge of the drop and hung his hand down as low as he could, and then flicked his lighter to see what was down there. Lorne's eyes widened as he saw what looked like a natural staircase dropping into further darkness. Lorne turned off his lighter and looked back toward the tribe. He only saw Kanin and Orn.

Shit! He thought. Lorne put his lighter back in his pocket and started to quickly crawl back.

Suddenly, there was a distinctive odour inside his nose. Lorne looked behind to see Ekorn standing above him. Lorne froze in mid-crawl. Ekorn looked down with an odd look, cocked his head to the side, and then looked at Lorne like he'd been a bad dog. With one hand, he grabbed Lorne by the back of his pants, picking him up like a bag of luggage. He carried Lorne back to where Walter lay and dropped him by his bed. Ekorn gave Lorne a disappointed scowl and walked away. Lorne, a little startled, looked at Walter, who wrote, "Shit yourself?" in the sand.

Lorne sighed and replied, "I might need a new pair of brown shorts."

Chapter VIII

As the sun rose, Lorne woke up with a peaceful smile on his face as he saw Joan sleeping beside him in his hospital bed.

Joan woke abruptly to Lorne flicking her boob over her bra. "Ouch! What the hell?"

Lorne looked at her. "Did I wake you?" he smiled. "It's morning. Let's go!"

Joan rubbed her eyes and asked what time it was.

"6:30 a.m."

She stretched and noticed her clothes were already set out and the bags were by the door. She stared at Lorne. "You're unbelievable. How long have you been up for?"

"Since 4:00, 4:30, 5:10, and 5:20 a.m."

"You're lucky you didn't wake me, then."

"I'm stupid, not suicidal."

Joan rubbed her eyes again, then got out of bed and grabbed her clothes on the way to the bathroom, mumbling words Lorne couldn't hear but understood well. Lorne watched the television on mute, changing the channels every two seconds until Joan was ready. When she came out dressed, she looked at Lorne blankly watching the television and twiddling his thumbs. She sighed and said, "You realize we can't go anywhere until Dr. Sale comes and check on you."

"This is bullshit. I have legs, I can just walk out of here."

"Hold your horses. She said she'd be here first thing. So she should be here soon."

"Well, let's get ready and leave this hole as soon as possible."

"Yes, yes. Settle down, and I'll help you." He still had trouble bending, so Joan helped him tie his shoes. She finished up as they heard a tap on the door.

Dr. Sale popped her head in, noticing that Lorne and Joan were already dressed and ready to go. "I guess I got here just in time. It's amazing you're not trying to climb out the window."

Joan looked at Lorne as she replied back to Dr. Sale, "If he were healthier, he probably would have, and left me here in the process."

Dr. Sale looked at Lorne. "Well, let's give you a once-over and get you out of here, shall we?"

When he heard that, Lorne couldn't hide the smile on his face, even if he had tried. "What do you need me to do?"

"Just relax, and let me check you out." As Dr. Sale examined Lorne, she knew in her head that Lorne was going home no matter what. She said, "Like I said before, you need to get rest and keep off your feet as much as possible, so *we* will get a wheelchair and *you* will get pushed out of here to your vehicle. No whining about it."

Lorne bowed his head. "Yes, ma'am. Whatever you say."

Joan and Dr. Sale smiled at each other. She walked back to the door, opened it, and brought in the wheelchair. Joan and Dr. Sale helped Lorne into it.

Dr. Sale then said to them both, "You both take care and get out of here." She looked directly at Lorne and continued, "I want to see you back here in two weeks, no matter what."

Lorne gave her a big salute and then shook her hand. "Thanks for everything."

Smiles were exchanged by all as Lorne and Joan left through the back entrance in case the reporters were still lurking. Joan unlocked the car and opened the passenger door for Lorne. He slid into the seat slowly and sighed as he got comfortable. Joan got into the driver's side and started the car.

"How are you feeling?" she asked.

"Like shit, but happy to get out of this place."

"You might want to get some sleep. I'll wake you up at the truck stop for that chilli burger you love so much."

"Oh, how do I love you, let me count the ways." Lorne reached for her hand, kissed it, and then closed his eyes and was asleep before they even left the parking lot.

Typical, Joan thought to herself. *He wakes me up early just in time for him to go back to sleep.*

* * * * *

Three hours had passed by the time Lorne woke up. He found the car parked on the side of the road and Joan asleep in the driver's seat beside him. Lorne put his chair into the upright position and looked outside. He noticed Joan had driven only about half an hour out of town before she'd pulled over for a nap. Smiling, he quietly opened the car door and got out, feeling his body creaking in almost every joint and bone. Lorne stretched and then hobbled around like an eighty-year-old.

The sky was blue with little white clouds floating here and there. Lorne took a deep breath. The morning air felt good. He limped to the bank at the edge of the road and looked over. He caught a whiff of something that wasn't the fresh morning air. Lorne's heart started to race. He began to sweat and breathe faster. He stood there, scanning the bank and the trees on the side of the road cautiously and intensely. It was a smell that reminded him of the death of his friends. His eyes located a bag of rotting garbage and two dead crows lying beside it. Lorne settled down but still stayed on guard as he walked a little faster back to the car. He got back in the car and awkwardly shut the door, trying to be quiet and inflict minimal pain on his body. He locked the door and then sighed and settled back into his seat.

Joan, still with her eyes closed, reached over and stroked his arm, not noticing his anxiety. "How are you feeling?"

"All right," Lorne lied through his teeth. "Needed to stretch the legs a little bit, but I feel better now. How was your nap?"

Joan smiled with her eyes closed. "I figured it was better to pull over than to pass out and wake up with you in the hospital again."

Lorne looked out the window. "If you'd ditched it, we probably could have just walked back to the hospital." They both chuckled. Lorne looked out the back window. "If I look hard enough, I think I can still see it from here."

"Very funny, smart-ass." Joan began rubbing her eyes open. "What time is it, anyhow?"

"It's time to get up. That burger is calling my stomach as we speak. But otherwise it is 10:35 a.m."

Joan opened her eyes wide and then looked at the clock for herself. "Holy shit! It didn't seem like we slept that long. That's going to work out better than I hoped." She quickly put her hands to her mouth and looked at Lorne, hoping he hadn't heard.

He had. Lorne looked at Joan. "*What's* going to work out better than you hoped?"

She tried to change the subject. "So, you're hungry for that burger, eh?"

"Joan!"

Joan sighed and threw her head back in frustration.

"Shit. You know your family and friends know you're coming home—"

Lorne stopped her mid-sentence. "I don't want a party."

"And I don't want to get old and grey," countered Joan, "but we both know we can't stop it, even if we tried."

Lorne put his head back. "Uhhh, I know. I just want to go home, see the kids, and sleep in my own bed. And be left alone."

Joan brushed the side of his face. "You know our friends and family. That's not going to happen."

Lorne sighed and rolled his eyes. "Fine! Let's go get that burger, and I'm going to get a milkshake, also." He looked closely at Joan. "The party isn't there, is it?"

"No, no, just when you get home."

"All right then, let's get out of here."

Joan sat up, adjusted her seat, and started the car. As she pulled back onto the road, Lorne looked out his window. He scanned the tree line, looking to see if anything was out there that didn't want to be noticed. He sat and listened happily to Joan talk about the kids and what they've been up to until they got to the burger joint. Joan pulled into the dirt parking lot. Lorne saw a couple vehicles already parked there.

"Can you park in the back please, hon? And if you don't mind, I'll just wait in the car. I know that truck parked out in front, and I don't need to talk to anyone right now. You go and order, and we'll eat in the car."

"Sure, no problem. What kind of shake do you want?"

"Chocolate, please."

"Be back in a few."

Joan kissed him and headed into the restaurant. Lorne put the seat back and slumped low, just high enough to peek through the window to see if anyone walked by.

Twenty minutes passed. Lorne started to get fidgety. He checked the ashtray, glove compartment, sun visor, and console for no reason. He started to play with the automatic door locks and mirrors, wondering what was taking so long. He thought about getting out of the car to see what was going on. He stared intensely at the corner of the building, waiting for Joan to come around with the flame-broiled treasures. Five minutes and a couple stomach growls later, Joan finally emerged, but she had nothing in her hands. Lorne's face filled with disappointment as she came to his window.

"It's a good thing you didn't go in. I just ordered now. I've been answering everyone's questions. I told them I had to use the washroom just to get out of there."

"Sorry about that," Lorne frowned. "What did you tell them?"

"Mainly that you're alive and awake and that you're still at the hospital for another week."

Lorne smiled. "That's my girl."

Joan put her hand on his. "It's going to be a little longer, so just sit tight and keep down like you're doing. I'll be right back—and put the mirrors back to where they were before."

Lorne wondered how the hell she noticed the mirrors were moved. *Who notices that shit?*

Ten more minutes went by before Joan came around the corner again. She hopped in and handed Lorne the warm bag, quickly starting the car. She popped it into reverse then, just as fast, put it in drive. Gravel spat out from the tires as she left the parking lot. Lorne looked back at the truck stop to see if anyone was running out and chasing them.

"Did you just rob the place for some burgers and fries?"

"No, also a couple milkshakes," she answered. Lorne laughed, then she continued, "I just had to get out of there. The natives were getting restless. They were starting to ask questions I didn't want to answer."

"The same as the ones Copeland asked? I know the feeling."

"Well, it's over for now, so open that bag up and let's dig in."

Lorne eagerly agreed and started dividing the food up for both of them. Lorne stared at the milkshakes. "We have to go back. There're two vanilla milkshakes, no chocolate one."

Joan replied without taking her eyes off the road, "The hell we are, mister. Vanilla is now your fav."

Lorne took a sip. "Mmmm, fantastic."

As they were eating, Lorne started to think out loud. "Maybe I'll pretend to be worse off than I am. I'm pretty sure I look like shit, so might as well take advantage of it, eh?"

Joan choked a little on her milkshake, chuckling. "Sorry to tell you, but your acting sucks. Just eat your burger and try to enjoy the party when we get there."

"About this party, what about the press and other uninvited guests?"

"Don't worry about that. We're actually going to your Dad's ranch just outside of town. He said Uncle Jerry and Uncle Jack had everything under control at the gate."

Lorne raised his eyebrows.

"They let the Twin brothers guard the gate? I can only imagine what that means."

"I didn't ask, and your Dad didn't say."

They kept eating. Lorne finished up, letting out a huge burp followed by a grateful sigh because he'd stayed awake to finish the whole thing. He started feeling drowsy.

Joan put her hand on his knee. "Just go back to sleep. I'll wake you before we get to town."

Lorne yawned and rubbed his eyes. He didn't deny he wanted to sleep.

* * * * *

Joan nudged Lorne awake. He opened his eyes just in time to see "Welcome to Edwardson" pass by his window.

"Couldn't you have waited twenty more minutes and just have woken me up at Dad's door?"

"You've got to get your acting skills up to par. Don't want the fam to notice you faking it, do you?"

"Hardy-har-har. I'd laugh harder, but I don't want my sides to split."

"Now, now, brown cow, take those grumpy pants off and put the happy ones on."

Lorne looked at Joan and started to undo his pants.

"Hey now, none of that," she stopped him. "You do not have the energy to go the distance. I'd probably kill you."

Lorne gave Joan a mischievous smile. "What a way to go, though."

"Just think about your Uncle Morton and his rotten toe until we get to your dad's house."

Lorne's face turned a little pale and his frisky smile quickly went away. "Yup, that did it. Thanks honey, that image is going to stay there for a while."

Ten minutes later, they pulled up to a closed metal gate. There was a jacked-up truck on either side, both with their tailgates down. In the back of each truck was a lawn chair, a case of beer (minus a few bottles), one 12 gauge shotgun, and a man built like a brick shithouse. As Joan parked in front of the gate, both men got out of their chairs and jumped down, and their respective trucks rose back up half an inch. They hunched next to Joan and Lorne's windows. As soon as they saw Lorne, both men welled up inside. Holding back a tear or two—but still trying to appear manly—the one man leaned into the window on Lorne's side and with a monster of a hand shook his. In a deep, low voice the man said, "Glad to see you, boy! It's about time you got here, you look like shit."

"Good to see you guys, too. Any strangers try stopping by?"

"There were some snoopy folk that weren't from around here at the beginning, but you fire a couple shots in the air and news travels fast."

While Lorne and Jack were talking, the man on Joan's side leaned in and hugged Joan and then reached over her to shake hands with Lorne. In a similar voice as Jack's, Jerry replied, "They'd all just kind of slow down at the gate, and then speed up and keep going."

"It wasn't because there were two beasts guarding the gate, was it?" Joan asked. Both Jack and Jerry chuckled.

The two men stepped back from the car and Jerry said, "I'll open the gate and let you in. We'll park the trucks and be up in a bit."

Lorne looked at the two guys. "Sounds good," he said. "What if people we know want to come up?"

Jack smiled and replied, "Everyone you know is already up there, boy. Now get going."

Jerry opened the gate and Joan drove through. There was a row of parked cars flanking each side of the driveway. Joan looked over at Lorne, his mouth open in awe.

"I hope you have your game face on," she said.

Lorne could only muster two words: "Fuck me."

"Elegantly put, honey."

"I didn't realize we knew this many people. Don't they know how to carpool?"

Joan laughed. She pulled up right in front of the doors to the house and stopped. People were everywhere, mingling. Slowly, the crowd recognized the car, and surprisingly, they waited for the couple to come out.

Lorne sat quiet for a moment, and then said, "This is going to suck the big one. It's going to take forever."

"Be thankful you have this many people who like you, though I'm not sure why. It could be worse—there could be *no one* here."

Lorne rolled his eyes. "Yes, mother."

Lorne hesitantly opened his door and slowly got out of his seat. The crowd gasped a little at his appearance. Lorne gave a small wave and nodded at the crowd. Everyone was quiet, not sure what to say or do. Standing at the front door of the house was Walter's sister, along with Lorne's eight-year-old daughter Kimberly and five-year-old son Adrian. On their cheeks he could see tears of joy, and on their faces, maybe a little bit of fear. Lorne immediately stood tall and pretended the pain didn't exist.

Kimberly and Adrian ran up to hug their dad. Adrian asked, "Are you okay, Daddy? Are you broken?"

Lorne choked back tears. "Nope. The doctor fixed me up! Just a little tired, son." Lorne looked down at his daughter. She was clinging to him and didn't seem to be letting go. He bent down to hug her back just as hard. There was no way he could hold his tears back. Joan immediately ran over and hugged all three for what felt like forever, yet somehow that wasn't long enough. The whole family was reunited once more.

The crowd cheered and clapped. Lorne had forgotten he'd initially not wanted to see anybody. He began looking for people he hadn't seen for some time.

Suddenly, a gruff but familiar voice came through the air and said, "You're walking more feebly than your old man."

Lorne looked up to see his dad, Max, leaning on the railing of the front deck. If the Marlboro Man were at this party, Lorne's old man would have stomped him with his boot for being a pussy. Max sauntered down the stairs. When he was about ten feet away, he stopped, lit a cigarette, and put it in his mouth. Lorne kissed his wife and kids, squeezed out of the group huddle, and stood up as straight as possible. He said to his Dad, "I could still kick your ass, old man."

Max looked Lorne straight in the eyes and took a puff of his cigarette. "You couldn't kick my ass even when you were in top condition, boy."

They stood looking at each other. For a moment, not even the crickets said anything. Seconds passed before both Lorne and his Dad each cracked a smile. Lorne limped over into his dad's arms for a hug. The crowd started to laugh and commenced with cheer and conversation.

"How you doing, boy?" said Max.

"All right, but you know me and crowds."

"Yup! Just like your old man. Hungry?"

"Not really. We ate at a truck stop on the way."

Max looked straight at Lorne. "Thirsty?"

Lorne smiled. "Is that even a question?"

"Well, let's stop with the mushy shit and go get a beer, god damn it."

Lorne looked over at Joan, who looked back at him and sighed. "Don't look at me," she said. "Have you ever argued with your father and won?"

Lorne grinned and turned back to his dad. "I promised the doctor I'd take it easy."

"Well, it's a good thing I got a reclining chair in the house." They put their arms around each other's shoulders to help themselves up the stairs and into the house.

The food and good times started. It was like Lorne had never been missing. His friends and family kept their questions to a minimum, purposely avoiding the big one: *What happened?* This party was for Lorne's coming back alive. He mostly just said "Hi" to a person and they would tell him how they were doing. He liked that because he didn't have to talk much.

In the back of his mind, he was dreading his inevitable talk with Walter's sister, Rebecca. Talking to Dan and Lee's family was hard, but at least they'd had closure and more time to deal with what had happened. Rebecca, on the other hand, had just found out that Walter was dead. She had now lost all hope that he could have been alive.

As Lorne saw many of his friends and family, surprisingly, the one guy he wanted to see wasn't there. Lorne looked around for Officer James Haul, but found out that James had gone out of town for his court case for a couple days. He wanted to thank James for all he'd done, both past and present. He now knew that James had allowed Walter and their crew to continue camping in their favourite spot. Lorne wanted to apologize for not being a better friend, but he knew it would have to wait for another day.

Time, beer, and laughs had passed by when Lorne saw Walter's sister talking to Joan in the kitchen. He got Joan's attention, and then motioned that he'd be on the back porch. Joan nodded her head and whispered into Rebecca's ear. Lorne slowly got up from his chair and hobbled outside for some fresh air. Rebecca walked down the hall and onto the porch where she found Lorne looking like he'd just dropped his mother's wedding ring down the drain. She walked towards him.

"I don't know what happened," she said softly, "and I might never know, but Joan told me you were with him when he died, and that's really all I need to know. Walter's friends and family were the most important things in his life. If he died with you around, then I know he died happy."

"He saved—"

Rebecca cut him off. "Don't say anything now. We'll talk another time. Right now, this is your day. You're probably tired and want to be left alone, also. I'm so glad you're alive and back, but I'm going to leave. Take care, and I'll see you all later." Rebecca hugged Lorne, who started to cry.

"I'm sorry," he apologized.

"I am, also. I'm off to the hospital now to go see mom." Rebecca kissed Lorne on the cheek and quickly slipped away to her car. Lorne just stood there, not knowing what to do. He felt two arms wrap around him from behind.

"Go get your jacket and sneak into the car," said Joan. "I'll grab the kids and tell your dad we're leaving. Everything is going to be all right."

Lorne gestured after Rebecca. "She ran off before I could ask her about her mom. Why is she in the hospital?"

"When her mom found out Walter was dead, she collapsed. I just found out tonight."

"Could her day get any worse? I can't believe she still came. Rebecca is one strong woman."

"She knows Walter would have wanted her to come and see that his good friend was doing all right."

Lorne turned around and kissed Joan. "I love you so much. Thanks for the party, even if I didn't want it," he said, smiling.

Joan wiped the tears from his face, then hers, and pointed Lorne toward the bedroom where all the jackets were. Lorne winked and held the porch door open for Joan. He headed down the hallway to retrieve their coats.

Joan steered herself through the party until she found Max. "Hey, Dad, how're things?"

"This takes me back when that bastard was about sixteen and had a party here. I came home to find him and a bunch of other bastards drunk and passed out on my floor."

"Well, I'm going to have to leave you with the drunk bastards again. I'm taking Lorne and the kids home. He wants to sleep in his own bed tonight."

"So you're going to leave me to take care of all these hooligans by myself, eh?"

Joan laughed and kissed Max on the cheek. "Thanks, Dad. I'll come back tomorrow morning for clean-up."

Max looked at her. "You'll do no such thing. You take care of my boy. I'll clean this place up. Probably make some of these Nancy boys—who can't hold their liquor—help me."

"You know they'll never say no to you."

Lorne's dad smirked. "I know."

"Love you," said Joan, "and thanks once again. I've got to get your son to bed."

"Take it easy on the boy, he still looks a little tender."

Joan smiled and disappeared into the partying crowd. She snagged Kimberly and Adrian and then got into the car where Lorne was already waiting.

* * * * *

The ride home was quiet. Everyone had fallen asleep except Joan. She pulled up to their house and shut off the car, quietly nudging Lorne.

"Wake up and go back to sleep in the house."

Lorne opened his eyes. "I'll grab Adrian."

"No, you won't. Go get ready for bed, you're not lifting anything."

Lorne looked at Joan with his eyes half-open. "Have I ever told you you're my best wife out of the bunch?"

"You can barely handle this wife. No way you could handle more than one. Now get going."

Lorne staggered to the front door, unlocked it, and left it open while turning on every light in the house on his way to the bathroom. Outside, Joan picked up both kids out of the car and put them over each shoulder like a fireman. She kicked the car door closed with her foot and walked into the house, and then kicked the front door closed the same way. She carried the kids upstairs and put them in hers and Lorne's bed. She tucked them in and kissed them and then walked downstairs. She found Lorne standing at the sink with his pants undone and missing a sock. His shirt was half on and a toothbrush was hanging from his mouth. Lorne's eyes were closed.

Joan giggled. "Honey, you awake?"

Lorne quickly opened his eyes and continued to brush his teeth like nothing had happened. "Yeah. Just brushing my teeth."

Joan walked up to him and kissed his shoulder.

"Get into bed, the kids are already there waiting for you. I'll handle everything down here."

Lorne clambered upstairs to the bed. Joan turned out all the lights Lorne had turned on and then headed upstairs to find him still awake, half-dressed and holding their kids in his arms. She snuck into bed and cuddled her family while staring into Lorne's eyes. As her eyes filled up with tears, she said, "I'm so glad you're back."

"So am I, hon, so am I."

The four settled in and drifted off to sleep. It was a good many hours before Lorne started to toss and turn painfully in his sleep remembering his friend in the cave.

Chapter IX

Lorne walked over to see Walter at the wall of the cave lying in his cedar branch bed. He squatted and said quietly to him, "I was hoping you fell asleep. It looked like you needed it."

Walter blinked once for "No," seeing as how he had lost his voice.

"Are you hungry? Thirsty?" asked Lorne.

Walter blinked once again.

"We might as well get comfy and settle in."

Walter looked directly at Lorne and blinked again slowly. Lorne knew Walter knew something wasn't right. Lorne sighed and started to tear up because he saw Walter fading away.

"You were always too stubborn for your own good." Lorne gripped Walter's shoulder. "I'm so sorry, buddy. I wish we could have gotten out of here."

Walter struggled and pointed his finger at Lorne. He whispered, "You . . . out . . . of . . . here."

Lorne struggled to hold back tears. He shook his hand and brushed Walter's head with the other.

"It was a good ride, though," said Lorne. "I'll never forget sitting in the park when I was twelve and watching this small, skinny kid scoot up to the top of a forty-foot tree in mere seconds while two bullies wondered where the hell he went. It was an honour to grow up and hang out with you, my friend."

Walter blinked twice, smiled, and whispered, "Good . . . ride."

Ekorn walked over and looked at the two men, and then put his hand on Walter's head. "*Draga Anda*," he said to Walter. Lorne helped Walter and Ekorn shake hands.

Walter smiled, and then looked at everything around him. "This . . . . was . . . cool too, . . . con . . . sid . . . . er—" Walter's hand went limp in Lorne and Ekorn's hands. The rest of him followed. Ekorn was still brushing Walter's hair back. Lorne broke down and cried.

Ekorn slowly separated the two men and nudged Lorne to walk over to the fire. Ekorn calmly wrapped his hands around Walter's body and quickly snapped his neck. Lorne put his fingers in his ears before he heard the bones crack and snap out of their sockets. Ekorn continued with each limb until Walter's body was cube-shaped, then he placed him onto the waiting fur. Orn and Kanin together with Lorne finished with the preparations, putting Walter with the fallen tribesmen. They all sat in silence.

Lorne was upset, but also shocked that they'd put a non-tribesman in with their own kind. Lorne wondered if there were more human bodies than just Walter's down the crevasse, or if Walter was special. Lorne thought Walter would have liked this gesture. He gave a small smile of gratitude and then walked to his bed and lay down, looking at the empty bed beside him. Lorne stared at it until he fell asleep.

* * * * *

The hours and minutes slid away into the past as Lorne slept. When he awoke, it was just in time to witness the sunrise. He was alone. There wasn't a soul in sight. He had only his own voice as company. The clan had no problems leaving Lorne alone in the cave these days; they knew he couldn't leave without falling to his death. Lorne had created a small friendship with Kanin and Ekorn. He hobbled around during the days, working on getting stronger. Sometimes he reached the edge of the cave and the drop-off. He had a feeling it would be worth his while to find out what was down there. One day, he stretched to look further over the edge, hoping to see something more when he felt himself slip and fall onto one of the ledges. He could feel his wounds. Lorne awkwardly shimmied back up into the cave and crawled back toward his bed. As he lay in the fetal position in pain, he again saw Walter's empty bed. He stared, wiping a tear from his face. Lorne rolled over to stare at the wall.

Some days Lorne didn't say a word. He only helped out when the clan needed him, then he went back to bed. One day, Ekorn had a spring in his step and came quickly over to Lorne. He motioned for Lorne to stand, grabbed his hand, and then took an unlit torch from the floor and journeyed to the back of the cave. Ekorn went to the edge where Lorne had made it a few days ago. Ekorn jumped down. Lorne lost sight of him. Suddenly two arms came up, reaching for Lorne. Humbly, Lorne swung over and let Ekorn pick him up and set him down on the floor of another ledge. Together they crept down within the cave, around boulders and ledges until they came to an open space. Ekorn grabbed the torch and pointed to Lorne's pocket. Lorne reached in and snagged his lighter, and then lit the torch. As the flame grew bigger it lit up the cavern.

Lorne discovered he was in a very old but man-made tunnel. A lot of rubble and some timbers were pushed to the side of the wall. He spotted more drawings on the cave walls, as well as human artifacts scattered in different places. It reminded Lorne of an organized storage locker. He looked to the left and saw about ten spears stacked against the wall and five rifles next to them, each looking older than the last. There were three helmets in the other corner that looked to be from the Spanish war era. Lorne gazed around in wonder. Ekorn handed him the torch and left, scurrying back the way they'd come.

Lorne noticed some ledges and chunks of timber that resembled a trophy case display. On one he saw a chainsaw and a hardhat. Beside that was a pilot's helmet and a World War II pistol. He searched further and noticed three more displays. There was an Indian chief's headdress, a Viking helmet and shield, and another helmet and spear that looked older than everything else. All the artifacts on the shelves had words carved over top of them on the walls. Lorne figured they were like tombstones. He wondered why only a few would be mantled, and others thrown to the side.

As Lorne was pondering, Ekorn came back. He took Lorne to an empty ledge ahead of the faller's chainsaw and hardhat monument. Ekorn took the torch and wedged it in a crevasse above him. He then grabbed an old spearhead and rock and began to chisel something into the cave face. Lorne watched as the letters *Draga Anda* were engraved—the same words Ekorn had said to Walter before he died. When he finished, Ekorn put Walter's cowboy hat and the stick Walter had used to write in the sand on the rock ledge underneath the words. Lorne started to tear up, and then smiled.

"You found and brought Walter's cowboy hat back. Thanks, that would have made his day, Squirrel—sorry, Ekorn."

Ekorn smiled. "Squirrel good, Elder Cap."

Lorne smiled back. Ekorn grabbed Lorne into a bear hug and started petting his head. Lorne gasped for fresh, hairless air, and then replied, "Okay, okay, that's good, Ekorn, I'm a happy camper again."

Ekorn released him, and Lorne could breathe easier again. He then said to Lorne, "*Draga Anda gott moarte.*"

Lorne nodded. "I agree, Ekorn, our friend Draw Words did die a good death, thank you."

Ekorn smiled and gave Lorne the torch, and then pushed him further into the cave. Lorne continued looking around at the ancient drawings and artifacts. Ekorn had once again left him alone. Lorne walked another thirty feet when he noticed a room he later wished he'd never seen. There were coolers, tents, lanterns, rifles, camera equipment, and other treasures that were useless to a tribe like this. There were also a lot of bones. They had been tossed into a pit. Some lay scattered like paper around a wastebasket. Lorne went over to examine them. They resembled deer, moose, bear, wolf, squirrel, and there was even a mammoth tusk. Among them were also human bones. Seeing this with the camping gear and other equipment made it pretty clear to Lorne where the other missing people had gone. He wondered why some bones were tossed like garbage and others were saved in the crypt like their own, but he figured it out as soon as he had the thought. Of course some bones were different than others. The people must have treated the Clan like family—with respect or without fear—or maybe they had taught them something useful.

Just then, he heard a whistle and a squeak come from down the cave. Lorne started hobbling up the trail and saw Ekorn waving him to come along. Ekorn met him halfway and hoisted Lorne onto his back. Taking the torch, he piggybacked Lorne swiftly back to his bed. Lorne was embarrassed. He was a full-grown man being carried effortlessly by another male, even if it was an enormous one. Ekorn went back to his chores. A few minutes later, the others came back to the cave unaware of Lorne's adventure. He sat back and watched the tribe do their thing, communicating, helping out, laughing, crying, and everything else the human race does—just with a shitload more hair.

* * * * *

Four days and nights of awkward rest and relaxation went by; each time Lorne would sneak out of bed, trying not to wake his wife and two sleeping kids. He walked downstairs into the kitchen and put on a pot of coffee and then sat at the table and stared out the window into the darkness. As the night rolled on, Joan woke to find Lorne missing again. *I should put a bell on that boy,* she thought to herself. The clock said 3:15 a.m. She rolled out of bed quietly and peeked downstairs. The bathroom light was on. Joan tiptoed down, trying to avoid creaking the stairs. She found Lorne sitting at the table in the kitchen, staring out the window.

"Couldn't sleep?" she asked. "Are you hungry? I can make some breakfast if you want?"

Lorne just sat there, not saying anything. Joan swallowed a lump in her throat and tapped Lorne on the shoulder. She asked him again if he were hungry. He turned to Joan with a look of guilt, fear, and doubt combined.

Joan's spine tingled. "What is it, Lorne? What's the matter?"

"Do you want to know what all happened out there?" Lorne asked.

She almost said, "Yes," but the look on her husband's face stopped her. "I'll make some coffee," she said instead.

"I already made some."

It was then that the smell of the strong brew hit her nose. She saw Lorne's empty cup on the counter and walked over to pour him another cup. She noticed the pot was still full and already half cold. Joan looked toward Lorne. He had turned back to the window and was staring out of it once again. She poured the pot of coffee into a saucepan and let it warm up on the stove. They sat together at the table, not saying anything, waiting for the coffee to heat up. It seemed to take forever. Ten minutes later, they had two cups steaming between them on the table.

"Did everything come back to you in your sleep?" Joan asked.

"I never forgot it in the first place," Lorne replied, nearly monotone. "I just figured you should know before the whole world found out and decided to lock me up and throw away the key."

Joan's heart rate kicked into high-gear, but her devotion and dedication to Lorne outweighed her worries. She took Lorne's hand across the table and held it between hers. Lorne sipped his coffee, sighed, and began his story.

* * * * *

A couple hours went by, along with four cups of coffee each, as well as the three cigarettes Lorne smoked. He was finished talking and felt somehow relieved. Lorne swallowed his coffee and looked at Joan to gauge her reaction. He hoped she believed him. She could jump up at any minute and call the cops or the guys in the white coats. Joan stood without saying a word. She walked around the table over to Lorne and put both hands on either side of his face. She kissed his forehead and looked him straight in the eye.

"If it were some random person on the street," she said, "or even some members of your family, I'd think you were off your rocker. I'd be grabbing the kids and running out the door right now. But I know you, and I know that look on your face. I didn't marry a murderer or a liar, so yes, I believe you."

Lorne let out the biggest sigh of relief he had ever had in his entire life. He grabbed his wife and hugged her hard. "You have no idea how much that means to me," he said into her hair, and then pulled back. "At least one person knows I'm not cuckoo for Cocoa Puffs. I wasn't quite sure what to say to you. I didn't want you to leave me, or not believe me."

"We've been through a lot, you and I. This is just another bump, but I will be with you through thick and thin, 'til death do us part."

Lorne rubbed his face with his hand. "If I'm convicted of my buddy's death, death will part us."

Joan brushed Lorne's head with her hand and told him, "You know you have to tell Detective Copeland your story. If you don't, they're going to question you their way, and make conclusions. I'm not losing you again."

"You know he's not going to believe a word I tell him, and I'm going to get locked up."

"Michael seems different from the others," Joan offered. "He also helped me out with the press and other crap while you were in the hospital. Not to mention, he let you come home even after you gave him all the attitude."

"Sounds like you should've married that guy instead," Lorne answered sarcastically.

"Look," Joan sighed, "I'll be with you when you talk to him. I'll get my mom to watch the kids for the day, and we'll deal with this together. Considering the circumstances, I also think if you get James over here, you'll have a better chance. He really needs to know. He's been the most helpful through all of this, and he still is one of your good friends."

Lorne sat for a second, and then replied, "If that's true, then he's the only good friend I have left." Lorne drank some more coffee and lit another cigarette. Joan looked at Lorne, and then hesitated. Lorne quickly asked, "What is it? You want to say something."

"You might want to ask one more person to listen. His name is Professor Will Robson."

"Who the hell is that?"

"He's the bear expert that came down and helped with the case. He moved down here a month and half ago to investigate the huge grizzlies that 'attacked you' and is possibly putting his reputation on the line to find them."

"How is that my fault? I didn't make him change his life around to find fuck-all."

"In a way you did, but that's not the point. You know more information that could ruin his career, and he came down to help."

Lorne sighed, but hesitantly agreed. "Fine. I'm not going to help him pack up his shit when he finds out he moved here for nothing."

"Well, that wasn't the only reason. He also met Officer Twin and they've been seeing each other for over a month now."

Lorne snickered. "Now, that makes more sense. He moved for the bear *and* for the beaver."

"Lorne!"

"What? You can't say I'm wrong ... I can't blame him, Gail's hot!"

Joan playfully squished his face with her hands and then kissed him. "You're unbearable."

Both laughed as he looked at the clock on the wall click to 5:55 a.m. He came up with a plan. "James is probably the only other person — besides you and Chief Gramps, if he were still alive—who would give me the benefit of the doubt." Lorne thought for a minute. "How's this? You make breakfast and we'll eat together with the kids first, then I'll call your mom and you call James and your 'Dick' friend." Lorne smirked, recalling his own nickname for Detective Copeland, but Joan gave him a dirty look. He nodded, knowing not to push it.

Lorne got out of his chair and headed upstairs to wake the kids. The four sat at the table and ate together, enjoying each other's company. It was a Hallmark moment. Joan cleaned off the table while Lorne sent the kids back upstairs to get dressed. He then went to phone Joan's mother. After the call, Lorne limped upstairs to help the kids, knowing they were playing instead of getting ready.

"Guess what, kids? Grandma and Grandpa are coming to pick you guys up."

His daughter put out her lip. "But we want to stay here with you."

Lorne smiled. "Your Mom and I have to do some things, but I promise afterwards we'll come rescue you from the old geezers and do whatever you two want to do."

Adrian piped up. "Monster truck ride!"

Not to be outdone, his daughter replied, "Pony ride!"

"Okay, sorry, I promise we will do something fun together that me and your mom will pick out."

The kids groaned, but agreed. Lorne slowly walked down the stairs to help Joan clean the dishes.

"As soon as your mom leaves with the kids, we'll phone James and Copeland," he said. "Who knows how long your mom will linger."

"Just say hi and run upstairs, or to the garage like you usually do. You don't want to start confusing the lady by acting differently."

Lorne rolled his eyes and continued to dry the dishes. They finished just in time to hear the doorbell. Joan went to the front door as Lorne headed upstairs to get the kids.

"Morning, Mom, how are you and Dad?" Joan asked.

"Oh, just fine. Your father stayed at home and is snowblowing the driveway. He says hi."

"Thanks for taking the kids on such short notice."

"Not a problem, did he tell you what happened yet?"

"No," Joan replied, raising her eyebrow. "And he's doing fine, thanks for asking."

"Oh, yes, of course, I was just going to ask that. Where is he now?"

"Upstairs getting the kids ready."

"Avoiding me already, is he?"

Joan avoided the question. "He just needs some more sleep, and the kids would just be too loud for him. The more sleep, the better."

"I understand, I'll just take the kids and get out and we'll be on our way."

Joan leaned over and kissed her mom on the cheek. "Thanks, Mom, you're a lifesaver. Hey kids! Grandma's here!"

The sounds of feet came barrelling down the stairs. Kimberly and Adrian hugged their grandma at the door.

"Hello, my little dumplings. Let's go see Grandpa and leave your parents alone for a little while."

"Yeah!" Kimberly answered with a big smile. "And then Dad will come rescue us from the old geezers and go do something fun!"

Joan's mom looked up at her daughter. "Oh, really?"

Joan mouthed "Thank you" and watched as her mom smiled, and then she said to the kids, "Let's get going."

Joan kissed and hugged both kids and then waved at her mom as she closed and locked the door behind them; then she leaned against it, sighing. She looked up the stairs to see if Lorne was hiding at the top. "The coast is clear, Lorne, you can come down now."

Lorne emerged from the kids' bedroom and made his way halfway down the stairs before replying in an innocent boy's voice, "Oh, I was just on my way down, I can't believe I missed her." He coughed back into his regular voice. "How is the old bird?"

"She's fine, and dad is snowblowing, but he says hi."

"See, your dad gets that I want to be left alone right now."

"My dad would make any excuse to stay home, but we have more important things to do than talk about my parents. Are you ready to do this?"

Lorne looked at his wife. "Through thick and thin?"

Joan stared back. "'Til death do us part."

"All right, then. You make the calls, and I'll go take a shower. Unless you want to join me?"

"Do you think you're strong enough for me?"

"Strong like bull!"

Joan rolled her eyes. "Just get in the shower, I'll make the calls."

Lorne sighed and dropped his lower lip down as far as it could go. He slowly dragged his feet up the stairs toward the bathroom, and then turned to make sure Joan saw him pouting, hoping she would reconsider. His wife just waved him off and laughed. As soon as Lorne disappeared around the corner, Joan's smile turned back to fear and worry. She went into the living room and made the call to Detective Copeland.

"Morning, Mr. Copeland, this is Joan McKenzie." She paused. "Yes, he's feeling better, thank you. Could you possibly come over today? Yes, he says he remembers some things. He said he'd tell you everything, but not without James Haul. Can you call James and Professor Robson, and then can you be up at the house in about two hours? That will be great. Thank you, and see you when you get here."

Joan hung up and listened to make sure the water was running in the shower before she covered her face with her hands. She then broke down and cried. She lay on the couch until she heard the water turn off, then quickly ran to the kitchen and washed her face in the sink.

Lorne came downstairs still drying his hair with a towel. "Could've helped me up there, being wounded and all."

Joan kept staring out the kitchen window above the sink. "Had to do a little more cleaning before people came over, don't want them seeing our mess."

"So you got a hold of your boyfriend, then?"

"Everyone will be here in about two hours. Speaking of messes, I should also have a shower before they get here."

"You should have had one with me—waste not, want not, you know."

Joan nodded with a smile. "Just make sure you answer the door when they knock."

"Got 'er. And I'll be on my best behaviour."

"I'll bet."

Joan started upstairs while Lorne walked to the front room and grabbed the remote to turn on the TV. He yelled up at Joan, "When are they coming?"

"About two hours!" she called down.

Lorne looked back at the TV and thought, *Take your time, why don't you . . . Wait, two hours!* Lorne got up from the couch as fast as he could and hobbled toward the stairs, taking his clothes off on his way back to the bathroom.

* * * * *

Lorne was dressed once again and sitting in the kitchen. Joan was still getting dressed. Lorne heard the doorbell and got up from his chair to answer the front door.

"Morning, Copeland, come in."

"Thank you, you look better and well rested today. Call me Michael or Mike, by the way."

"All right, Mike. I don't know about well rested, but I'm definitely feeling a lot better. Come in and have a seat. Joan is just upstairs getting dressed . . . and stop thinking about my wife that way."

Mike stepped back a bit and paused in surprise. "I wasn't—"

Lorne cut him off. "Don't worry about it, I'm just fucking with you."

"I see you're in good spirits this morning. It's good you're happy."

"Have to be. I have no clue when I'm going to have another good day. Coffee?"

Mike sat down at the table, noticing Lorne's attitude had suddenly changed when he had said that last comment. Mike was curious, but answered "Yes please" to the coffee offer. Then he asked, "So . . . you remembered something then?"

"That's why you're here, but I want to wait for Joan to come down, and I also want my friend James here." Lorne passed Mike his coffee.

"I remember you telling me he was suspended, but he's coming up as my friend."

"I figured as much. That's why I called him for Joan." Mike took a sip. "I was going to pick him up, but he had to pick up Professor Robson first," said Mike. "He should be here shortly, but this is your show right now. I've waited this long, I can wait a little while longer."

Lorne poured a cup of coffee for himself and then sat down at the table. "Good. So how's the town treating you?"

"Very well, considering the way we had to come into it."

"Yup. That'll happen."

The doorbell rang again. Lorne got up from his chair and slid the sugar and cream towards Mike. "Just amuse yourself until I get back."

Lorne opened the door to find James with Will and a huge gift basket by his side. "Morning, James," Lorne smiled. "Sorry for the short notice."

James peeked around the basket and both stared at each other in silence. Finally, Lorne spoke again. "Been awhile, hasn't it. Good to see you, man."

"You too. Thanks for getting a hold of me—it was a little unexpected, though. Sorry I couldn't make your party. Had some business to take care of."

"I heard. We'll have to talk about that."

"We'll have to talk about a lot of things. By the way, this is Will."

The men shook hands. Lorne and James realized they hadn't done that in a long time. Lorne looked at the basket once more. "That's quite the basket you got there."

"It's the only way I could hide this." James reached through the flowers and lifted out a Texas mickey of whiskey. "I figured it was this or cookies."

Lorne laughed and replied, "Good pick—cookies can go bad."

"So can we come in now?"

"Oh shit! Yeah, come in, come in." Lorne stepped aside and then closed the door behind them. James put the whiskey back in the basket and put it beside the table in the living room. They both gave each other a hug, then Lorne pointed James and Will towards the kitchen. James saw Mike sitting at the table.

"Morning, Mike, how's it going?"

"Good, thanks. Nice to see you both again. I see why you were late."

"The liquor store should open earlier."

The men chuckled. Lorne grabbed three more cups and put coffee into both. Joan came down the stairs and grabbed the last cup of coffee.

"Morning, James, long time no see."

James smiled. "It's under better circumstances now."

He got up from the table to hug Joan and then sat back down. Joan then shook Will's hand and said, "Nice to see you as well, Professor Robson. How are you?"

Will smiled and replied, "Very well, but you all can call me Will. Thank you for the invitation."

Lorne quickly answered, "Joan told me you helped out a lot, and that you have a career riding on this information. I don't want to ruin a man's reputation, so you need to hear this also."

Will wasn't quite sure what that meant, so he just nodded and quietly sat at the table. The warm feeling of welcome drifted away when Lorne said that, but Joan quickly tried to get it back and shook Michael's hand. He would have gladly taken a hug like the one James had gotten, but he happily settled for the handshake.

"Morning, Michael, how are you?" Joan asked.

"Very well, thank you, but to tell you the truth, I'm starting to miss home. The sooner I can close this case, the sooner I can get back."

Lorne looked at everyone around the table. "Well, now that every-one's here, we can get this show on the road." Joan held Lorne's hand. Lorne took a sip of coffee and then a deep breath. "I called you here, Mike, because I'm only going to tell this story one more time. I don't really know you, but you seem to be one of those determined bastards who doesn't give up easily. Also, you've been good to my wife and family through this whole thing, so I owe you something."

Mike raised an eyebrow. "Thanks, I think."

Lorne nodded and continued. "I called you in, James, for three reasons: One, you should know the truth about what happened to our friends and your cousin. Two, Walter told me you let us go to the cabin for many years, and I want to thank you for that. Besides the circumstances, most of our good times were up there. We would have gone up no matter what, so don't blame yourself for not stopping us. Three, besides my wife and your grandfather Chief Gramps, you're the only one who might believe me and convince this guy—" Lorne jabbed a thumb in Mike's direction, "not to lock me up."

James looked at Lorne with a wondering look.

Mike spoke up. "You might not know this, but I have been accused of having an open mind."

"Dude, if someone I didn't know told me this story, I'd be phoning the cops or the loony bin." Lorne looked at his wife with love. "I told Joan what happened this morning. If she hadn't believed me—or if she'd thought I would go to prison—this story would have gone to the grave with me."

"Well, let's hear the story, and then we'll conclude if you're insane or not, shall we?" Mike replied.

Joan stood to top up everyone's coffee and put on another pot.

Lorne lit a cigarette. "While you're up, honey, James brought you a basket of flowers. They're in the living room."

"Well, thank you, James."

"Not a problem," James answered.

Lorne cracked the window, took a big puff off of his cigarette, and blew the smoke outside. "You might want to go grab the other thing that's in there with the flowers. We might need it."

James waved Joan off. "Don't worry about it, Joan, we'll get it later."

Joan wasn't sure what the inside joke was, so she shrugged and sat down beside Lorne. She kissed him and took his hand in hers. "Are you ready?" she asked.

Lorne curled his lip and put his cigarette back on the ashtray. "Ready as I'll ever be." Lorne sat upright as the detective and the professor got out their pens and papers. "Do you want me to start and stop to wait for you two to write? Because there is no way in hell you're going to get me to record this," Lorne said.

Robson and Copeland shook their heads as Mike replied, "I can write as fast as you can talk."

Lorne shrugged, took a sip of his coffee, and then started. "Me and the boys went on our hunting trip countless times before, so closing access to the camp wasn't going to stop us. On this trip, we headed up to Pinkston Peak and set up at the cabin, like always, then celebrated, like always. Of course, we drank and partied more than we should have. We were all pissing ourselves laughing at Lee, who'd just done a nosedive into the dirt, when we heard a noise. Looking into the woods, we saw something staring at us. All of us were too drunk to run. We knew our guns were packed in the truck. I thought about throwing a burning log at whatever it was, but there was the whole forest fire argument from Walter." Lorne smiled, remembering his friend going on about how quickly fire could spread. "Lee, Dan, and I were thinking this thing was going to come out and kill us at any time, and there's Walter thinking about damage control. That was Walter—the group's collective conscience. Anyways, we kind of jumped to conclusions a little quick. We'd been telling creepy stories just before we saw the glowing eyes in the bush, so of course we were a little antsy-in-the-pantsy."

James nodded, knowing the feeling from when he used to run with the guys.

Lorne continued, "The eyes suddenly popped out of the woods into the light of the fire." Both James and Mike shifted forward in their seats. "It was two fucking pack rats; *big* fucking pack rats, but rats nonetheless. They rolled out wrestling an empty beer can. Being as how alcohol and intelligence works so well together, we decided to try and catch them. It seemed like a good idea at the time."

James shook his head. "Sounds like the time we tried to rope that deer twenty years ago at the cabin also. That didn't work out too well, either."

"Yup, similar conditions. Wildlife, wild guys, and too much alcohol."

Lorne, James, and Joan laughed while Mike and Will just smiled, not knowing the story of the deer.

"We surrounded the two rats," Lorne continued. "Lee tried to corral them. Walter tried to lasso one with a tarp rope. I tried kicking one into an empty beer case, and Dan sat in his lawn chair laughing his ass off."

Mike found it hard to keep a straight face thinking about airborne rats.

"After a few minutes, we got tired. The rats were scared off, obviously, but not before one of them bit Lee on his forearm. We just poured some whiskey on it and wrapped it up. No way were we going all the way home for a stupid rodent bite. Some of the chicks that guy slept with had worse diseases then that pack rat did."

Joan whipped her hand out of Lorne's and backhanded him across the chest.

"Sorry, honey. Anyway, in hindsight maybe we *should've* come home because of the stupid rodent bite. After a few more drinks, we called it a night and passed out 'til about 10:00 a.m. the next morning. It was a decent day. I shot a massive deer, and we got it back to the camp. We had a good night and only drank half as much as we had the night before. We used to make our hunting trips three days or longer because the first day and a half was always a write-off. After a good breakfast and some stomach-settling, we were all pretty spry, considering how much alcohol we had drunk."

"What day was that?" asked Copeland, his pen poised mid-air.

"Sunday. That's when it started to go ugly . . ."

Chapter X

The sun rose up with the smell of morning dew, stale beer, and man, each one having woken up more hung over than the other. Dan rolled over and sat up on the side of his bed, kicking some empty beer cans out of the way so that when Walter woke up and jumped out of the top bunk, he wouldn't break his ankle. Lorne and Lee woke up from their beds and cracked their backs and neck.

Lee stared at the ceiling, and then at Dan. "So, what are the odds of you guys trading beds for the last night?" Lee asked.

"This better be the best offer in the world, whatcha got for us?"

"I'll make breakfast, lunch, and dinner today and breakfast tomorrow, and do the dishes."

Walter turned over and said to Lee, "Sold! You can have my bed." Dan kicked the mattress from the bottom and launched Water into the air and back onto his bed. Walter quickly gave Dan the middle finger and asked, "Why does it matter if I trade my bed without you?"

"Because I have to sleep below the person who has top bunk, and you're lighter than all of us," Dan replied. Walter smiled as he nodded to Dan's logic. Dan then said, "That was pretty good, Lee, but how about you Lorne—what do you have for us?"

"I'll drive the rest of the time we're out here, and I'll gut whatever you kill today."

"Now we say sold."

All got out of bed and shook hands. They got dressed and headed outside to quarter the deer—except for Lee; he stayed in the cabin and started to make breakfast.

All three got to the buck and looked at Lee's homemade contraption. Lorne scratched his head still in disbelief of what had happened last night, but nodded to himself and said, "Well, it looks like Lee's booby trap worked—no signs of anything coming near this thing."

Water backed up a smidge and warned Lorne, "Just be careful disarming that thing. We can still use it tonight for the rest of the kills."

"The rest of the kills? You think you guys are going to get more than one?"

Dan looked at Lorne and said, "We better, or the offer for the beds only became *half* worth it."

Lorne bent down by the home-made alarm system and carefully unplugged the nine-volt battery and then moved the cans away. Walter and Dan grabbed two massive bone saws and started to quarter the deer. As each chunk came down, Lorne wrapped it in paper and tossed it into the freezer on the cabin porch.

Lorne, Dan, and Walter finished up and headed into the cabin. They were about to give Lee the gears about not helping, but then they saw that he had the table full with everything: plates, forks, knives, spoons, eggs, bacon, pancakes, toast, sausages, ham, and steak. All three just stared at the table in awe.

Lorne looked around, under the bed, and then at the ceiling. He then asked Lee, "Where did you hide the bitch that helped you with this? This all looks fantastic."

Lee smiled and replied, "Now you know why the ladies love me so much."

Walter wiped his mouth with his sleeve. "I'm way too hungry and impressed right now to mock you, dude—you did good."

Everyone washed up and sat down at the table and started to dig in.

Dan tipped his cup towards Lee. "Good job man, this tastes great, but why the big spread, anyways?"

"Because I know all of us and our last night here is going to be a hard one; I'll be too hung over to make breakfast tomorrow. This way, whatever we don't eat now we can wrap up and have as dinner and breakfast whenever we want—the world is our oyster."

Lorne leaned back in his chair and replied, "The man's right. When he gets an idea, it's usually a good one—we just have to wait a long time to get one from him."

Dan and Walter both chuckled, while Lee looked at Lorne and replied, getting quieter as he spoke, "Very funny, ha. ha. Shut up and eat . . . a dick."

"What was that? You kind of drifted off at the end of that sentence."

"Nothing important, just keep eating."

Lee got a smirk across his face, as did Walter, because he heard what Lee had said.

Everyone continued to eat away until their bellies were overfilled. They pushed themselves and their chairs away from the table and leaned back. Lee grabbed an old newspaper that was sitting on the countertop and started reading it; Lorne and Dan grabbed some toothpicks and cleaned their teeth; and Walter put his head back and closed his eyes.

Lee started telling the boys about an article in the paper. "Hey, get this. They say in the paper that this thing called the "Internet" is going to be the wave of the future."

Lorne instantly replied, "Sounds like a hoax." All just smiled.

After fifteen minutes, Lorne made the first move and started to clean off the table. Seconds later, everyone followed suit. Lee washed the dishes, Dan wrapped the leftovers up and put them into the fridge, and Walter and Lorne got the truck ready for one last expedition. Everyone finished with their duties and hopped into the crew-cab once again. Lorne, now in the driver's seat, looked at the clock on the dash: 9:45 a.m.

"All right boys, let's make history, and let's get everyone to shoot something today. Walter, try to stay up for at least half an hour this time."

About ten minutes went by before Walter fell asleep, and then an hour later, they made it to the clearing at the base of Turtle Hill. As soon as the truck stopped Walter woke up, opened his door, hopped out, and grabbed his rifle and packsack. He was spry as ever, and ready to leave before anyone else had gotten their hand on their door handles.

Walter, with a chipper voice, asked all three, "So, where am I going, and who am I going with?"

Dan replied, "You're going the same way as yesterday, but you're going with Lee this time."

"All right then, let's get at 'er. I got your pack, Lee." Walter grabbed Lee's pack from the back and closed his door, then started walking towards the trees. Lee downed the rest of his coffee and quickly filled it up again with fresh hot coffee from the thermos, grabbed his rifle, and jumped out of the truck. He waved at Lorne and Dan, and then ran and caught up to Walter and took his pack.

Lorne stared out the window and watched the two disappear into the woods. Then he said to Dan, "I don't get it—how can a guy who goes into a deep sleep at the drop of a hat wake up like he's had eight cups of coffee without skipping a beat?"

"We don't explain him, we're just friends with him," Dan answered. Lorne just shook his head in agreement as he got out of the truck and grabbed his gear. Everyone then headed off to their destinations.

* * * * *

The sun went higher into the sky as the time passed by. Lorne and Dan had walked up one of the draws for about an hour when they decided to take a break. Dan scoured the ridge and then said, "Let's pop a squat here for a bit; we got a good view if anything comes around, and I'm sweating my bag off right now—*and* sweating the alcohol out of my system. Man, we drink too much."

"That was us priming ourselves up for tonight—we aren't bringing any of that booze back with us," Lorne replied.

Dan wiped the sweat off his face. "We might have to keep some of it here and keep it chilling until next weekend for the bachelor party you guys are throwing for me."

Lorne's face dropped in confusion and surprise. "Bachelor party? What the hell, man?"

"Oh yeah, I asked Marie to marry me two weeks ago, and we're eloping at the end of the month. I was hoping you and Joan would stand up for us."

"Fuck yeah! But why didn't you say something sooner? We could have made this your party and go all out."

"Because this is Walter's weekend bash with us, and I didn't want it to become mine and ruin it for him. Also, if I said anything sooner, our friends are like family, so you know they would blow everything out of proportion, and then the gong show would follow. Marie and I just want to do something simple and quick, and as quiet as possible. We'll have a get-together later."

Lorne lit a cigarette, took a puff, and then said, "You know, Walter wouldn't have minded."

"I know, but why risk it? Plus, we're guaranteed to have *two* good bashes in one month."

"Good point. Well, if you want to keep it quiet I won't say anything, until you give me the go-ahead."

Just then, Lorne stopped talking, nudged Dan, and pointed at a four-point buck walking out of the tree line and into the open. Lorne quickly put his cigarette out, stuck it behind his ear, and whispered to Dan, "I already have my buck and used my tag, so if you want it, you can have it."

"Sold!" Dan quickly sighted it in his scope and then thought about the day before, making sure there was no one else looking at the same deer. He pulled the trigger and hit the beast. The buck jumped and started to haul ass back into the bushes.

Dan cheered, "Yes! That was an awesome shot. I think he left his heart on the ground."

"Nice shot. Let's go retrieve that beautiful beast."

Both headed down to the spot where they last saw the deer to follow the blood trail. It didn't take too long to find the trail and the buck dead on the ground. Lorne and Dan stood above it and high-fived each other. Lorne then handed the walkie-talkie to Dan, and Dan called Lee.

"Hey boys, one down. You two are up, because I just got a four-pointer, over."

"Are you guys going to need help? Over."

"You two just keep hunting—we'll get this bad boy back to the truck. You both get your bears, and we'll keep our eyes out for them also. Over."

"It must be pretty small to deny free help. Over."

"I'm happy right now, so don't piss me off. You guys just carry on, and we'll talk to you both later. Over and out."

* * * * *

Walter and Lee chuckled as they continued on, strictly searching for signs of bear now. An hour went by without signs of anything, and both Lee and Walter lost momentum and motivation. They were half-assedly tracking and looking around when they got a call from Lorne.

"Any luck over there yet? Over."

Lee answered this time. "No hide, no hair, no shit of any kind. Over."

"Well, we're about fifteen minutes from the truck," said Dan "and we just came across some grizzly bear tracks less than a day old. So if you want, you can meet us at the truck and we can load this deer into the box and then all four of us go back and look for it—or do you two want to keep searching up there? Over."

"You two keep doing what you have to do. We have lots of daylight, so let's keep our search spread out. Over."

"You got it. We'll load this bastard up and then head back and look for a bear for ya, and we'll touch base after a while. Over and out."

* * * * *

The two had been walking for another hour when Lee suddenly stopped in his tracks, smelling something.

"Wow!" Walter said, looking ahead. "That's what I call fresh, dude. That shit is still steaming."

"And those prints are huge. Looks like it's headed west. Let's be on guard for a while."

Lee and Walter felt a sudden second wind. They followed the bear tracks through the shrubbery and up and down a couple of draws for about twenty minutes before they realized they'd gone in a complete circle. Lee noticed both their footprints and the bear's on top of each other.

"Holy shit, Walter, are we tracking him, or is he tracking us?"

"I'm not sure, but if we're going to do laps all day we might as well find a tree to climb and wait for him to come to us."

Lee looked up at the trees and said to Walter, "We could sure use a tree stand right about now."

"Tree stand?" Walter gave himself a Mexican accent. "We don't need no stinkin' tree stand."

Walter dropped his pack, grabbed the rope from inside, and then tied a baseball-sized rock on the end. He tossed it over a limb on a tree and let the end drop back to him. Lee cupped his hands. Walter stepped into them and was boosted halfway up the rope. Walter shimmied up the rope until he got a hold of the limb. Walter tied the rope firmly to the tree so that Lee could also climb up after he'd tossed the rifles and packs up. Lee climbed up the rope halfway until Walter grabbed his hand and helped him the rest of the way. The two men settled into the tree like two cats staring into a birdhouse. They played rock–paper–scissors to find out whose kill it would be. Lee won, and he smiled.

Some time went by without a sound. Walter and Lee crouched quietly and uncomfortably on the limb until Lee broke the silence. "I think I hear something."

They both sat silently listening for sounds of movement from below. Lee pointed towards a clump of small willow trees where they'd left footprints a while ago. The willows moved slightly and then parted. A black, shiny nose sniffed at the footprints. The trees made way for the nose, then the face, the head and then the rest. The black bear tracked the men's footprints walking very slowly, cautiously. He was alert, sniffing at the air and ground, searching for the men. He was a good-sized bear; from their perch in the tree, Walter and Lee guesstimated the bear weighed in around five hundred pounds, give or take. Walter passed Lee his rifle. Lee raised the gun and sighted up the black mammoth. The bear sniffed around and then stopped moving. He appeared confused as to where the men were. Lee knew as soon as he pulled the bolt back on the rifle the sound would startle the bear, so he'd have to shoot just as quick. Lee breathed long and slow to calm himself down. Walter gripped the tree and froze like a statue. Lee put a bullet in and pushed it back in.

Click. The bear's ear twitched. He began to bolt back to the bushes. Lee took his shot. There was a painful yelp, but the bear didn't slow down. He was quickly out of sight.

With the excitement, Lee forgot he was in a tree and lost his balance. The rifle dropped and crashed to the ground. Lee felt the limb crack and started to fall; he reached out to grab for something to slow himself down. Walter grabbed Lee's arm to stabilize him, but instead they both started to go down. Walter locked his legs around the base of the tree and gripped it hard. Both bodies swung and smacked the trunk of the tree.

Walter looked down at Lee. "Ouch! Dude, whatever you do, don't look down."

"Holy shit man, why?" Lee asked with his eyes opened wide. "How far from the ground are we?"

"A good four feet, but your rifle is toast."

"Shit."

Walter dropped Lee and then made his way down the rest of the tree. Lee picked up the pieces of his rifle. "Son of a bitch," he mourned. "There goes my next two weeks' pay, but I hit that bastard."

"You more than likely killed him. Just about got yourself, also."

Lee wiped the sweat and dirt from his face. "Yeah, nice snatch-up there by the way—thanks."

"No prob. Shitty deal about your rifle, though."

"Well, it could have been a hell of a lot worse, but I did shoot that thing, and now we've got to go retrieve that son of a bitch. In case we have to shoot it again, we'll just use yours."

Walter sat down on a log.

"Let's calm down a bit and have a coffee and a snack first," Walter suggested. "My nerves are a little shot, and I feel a little lightheaded. We have lots of daylight. The bear will bleed out and slow down. He'll be a lot less angry, also. I'll call up the others and tell them the plan."

Lee smiled and grabbed the thermos. He poured coffee while Walter radioed Dan and Lorne. After their break, both trekked through the bush until they finally came across a huge pool of blood. They saw the blood pool, and then they looked at each other with the same confused expressions on their faces at what they found—or rather, *didn't* find.

Walter stood there for a second and then asked Lee, "Riddle me this, Lee. We have a massive pool of blood where your bear should be lying, and yet, there is no bear. What the fuck, over?"

"You're not on the radio anymore."

"Sorry—what the fuck?"

Lee started walking around in circles, looking for evidence of where the bear could have gone. Walter stood there watching Lee, who reminded him of a chicken running around with his head cut off. Lee started to wave his hands in the air and then shouted, "Bullshit! It's dead, this is its blood, it didn't just vanish into thin air, it couldn't have climbed any tree around here, where the hell did it go?"

Walter started looking up and looking into the trees. "We climbed the trees, maybe he's trying our technique and is going to get the drop on us."

"Yeah, right. He's probably sighting us up right now, ready to attack without any blood in him. Shit, maybe it's a zombie bear."

"Let's keep looking around a little longer and keep alert, just in case it's still alive and is pissed off. Dan and Lorne said they'd come and help, so they should be here soon, and then they can help us figure this shit out, because I ain't leaving this spot until we find it."

* * * * *

A lot of time passed by the time Dan and Lorne met up with Walter and Lee. They showed up to the sight of Lee and Walter sitting on a log drinking a cup of coffee. Both walked up and Dan asked, "Are you in a union? What's taking so long? We figured you'd be at least halfway to the truck by now. We said we would help you, not do it for you guys."

Lee kept staring right in front of himself, replying with little emotion in his voice. "Don't piss me off right now, I'm not in the mood."

Dan replied, "Sorry, Nancy. What's his problem?"

Walter answered for Lee. "We can't find it. Lee definitely shot it, but it's gone."

Lorne looked at Walter with a confused look on his face. "What do you mean, you can't find it? A blind man could see the blood trail it left. Did it fly away on you guys, or what?"

Walter and Lee both looked at each other.

"Funny you should mention that," Walter replied, "but pigs fly, not black bears."

Lee looked at both and then pointed to the blood trail. "You two follow the trail the rest of the way and then come back and tell us what's going on, Sherlocks."

Dan looked and pointed at Lorne. "He's Sherlock, I'm Watson."

Lee replied back, "Well, we're going to need all you guys to help."

Dan and Lorne slowly started walking into the bushes where the blood trail led, looking back at Walter and Lee and waiting to deliver the punch line and the laughter to follow, but to their dismay, it never came. About twenty minutes went by when Dan and Lorne came back.

Dan had the same look that Lee had on his face. "If you guys went through all that trouble to hide the bear, you two should have also cleaned up the shitload of blood out there," Dan said.

Lee looked back. "That's the problem—we didn't touch anything. That's what we found also. It should have been there—dead, and waiting for us to pick it up and take it home."

The Clan

Lorne quickly coughed and said at the same time, "Bullshit." All three looked at him; Dan smiled, but Walter and Lee didn't. Lorne then continued, "There's no way in hell your bear could lose that much blood and get up by himself and walk off—there's no way."

Walter looked at Lorne and Dan and then said, "Now, curse a little more, look up and down, back and forth, run around in friggin' circles for about ten minutes, and then you'll be in the same place we were about an hour ago."

Neither Lorne nor Dan said anything, still just waiting for one or the other to crack a smile or start laughing, but when no one did, Lorne started to get concerned. "You two aren't kidding, are you? You guys can't really find this thing?"

Lee looked at them both like they were idiots, and then quickly snarled, "No! We've been looking for this bastard forever, man. We have absolutely no idea where the hell it went."

Dan tried to help and organize a solution. "Well, you have two more sets of eyes here now, so let's all pick a direction and each go our separate ways and see if we can find any trace of this thing, and then we'll meet back here in half an hour."

Everyone agreed and headed out in their direction. Dan, Lorne, and Lee took off quickly into the wilderness, while Walter got up slowly from the log he was sitting on and sauntered his way into the bush with very little motivation.

* * * * *

Thirty minutes went by, and three of the men came out of the bush and saw Walter sitting on the log again, cooking smokies over a small fire.

Lee asked Walter, "Did you even leave?"

"Yup. I got the direction where all four of us had scanned forever, so I went and looked for about ten minutes, and then I figured I might do something useful and get a fire going, make some fresh coffee, and get some food set up for us. Let me guess—you all came back with the same useless results."

The three men looked at Walter and nodded. They sat down by the fire as Walter poured them fresh cups of coffee.

Lorne lit himself a cigarette, and then broke the silence. "I don't know what to tell you, Lee."

Dan knew what to say: "You got screwed."

Lorne nodded back. "Yeah, that pretty much explains it."

Lee also nodded. "You're probably right, but you all agree that I hit it, and it should have been dead, and that it landed over there?"

All three eagerly agreed. They were sitting there quietly, thinking about the situation, when Walter asked, "So, what do you want to do?"

Lee replied, "Well, I'm pissed off right now, so I'm done. If it were up to me, I say we might as well call it for the day and go back to the cabin and get shit-faced."

Dan raised his cup of coffee. "Sounds like a good plan to me, I second that motion."

Walter shrugged his shoulders and replied, "I could go back to the cabin as soon as I finish my smokie, actually."

Lee also nodded and said, "I don't give a shit anymore, let's go."

Dan smiled, and Lorne sighed, "So be it."

With that, all four men agreed and finished up their snacks and coffees. Then they packed up as Walter put out the fire. They headed back to the truck, with Lee walking behind the others a little more slowly, but still keeping up. Eventually, they saw the crew-cab peeking through the trees.

Dan smiled and said positively, "The good news is that we didn't get skunked today—at least one of us has something to show off."

As they got closer, Walter saw the back of the truck and asked Dan, "I thought you two said you loaded it up already—you guys left it up there? Were you guys born stupid, or did you just work at perfecting it? Now we all have to go hiking into the bushes before it gets dark and go get it."

Dan looked at Walter like he was new and asked, "What the hell are you rambling about?"

"I thought you guys loaded up your buck, and then went looking for the grizzly tracks."

"We did, dumbass."

Walter went back to his sarcastic dopey voice. "Okay, dicksmack."

Dan just replied in his own voice, "Don't make me beat your ass."

As Dan and Walter bickered at each other, Lorne looked into the box of the truck and noticed what Walter were talking about—their buck had gone missing, as well. Lorne ran towards the truck. "What the fuck?"

Walter and Dan stopped arguing when they heard Lorne say that. Dan ran towards the truck, and then also yelled, "Who the hell took it? Someone stole my deer!"

Lee got to the crew-cab last and quickly started to laugh hysterically. "That's frickin' hilarious."

Dan, on the other hand, did not find it amusing at all, and he looked at Lee with daggers in his eyes. "How is this hilarious?" he asked.

"I lost my kill, and now you know how I feel—that's how."

"At least I know for sure I killed mine—at least I got to see and drag mine into the truck."

Lee laughed again and replied, "Sounds like a lot of useless effort to me."

Dan snapped back, "You sound like a lot of useless effort to me! Mine wouldn't have gotten stolen if I didn't have to come over and help you pussies look for your shit."

Walter cut in, "Hey! Shut up, all of you. This ain't helping anything, god damn it. Now everyone, calm the fuck down." Everyone stopped yelling and silence commenced once again.

Lorne then broke the uncomfortable silence once more. "Is everyone good now?"

Walter and Lee said at the same time, "Yes."

Dan waited a couple of more seconds, and then replied, "Maybe."

Lorne nodded and said, "Good enough. Let's figure out what's going on here, and then and find out what happened to Dan's deer. We know for sure it didn't get up by itself and walk off, so don't even suggest it, Walter."

"Fine."

Dan said, "All I can think of right now is we do the same thing we did today and take a direction each and meet back in fifteen minutes, but this time, let's find something."

Everyone agreed once more and then picked a direction and headed out searching for clues. Once again, they all came back with the same information: absolutely nothing but confusion and anger.

As they all got back to the truck, Walter sighed, "Dude, I haven't found shit, and it's getting way too dark so see anything out here."

Lorne agreed. "I couldn't find any other tire tracks around except for ours, so someone didn't pull up and take it."

Dan went next. "And I couldn't find any other footprints around, except for ours."

Lee finished with, "I looked around for other animal tracks to see if something came and snagged it, but no luck that way, either."

Lorne shook his head and said, "This sounds like a shitty Scooby-Doo episode."

"Well, let's just go find the groundskeeper or the hotel manager and kick their asses—they're the ones who are usually the culprits at the end," Walter said in a more a positive voice.

Lee rubbed both of his temples with his hands. "Well, this day just became the biggest write-off of all time. So, what's the plan, guys?"

"Fuck it!" Lorne replied. "We were on our way back to the cabin before this fiasco to get pissed, so let's just stick to that plan."

Everyone regrettably agreed. They threw their gear into the truck and hopped in. All the doors closed, and Lorne started the truck up and headed back to the cabin.

Lee looked out the window and said, "This is going to be quite the story we get to tell when we get back home."

Walter shrugged his shoulders and replied, "Well, one is still better than nothing. We still have Lorne's kill in the cooler."

Lee jokingly took the spin off and said, "That's only if it's still there when we get there." All three looked at Lee with the stare of death in their eyes. Lee quickly defended himself. "Just kidding, guys. It's just that you never know what's going to happen, with the way today's events are panning out. I wouldn't be surprised if it wasn't there, that's all."

Dan looked at Lorne. "Better haul ass and get back to the cabin, Lorne, just in case Lee's right." Lorne and Walter laughed while Lorne stepped slightly harder on the gas pedal and sped up.

Zipping down the road, the moonlight shone through the trees as the headlights of the crew-cab went up and down, lighting up and dimming down the road ahead of them. The truck bounced around left and right as the three guys watched Walter's sleeping head bob all over the place, keeping bad time. Lorne headed down an incline on the road and started to head back up the hill when he saw something black and roundish near the side of the ditch at the top of the hill. Lorne pointed and asked the boys, "What is that mound at the top of the hill?"

Dan looked ahead. "A boulder, maybe? It might have rolled down off the bank this morning."

"I don't think so, kinda looks like it's moving. Is it eating something?" Lorne asked.

Lee looked around Dan's head and out the front windshield. "Are you guys retarded? That's a fucking bear, dudes."

"I think he's right," Dan agreed, "but it looks pretty damn big. Slow down a bit."

With the anger and frustration the men had experienced for the day and with their "moral compass" sleeping, Lee lost his good judgement and replied, "Fuck that! High beam that asshole and speed up, we're doing a drive-by."

Lee grabbed a rifle and crawled halfway out the window. Lorne struggled to keep the truck in control as Walter woke up with the commotion and saw Lee half out the window. Walter instantly grabbed Lee's legs, thinking he was falling out. Lorne got about thirty feet away and then slammed on the brakes. The bear looked up. Lee took his shot—*Bang*. The bear let out a yelp and then darted into the bush. The truck skidded to a stop; the only sound was its idling engine. Walter picked himself up off the truck's floor. Lee sat back into his seat, holding his mouth with both hands.

"Dude, are you all right?" Walter asked Lee. Lee dropped his hands, which were bloody. Walter glared at Lorne. "What the hell, Lorne? You could have killed Lee." No one answered.

"Are you guys, all right?" Walter asked again. "What the hell?" He leaned over the front seat and looked at Lorne and Dan's white faces. Walter gave them both a shake. "Hey! What's wrong?"

Dan stared out the window. "You didn't see that?"

"All I saw was Lee's body half out the window, and then a close up of the fabric of the back seat. By the way, it wasmade in Japan." Lorne looked at Dan, ignoring Walter. Lee hung his head out the window and spit out the blood in his mouth, and then wiped it off with the sleeve of his shirt. "I already took the shot before it turned around," Lee said.

"That was the biggest thing I've ever seen," Lorne replied, "especially when it stood up."

Walter, still confused, asked, "How big was the black bear?"

They all looked at Walter.

"Black bear?" Dan said. "That was no black bear."

Walter asked, "Brown bear? Grizz? Koala? Panda? Teddy? What?"

The others carried on like Walter wasn't even in the truck.

"We have to go and look for it," Lorne said, and then to Lee, "You shot it."

"Fuck that," Lee replied. "I'm not getting out of this truck."

Dan peeked out the window and looked through the bushes where the headlights pointed. "I agree with both of you," said Dan. "Let's stay in the truck and go off-road for a bit."

Walter started to get pissed off. "You guys are messed up. What do you think you shot?"

Lee acknowledged Walter. "It wasn't a bear, that's for sure. He looked like he had a bear skin *on*, but he definitely wasn't a bear."

"You hit a person?" Walter asked, shocked.

"I don't know."

Lorne quickly said, "Keep your mouths shut and your ears and eyes open."

The four looked out their windows for the wounded animal. Lorne drove off the road and soon passed a deer carcass.

"Is that your deer, Dan?" asked Lee.

"Can't say for sure," answered Dan. "It has the same amount of points and is pretty fucking big, so I'd say yes."

Lorne made an astute observation. "That's quite the distance to here from Meadow Creek."

Dan agreed, but still said, "That means whatever Lee shot is either very fast, or very strong—or both, to be this far away."

Lorne drove between the trees with the high beams on. The three passengers held their loaded weapons, scanning the trees. Lee occasionally spit blood out of his mouth. Still skeptical, Walter kept his eyes open, which was a feat in itself.

Suddenly, headlights illuminated a furry mound hunched over and motionless on the ground.

"There it is!" shouted Lorne.

Walter burst out laughing. "You crack victims! That's just a grizzly bear. A huge one, I give you that, but it's just a grizz."

Lee glared at Walter. "Well, if you're so positive, it's *just* a grizzly, go out and see if it's dead. We'll back you up from our windows."

"All right."

Walter clicked the safety off his rifle and opened his door. Dan reached over the seat and slammed Walter's door shut.

"I know you don't believe us, but don't go out there."

"Whatever it is," replied Walter, "I'll be careful and make sure it's dead."

"Listen to Dan," said Lorne. "It's not your responsibility. We three were the ones that tried to kill it, so one of us should do it."

Lorne and Lee agreed with Dan. Lorne reached for his pack of cigarettes. He took out three and ripped one in half, put the half and two others in his hand, and then put the extra broken half in his mouth and lit it. Dan, Lee, and Lorne were about to hopefully pull the long ones when Walter stopped them.

"You all might think I shouldn't be part of this, but I am, so stick another cig in your hand, I'm picking also," Walter demanded.

Lorne looked at Walter, sighed, and stuck one more cigarette into his hand. The men each picked a cigarette and then opened their hands together.

"Shit," sighed Dan.

He double-checked his fully loaded rifle, grabbed one more clip and put it in his pocket, and then got out of the truck. Lee took Lorne's rifle and he and Walter sat halfway out their windows, aiming at the furry mound. Lorne was ready to hit it with the truck if he had to. Dan walked slowly toward the dark heap with his gun pointed at it, trying not to gag from the odour the carcass emitted.

"He should put a few more shots in it right now to make sure it's dead," Lee said to Walter and Lorne.

"A, he doesn't want to piss it off if it's playing possum," Walter replied. "B, he doesn't want to alarm anything else, just in case it's not alone. And C, if it's a trophy bear like I think it is, we don't need anymore holes put into it."

Dan had reached the mound of fur. He poked it cautiously with the barrel of his rifle—nothing. He jabbed it quite a bit harder. Again, it didn't move. Dan looked back at the truck and shrugged his shoulders, and then gave it a huge kick with his boot.

"I believe it's dead," he said. "It fucking reeks, but come on out. You guys have to see this, we're loading this puppy up."

"What is it?" yelled Walter.

"You're helping me load it, so come out and see for yourself," Dan replied. "There's a pretty good reason we thought it was a bear."

Lorne shut off the engine, keeping the headlights on. The men got out of the truck and walked over to the dead animal. Lorne grabbed his rifle back from Lee. Lee quickly picked up a large stick as a replacement. Inspecting the furry carcass, the men noticed it wearing a bearskin jacket and bear paws as gloves. Walter was speechless. Dan kicked it and rolled it over.

Lee yelled, "Told ya! We're going to be famous, bitches! I can't still believe it."

"That you shot Bigfoot?" Dan asked.

* * * * *

Back in Edwardson, sitting at Lorne's kitchen table, Will dropped his pencil and Mike paused writing as the visitors stopped and stared at Lorne. Mike blinked multiple times. "I'm sorry, but did you just say '*Bigfoot*?'"

"Did I fucking stutter?" Lorne asked abruptly.

Joan put her hand on his shoulder. "Calm down, Lorne," she said. "He's just making sure he heard you right."

Joan stared hard at Mike. "Right?" she said.

Mike quickly looked back down at his notepad. "Exactly, just making sure I'm writing this down correctly."

James and Will sat there quietly as Lorne looked all of them in the eye. "Yeah, I said Bigfoot. Sasquatch. Fucking Hairy Henderson. Now you know why I didn't really want to bring this shit up here, or at the hospital."

Everyone took a sip of coffee, wondering what to say. A long minute went by before James finally said, "Well, you would have made Chief Gramps happy. He would never let us live it down if he were still alive to hear this. He used to say sasquatch have been here for ages. I never believed it, but if you say that's what you saw . . . then I believe it."

Mike raised an eyebrow towards James but said nothing.

"So Mike," James asked, "shall Lorne carry on?"

"By all means, I need to hear the rest of it."

Will sat like a fly on the wall, keeping as quiet as possible, just listening to everything being said. It was like he was on one of his wilderness expeditions, observing and catching every detail that he could.

"All right, Lorne," said James, "carry on, but you might want to snag that 'Get well' gift I got you, first."

Lorne got up from the table to retrieve the basket. He came back and put it on the table, and then took the flowers and handed them to Joan.

"Here, honey, these are for you. This," Lorne raised the bottle of whiskey, "is for me. Well, *us* now."

Lorne cracked the bottle and topped up coffees around the table. Lorne slid one cup over to Mike. Mike waved no, hesitated, and then said, "Hell, why not."

Lorne downed his own cup, topped it up again, and then sat down. He lit a cigarette again and continued with his story.

* * * * *

Walter was speechless for the first time in his life

"Hey, Walter, no sarcastic remark?" asked Dan.

The others chuckled while Walter stared at the dead figure, dumbfounded.

"Hey," said Lee, "Earth to Walter. You still there?"

Dan walked over to Walter and gave him a shove. This seemed to spark something in Walter, who began rambling at the speed of sound.

"I can't believe we killed a Bigfoot! We shouldn't have killed a Bigfoot. No one has ever killed a Bigfoot before. If they did, they've never lived to tell the tale. We killed one, and now we have one. We shouldn't have one, we should just leave it and pretend we never saw one. We should just go home without one."

Lorne asked Dan and Lee, "Where did the ramblin' man come from? That doesn't sound like Walter at all."

Dan shook Walter by his shoulders and said, "Hey, man, snap out of it. What's the big deal? It's dead. Calm down."

"You know what?" Lorne said looking around. "The ramblin' man is right. We should just get the hell out of here."

"Bullshit!" Dan instantly refused. "This is our money ticket here, people. None of us are living high on the hog here. Hell, we're barely on the hog. This beats any trophy anybody has ever had. Do you guys realize how big this is?"

Lee agreed with a big smile. "I'm with you, Dan. This has got to be the coolest thing I've ever seen, and I've seen a lot of cool shit in my time."

Lorne tried to make his point. "I'm not arguing the fact that this is amazing by any means. It's just I have a horrible feeling right now, and I don't like it, that's all."

Walter cut in. "A horrible feeling? That's an understatement. We shot an endangered species. Also, if it's the only one around why do I feel like we're being watched by a thousand eyes itching to take us down at any time?"

Dan started to get irritated. "Because right now you're a paranoid baby bitch, and you're about to get smacked."

"Don't be a douche," said Walter. "All I'm saying is if we're going to take this thing, let's get our asses in gear, load this fucker up, and get the hell out of here, because I am scared shitless right now."

"That's what I'm talking about!" shouted Lee.

Lorne backed Walter. "I'm not liking this place either, so I agree with Walter one-hundred percent."

"So, we all agree, then," Dan replied. "Lorne and Walter are pussies, and we're taking this thing home." Dan and Lee high-fived each other.

Walter ran to the truck and grabbed some rope while Lorne kept an eye out with his finger on the trigger of his rifle. Walter came back to the dead body with the rope. Dan took it and hurled half of it over a tree limb.

"Hey, Lee," Dan said, "grab its hands and tie them together. We'll pull it up, and Lorne, get in the truck, back it up, and underneath the thing—then we can drop it in."

Lee tied the mammoth of a beast's hands together, and then the four men pulled with all their strength, heaving it upright. They were all shocked by how tall it was. With its body dangling from the arms, it was about fifteen feet in length, casting a shadow resembling a human. The men felt pity and guilt. Dan tied off the rope.

Lee looked at Dan and Walter. Lorne was about to head for the truck and turn it around, but Lee said, "Wait Lorne, I've changed my—"

From the bushes came a sudden high-pitched, blood-curdling howl into the darkness. Dan's head shot around. "What the hell was that?"

The others looked around nervously. The howl came again, but from the other direction. Lorne and Dan pointed their rifles toward the woods, each in different directions. Lee stepped away from the hanging bigfoot. Walter ran and jumped into the truck.

Lee looked over at Lorne, while Lorne looked back at Dan strangely, who was just standing in one spot, staring into the woods with his rifle cocked and by his side.

Dan slowly said to Lorne and Lee, "Lorne, start the truck, and Lee, fucking run. Now!" Lee darted towards the truck. Lorne jumped into the cab to start the engine while Walter opened the back door for Lee, who dove in. The vicious howl was gaining on Dan, who shot from the hip and hit a tree. There was a sudden silence. Dan turned and spotted a four-legged figure about twenty feet in front of him.

The huge, shadowy beast rose on two legs and looked down at Dan. Everything was quiet and motionless until shots rang out. Walter hung out his window, giving Dan an opportunity to escape by firing his rifle toward the beast. The giant did a 90-degree turn and vanished into the shadows. Dan did a 180-degree turn and hightailed it toward the truck. He dove, sliding along the hood and landing on the other side of the crew-cab. Rising quickly from the ground, Dan jumped into the passenger side as Walter rolled up his window. Just as fast as the locks clicked, Lee's door was ripped off its hinges and fired into the trees. Walter used his rifle to shoot through Lee's door at whatever was on the other side. Through the ringing in their ears, the men heard a painful yelp from outside.

"Go, man, go!" yelled Lee.

Lorne slammed the truck into gear and hauled ass out of the bush. In passing, he smacked the carcass hanging from the tree and smashed the windshield. Branches, limbs, and small trees scraped the sides of the truck as Lorne slalomed through the woods with his foot pressed firmly on the gas pedal, trying to find the road. Lee was frantically tugging on his seat belt, which kept triggering the quick speed safety lock. Walter grabbed the slack of Lee's seatbelt and held it on Lee for dear life.

Dan pointed out the window. "There's the road! On the left"

Lorne veered left, sideswiping a stump. He didn't slow down, even as the road came into sight. The truck hit a lip in the ditch and caught air, as did its passengers, and then the truck slammed back onto the road. Lorne straightened it out and began driving a little less frantically.

"Is everyone all right?" Lorne asked.

"I thought we were in an airplane for a bit there," Dan answered, eyes wide.

"What the hell was that sound?" asked Lee.

"You know damn well what that sound was," replied Lorne. "We just never heard it before."

"Hey, Lee," said Walter, "you're bleeding."

Lee looked at his shirt and saw blood. He pulled it off and found four claw marks across his arm. "Shit, I didn't even feel it. Kind of hurts now that you've mentioned it."

"It looks deep. Are you going to need stitches?" Walter asked.

"Naw, I'll just wrap it up with my shirt. It should be okay, could've been worse, that thing could have taken my arm off with the door, no doubt," said Lee. Walter let go of Lee and his seatbelt, and Lee took a breath of fresh air, regaining his circulation in his body.

Walter told Lee, "Make sure you put that seatbelt on, don't want you to fall out and bounce onto the road—we probably wouldn't stop to pick you up."

Lee pulled on the seatbelt and clicked it easily into place.

"Figures. Soon as we're out of danger and onto the smooth road, my belt fucking works."

"I can guarantee the manufacturers didn't plan for this scenario," replied Dan.

Lorne looked out the cracked windshield. "I'm not sure, but we've gotta be only a couple clicks from the cabin."

"That's if we're going the right way," replied Dan. "At the next wide spot, we should stop and get our bearings. We should also check out the truck. It seems to be riding a little rough."

Lorne laughed. "Are you nuts? I'm not stopping until we get home. Screw the cabin!"

"Dan's right," Lee said, "if we're taking the wrong road, we'll end up in the boondocks and run out of gas, or just keep driving in circles."

"You two sure team up a lot, don't you?" said Lorne.

"They sure do," answered Walter, "but eighty percent of the time, they make sense."

"Walter, you're still awake?" asked Lorne sarcastically.

"I have to be," replied Walter. "It's pretty breezy in here right now." Lee pretended to do up his window on his missing door.

Dan pointed out a wide spot on the road. Lorne pulled off and parked the truck. Everyone sighed while the dust slowly caught up

and settled down beside them, covering everything. There was smoke steaming out from under the hood. The truck was overheating. Lee undid his seatbelt and hopped out, holding his arm. Lorne got out and stretched while Walter leaned his head on the seat. Dan sighed and closed his eyes.

Lorne was assessing the damage when he asked, "Hey Dan, do you want the good news or the bad news?"

"Neither at this moment."

Lorne ignored him. "Your boss' truck looks like shit, and we have a flat tire."

"Who cares? It was a Ford, anyhow," Dan replied.

Walter piped up from the backseat. "If it were a Chevy, we'd be pushing it out of the woods."

Lorne asked Dan to pop the hood. Dan leaned over to the driver's side and flexed the hood release. As he did so, Walter reached and flicked Dan's hat off his head. Lorne walked over to the front of the truck and waved the steam away. Dan sat up, put his hat back on, and gave Walter the middle finger.

"What's the good news?" Dan shouted to Lorne.

"I don't know what we ran over, but besides this thing smelling like coolant and shit, I believe it'll still get us home," replied Lorne, "and we have a spare. We have to let it cool down a bit, though."

Dan didn't even have to turn around to know Walter was smiling that the Ford would get them home. "Don't say a word," Dan warned him, "or I'm coming over this seat to kick your ass."

Lee hopped into the backseat. "Shit, guys, I recognize this road. We're only about half an hour away from the cabin. We just have to go up a bit and take a left at the end of the switchback."

"Told ya," Lorne smiled. "I knew we were close. So, what do you guys want to do?"

"Screw the gear and the cabin, and let's go home." Dan said.

"I'm driving," Lorne said, "and two votes count as the majority, so let's get the hell home."

"How do you know Walter and me agree with you guys?" asked Lee.

"Because I actually don't care," Lorne countered. "I'm going home, and you're all coming with me." Lorne slammed down the hood. He looked through the cracked windshield and noticed all of his friends staring past him. "What now?" he asked.

The steam rising from the engine collided with the breath of a large silhouette standing right behind him. Dan tried to yell for Lorne to run. The beast let out a monstrous roar and backhanded Lorne, who sailed into the air and crashed into the trees.

Lorne lay motionless while the others sat shocked inside the truck. The monster let out another roar and started slamming its fists on the hood of the truck like a crazed ape. It shook and destroyed the front of the truck. The three men had started screaming, but they soon came back to their senses. Walter jumped out and ran to Lorne. Dan jumped into the back seat to grab a rifle, but before he could even get his hands on it, Lee was jerked from the seat by his feet and hurled onto the road. Lee looked up to see a different sasquatch baring his teeth at him. Dan darted out and pointed the rifle at the snarling beast. He suddenly felt himself being lifted off the ground. Dan had seconds to register the drooling, angry face looking back at him before he was tossed into the trees, as well. Dan hit the ground and bounced. He shook it off and noticed his rifle was only about five feet away. He quickly rolled to it and stood ready to shoot the big-footed beast down.

While Dan and Lee were having a duel between the two sasquatches, Walter was making sure Lorne was still alive. He noticed the Mexican standoff and shouted, "Stop! Put the gun down *now*, Dan!"

Dan kept sighting up one of the beasts. "Are you fucking nuts?" he asked.

"Trust me. Just put it down, *now*."

While Walter was warning Dan, the two sasquatches slowed their plan of attack, as well. Their look of anger had diminished and was replaced by curiosity.

Dan didn't care. "Fuck that. These assholes are going down."

"Don't do it!" Walter yelled again.

As soon as Dan cocked the trigger, a third sasquatch blew out of the bushes and swiped Dan from behind, gashing his side. It tore the rifle from Dan's hand and then picked him up and tossed him forward. Dan was airborne again, this time landing in the box of the truck. He stopped moving. The sasquatch turned their eyes to Lee lying on the ground. They surrounded him. Lee shouted at them.

"What the fuck? I didn't mean to kill your buddy, but if you want to dance, let's dance, assholes."

The sasquatch went to attack Lee when two shots rang into the air. The creatures stopped and looked at Walter with his rifle pointing at them.

"Leave Lee alone," Walter said calmly. "No one else is dying tonight. Now you three move over there."

He waved the gun to gesture them away from Lee. Lee was shocked to see that the sasquatch seemingly understood. Walter walked back to the truck and grabbed a first aid kit, still pointing the gun at the hairy group. He noticed Dan's motionless body. Walter scowled. He walked backwards slowly, pointing the rifle, and then headed back to Lorne. Walter made sure everyone could see him put the rifle down and then step away. He went to Lorne and started to wrap him up with bandages. The sasquatches looked at each other, and then at Lee, who yelled at Walter, "Are you insane? They are going to kill us!"

"I don't think so," Walter replied calmly. "We're not armed. I think we'll be fine."

"You *think*? Maybe in your rainbow-coloured world, but not in mine."

"Just don't make any fast movements," Walter said, "and don't pick up a rifle. I've got to help Lorne here, he's in pretty bad shape." Walter wrapped a bandage around Lorne's leg. The three sasquatches slowly walked towards Walter. Lee looked up. As the last one passed by him, it gave Lee a left hook and laid him out cold.

"Look," Walter said, surprisingly calmly. "I have no idea if you understand what I'm saying, but if you do, then let's call it even. We accidentally killed one of your guys, and you guys killed Dan. The sasquatch looked at Walter, confused. One of them made a couple grunts. Another kneeled down and looked at Lorne and his wounds. Walter noticed the two standing next to him showing more curiosity than anger. Walter also thought he saw a bit of sorrow. He watched the three communicate with each other with grunts and hand gestures. He heard a noise, looked around, and then jumped up quickly.

"Don't!" Walter shouted at Lee. He pushed one of the beasts down and rolled with it to the ground as the other two were startled from the noise of a rifle shot. Walter stood and stared at Lee, who had the rifle back in his hands. "You dumbass! You don't und—"

Walter felt his side and then fell face-first into the dirt. As he hit the ground, his breath blew the dirt away in front of him. Lee stood in horror; he'd just shot his buddy trying to save him from the beasts.

* * * * *

"Oh my god!" Will said, "Why would he have done that?"

Lorne calmly replied, "Because for some reason, Walter always had a soft spot for these things, even when we didn't believe they were real. In the back of his mind, he listened to Chief Gramps and always believed sasquatches existed."

James remembered Walter always listening with interest when his grandfather told his stories.

Lorne looked at Mike, and then continued, "So when you asked me at the hospital if I knew how many grizzly bears attacked us, I couldn't answer because there were no grizzly bears, ancient tribes, or anything paranormal that attacked us. It was all the same thing. A group of bearskin-wearing emotional bigfoot bastards. They were full of rage and hate when we were being attacked, but were totally different when they were helping us."

James quickly asked. "They helped you?"

"That's who kept Walter and me alive all this time. I was blind for a while, and Walter told me we were saved by an old Indian tribe. He figured I'd probably have freaked out and done more damage if I knew the truth at that time. I think he was right. They fixed Walter and me up and kept us alive as long as they could. I believe if Walter didn't try saving them that night, we all would have been dead."

"I think you're right about that," James said.

Will couldn't hide the disappointment in his face when he heard there were no grizzly bears. Lorne looked at him and said, "That's why you had to come. Joan told me you that's one of the reasons you moved here—to search for the monster grizzly bears."

"That was one of the big reasons."

"When I got away, I saw something that still might give you a reason to stay."

Mike asked, "How did you get away from them?"

"Well, that's where my secondary wounds came from." Lorne kissed Joan and smiled as Mike, Will, and James sat eagerly waiting to hear the rest.

Chapter XI

Lorne woke up slowly. For him and the five others in the tribe, the morning started the same way it had for many weeks. With the coldness and the leaves off the trees, Lorne figured it had to be December. There was still no snow that stayed on the ground, but it could come at any time. Lorne tightened up his own wolf-skin jacket that Ekorn had given him as a breeze sailed through the cave entrance. With his eyes half-open, he watched the one sasquatch sitting by the fire as it got ready to go hunting.

Dawn slowly crept into the cave. Lorne watched as Bear, now known as "Grobain," sat cross-legged and motionless like a statue. "Kanin," who was formerly named Badger, tied a set of bear claws to Grobain's hands and a bearskin around him as a cloak. Lorne was starting to understand why it was hard to ever see a sasquatch. They had definitely learned from the Indians—or had the Indians learned from them? Lorne watched in awe as Grobain got ready to out into the wilderness, so calm and cool. He could not say the same for Ekorn, formerly Squirrel. The ordeal was similar, but not as well conducted. Kanin tried putting the bear gear on Ekorn, but it was like watching a mother dress her kid in his snowsuit when he's just eaten a chocolate bar. Lorne chuckled to himself as Kanin sighed with exhaustion.

Grobain stood up as much as he could with his bear cloak and touched his hand on the tops of all their heads. He then disappeared out the cave's entrance.

Kanin and Orn (formerly known as "Eagle") grabbed handfuls of different berries, flowers, leaves, and a few other things Lorne couldn't discern into their own bowls. Ekorn stood with his arms out to his side as both Kanin and Sparrow (now known as "Vrabie") began to rub all of the ingredients into Ekorn's fur and all over his body. As the ingredients started to mix, a strange and powerful odour emitted from Ekorn. It wafted towards Lorne, who tried to hold in his gagging. A tear from the exertion rolled down Lorne's face.

The process of applying the rub onto Ekorn took several minutes, until finally Ekorn was let go. He was out the door like a bullet. Most of the smell went with him, much to Lorne's relief. Kanin and Vrabie put everything away then washed the lingering smell off themselves in the trickling water that leaked out of the rocks of the cave. As they finished up, Orn tapped Vrabie and Kanin on the head as well as she headed out. Both Kanin and Vrabie quietly went back to their beds and went back to sleep. Lorne, quite amazed, wondered why they made one deliberately smelly and then the other one not—was one going to be downwind and one up, or was one a decoy? Then why would one just go out naked, or unarmed, so to speak—just as a lookout, maybe? All he knew was that he was watching history being made, and he wondered if he would live through this to tell anyone—or even if anyone would believe him if he did.

* * * * *

The wind started to pick up to a slight breeze. Two deer finished grazing in the field. They sauntered to the edge of the dense forest and walked on the edge until they found an easy spot to walk into. The wind whistled gently past them and the trees as the deer stepped over old growth and foliage, carefully and cautiously making as little noise as possible. It was a slightly overcast day, still sunny, but inside the dense canopy of the forest it was significantly darker—a perfect time to have an afternoon nap after a full lunch.

The two deer made their way through to find a comfortable, mossy, but secluded spot under a tree. As they zigzagged on a faint narrow game trail, they saw an ideal spot. The one deer started to settle in and lie down as the other lifted his leg—and then stopped dead in his tracks. The deer's ears popped straight up and he slowly put his foot back onto the ground, and very slowly, he scoured his surroundings. The other deer became alert, but was still lying down. The standing deer stood there for about five minutes, only making slight movements as it searched and smelt the air. It had one of those feelings that it was being watched, but besides the sounds of birds and squirrels, everything was normal; it felt like something was off, but it couldn't place it. Cautiously, the deer settled down and found a comfortable place to lie down for a nap.

Twenty minutes went by before both were finally asleep, the breeze still blowing a couple leaves off the trees. A tweet of a bird and a squeak of a squirrel were still heard here and there—a little closer, but also a little faster. The two deer rested on the mossy ground, the leaves on the tree above them start to fall more frequently, and about five feet away, one of the moss-covered rocks started to move. As quiet as a mouse, the one sasquatch shimmied down the tree as the other rolled out of the moss that was covering him. The third one sat still in his perch, keeping watch. The two sasquatches crept up to the two sleeping deer and snapped both their necks in a flash; the deer never even knew what happened. The two sasquatches swiped and sliced the throats of the deer to let them bleed out, and then with some (but not a lot of) effort, they ripped off all the deer's legs off the carcasses. As they carried their food back to the cave, Grobain stopped them dead in their tracks and listened to hear what was tracking them.

* * * * *

Lorne, Vrabie, and Kanin had built some more food packs and were tying them up Lorne's way when all three heard a massive howl outside the cave. Instantly, the three stopped what they were doing, and Vrabie quickly jumped through the cave door just like a paratrooper, snagged the top of one tree and swung to another smaller one, arching it over until he touched the ground. As the tree snapped and broke halfway up the trunk, Squirrel was on the ground bolting towards the echoing howl. Kanin was just as fast, leaving Lorne by himself. Lorne wasn't sure what was happening, but he knew it wasn't good.

Ten minutes went by without a sound, until he heard the frequent squeaks coming closer and closer. Vrabie popped up first, and then started to pull up Orn with Ekorn behind. Lorne quickly helped pull up Orn and helped him lie down on his bed. As he moved his hands, he saw that they were all covered with blood. Lorne grabbed the metal pot he found in the "rubble" pile about a week ago and filled it with water and started to warm it up on the fire, while Ekorn tried to clean the dirt and hair out of Orn's wounds. Ekorn got some wraps and put them in the water. As they all surrounded Orn, she started talking. Lorne didn't understand it all, but what he got was that Grobain was still out there and needed help. Lorne could tell Vrabie wasn't going anywhere with Orn hurt like that, and he also knew Ekorn wanted to stay and go at the same time.

Lorne looked at them all with a serious face and strongly stated his opinion. "Let's go, Ekorn. I can move pretty good now, take me down with you and I can help." All looked at Lorne with an odd expression in their faces. Lorne got angry and continued, "Don't piss me off. I've been here long enough. I know you can understand some of the shit I say, and you know you can trust me, so let's get them back here before you're all found out, all right?"

Orn grunted as Ekorn got a huge smile on his face. Ekorn looked at Lorne and said, "*Fa Pe!*"

Lorne nodded and sighed, "Finally. I'll get on your back, but I got to get something first." Lorne quickly hobbled and jumped into the shadows in the back of the cave, and within seconds he came back holding a spear and with an old-looking dagger tied to his leg that he had found in the pile of "useless artifacts."

Lorne smiled and nodded, and then in an enthusiastic voice, he said, "Okay, let's go!" Ekorn patted Orn on the head and winked at Vrabie. He then grabbed Lorne by the arm and threw him onto his back. Lorne held on as tightly as he could, ignoring the stench as Ekorn leapt out of the cave and onto a tree. Ekorn swung from limb-to-limb like an orangutan and then landed onto the ground quite delicately, considering the speed and size of him. He dropped off Lorne and hushed him and then turned into stealth mode. Both were quiet and listened for sounds of the other two.

They hunched down and looked around. Lorne felt the ground and realized he hadn't seen it or touched it in a long time. Lorne smelt the air and took in the fact it was fresh and not stagnate like the cave. As he listened to the sounds of the wilderness, he looked around to see Ekorn nowhere in sight. As Lorne scoured the forest he heard a faint growl in the distance—a bear growl, but not Grobain's growl. Just then, Lorne heard a squeak come from his left about fifteen feet away. Lorne turned to see Ekorn waving him towards his direction.

Lorne went over and whispered to Ekorn, "God damn, you guys know how to blend in." Ekorn pointed, and they quietly headed towards the growling. After about ten minutes of slow and quiet stalking, they saw two wolves in the distance. They were growling and looking at an old log wrapped in moss. Ekorn nudged Lorne to stay put, and then like a ninja, he jumped up to a tree limb and crossed over to the next until he was over top of the two wolves. Ekorn started to squeak periodically and listened for something back. He finally heard a couple of faint badger cries coming from the moss-covered log. Ekorn looked over at Lorne and pointed at the log, then pointed at the wolves, and then at himself. Lorne watched as Ekorn looked around, and then at the two snarling wolves. Ekorn let out this huge, freaky-sounding howl and a roar at the same time that made Lorne cringe in fear as a chill went down his spine. The two wolves looked up startled, as Ekorn dropped down in front of them. As both stared at Ekorn, Lorne noticed that there was a third about ten feet beside them. Ekorn, not backing down quickly, smacked the one wolf in the face about three times with cat-like reflexes. The wolf wobbled back and then looked at Ekorn again. The second wolf howled right in Ekorn's face, who returned with a roar and then potato-punched the second on the top of its head. As the wolf dropped to the ground, the third launched himself at Ekorn. Without a flinch, he caught the wolf in the air and tossed it past him.

Ekorn quickly dropped on all fours and ran straight into the forest. The two wolves snarled and charged after him, crushing branches and brush with them. Wolf number two woke up, shook his head, and then followed the rest of them. Lorne was surprised once more when he saw a fourth wolf come out of the woodwork and chase right behind the rest. Everything went quiet, and Lorne didn't make a move for about two minutes. He thought to himself, *That should be enough time to see if anything else was lingering around. I'll try my luck and move.*

Lorne quickly ran up towards the log and quietly said, "Hey, Kanin, are you okay? We need to get you out of here." Lorne heard nothing coming from the log. Lorne thought for a bit, and then called out with his elk call. Seconds later, he heard a badger squeak come from the log. Kanin slowly rolled away from the log, peeling the moss from over top of her. Lorne ran over and helped her up. He noticed a huge gash on her leg. Lorne ripped a sleeve off of his shirt and tied it around her leg. As he helped her stand, Kanin used Lorne as a leaning post and both headed towards the cave as fast as possible.

They made it to the cliff's edge where the cave was without a trace of the wolves, or Ekorn. Kanin looked up at the trees and towards the sky. She then started squeaking repeatedly, and Lorne did his elk call once more.

Moments later, Vrabie came whipping down and hugged her. She looked at Lorne with gratitude. Lorne looked back.

"I'm going back for Ekorn and Grobain, get her out of here." Lorne didn't wait for permission and took off back into the forest. Vrabie put Kanin on his back and scurried back up to the cave.

Lorne tracked the pack of wolf tracks for about twenty minutes without a sound. As he watched the trail fade and appear, he noticed that the wolves split up into two pairs, but he also saw a different set of tracks following behind. The pack of wolves were tracking Ekorn, while the bear they had heard a while back was tracking the pack of wolves—and now Lorne was tracking them all. Lorne knew this was not going to go in his favour if he found them all at the same time. He was cautious, because now the tracks were on either side of him.

Lorne was getting tired and figured he would try a different approach. He grabbed a piece of his shirt and wiped the sweat off of himself; he then hung it on a branch. Lorne walked about thirty feet upwind and bunkered onto the ground and covered himself with leaves and moss. As he blended into the ground, he took some well-needed breaths and watched the rag blow in the wind.

Lorne made little sound of his own and listened for other ones. In the distance, he could hear a couple tweets and the rustling of leaves from birds and squirrels—definitely not from Ekorn. Another half-hour went by when Lorne finally heard something larger than a weasel. He sat there listening and waiting as one of the pair of wolves slowly walked up and sniffed around, heading for the rag dangling from the branch. Lorne saw some fresh blood in its fur, but it wasn't limping nor did it seem to be in pain, so he figured it must have been Ekorn's blood. *So should I try and kill them, or should I follow them and see where they take me?* Lorne wondered.

As Lorne watched the two sniff around, he knew they were being cautious. The wolves got to the rag and sniffed the shit out of it, made some odd snarls, and looked around. Lorne started to tense up as the one wolf looked towards his direction. Lorne figured that there were four of them, plus a bear, so he might as well take out as many as he could out as quickly as possible—plus, he had the drop on these two.

Lorne put his spear in front of him and torpedoed out of the leaves and rammed the spear into the wolf. The wolf howled in pain and dropped to the ground. Lorne fell with it and broke the spear as both hit the ground. Lorne got up quickly, and was looking at the other wolf with just a stick in his hand. The wolf snarled. Lorne whipped out his knife that was tied around his leg. Lorne stood in attack mode with a weapon in each hand as both him and the wolf stared each other down. Both started to circle each other; suddenly, Lorne stopped and stared at the wolf, realizing why it wasn't attacking him. Lorne could feel the other set—or sets—of eyes staring at him. Lorne sighed and just said, "Shit."

The two other wolves lunged out of the bush and towards Lorne. Lorne quickly and wildly started swinging the stick and his knife around. He hit one in the nose and one in the side. Both let out a yelp, and the third got onto Lorne's back. Lorne dropped his stick, but twisted around and fought the wolf's head back from biting his face. He put his forearm up and the wolf bit into it. As Lorne yelled in pain, he gripped his knife tightly and repeatedly started jabbing it into the wolf's side. Blood and fur flew off his blade and onto him. At a quick glance, it looked like two wolves were fighting each other, with all the blood covering both of them and Lorne wearing his wolf-skin jacket. The wolf on top of him started to weigh him down. As the wolf stopped moving, Lorne rolled it over and stood up, looking at the other two who were looking at him; Lorne was covered in their brother's blood, as well as his own. Lorne was cut, scraped, and bitten, and he stared at the other two while holding onto his arm.

Lorne spit out some blood and boldly yelled, "Now, who's next? Either way none of us are going home in one piece."

The two, standing side by side, started to growl—and then suddenly, both of their heads were pounded two feet into the ground by a force that was fifteen feet long and about 1,500 pounds. Ekorn had dropped out of a tree and onto the two wolves; then he rolled and fell to the ground. Ekorn combat-rolled back up, and was facing the wolves, whose heads looked like smashed pumpkins. He looked at the bleeding carcasses and let out a victory grunt. It wasn't the big one he had let out near Kanin, but it was more smug. Ekorn stood straight up, looked directly at Lorne, and gave him a smile.

Lorne looked at Ekorn, more pissed off than happy. Lorne staggered slowly and cautiously walked over to Ekorn. Lorne started to angrily whisper, "You asshole. How long were you up there? I was looking for you for about an hour. Were you watching me all this time?" Ekorn, still smiling, put his hand on Lorne's shoulder and tipped his head towards Lorne's rag. Then he looked back at Lorne and nodded at him with approval. Lorne lost his anger and calmed down. "Well, I felt I was running in circles, and thought I could put the odds in my favour by luring them with my smell, instead of being surrounded or ambushed by them. I'm still not sure if it worked."

Ekorn looked at Lorne with concern. Lorne just shrugged and said, "This is more of the wolves and Kanin's blood than mine. I'll be all right, Kanin is safe at the cave." Ekorn put his finger up as a number one and then pointed towards the north.

Lorne replied, "It's those bear tracks I saw a ways back, right?"

Ekorn nodded.

Lorne whipped his good arm as blood dripped from it. He then looked at Ekorn wounds. "Well, besides a couple scrapes, you look pretty good, so let's go get that bastard and find Grobain—but try to keep up, okay?"

Ekorn looked at Lorne with an odd look, and then paused. Lorne looked back. "You'd be laughing right now if you got my sense of humour." Lorne sighed, and then ripped the sleeve off of the other side of his shirt and wrapped it around his arm. Ekorn nudged Lorne forward about two steps, and then both started heading towards the bushes that Ekorn had pointed towards.

Both were tired and wounded. Ekorn tracked and led at a decent pace that Lorne could follow, until both heard the sounds of two beasts fighting. The two slowed down and zigzagged back and forth from tree to tree until they came to a clearing where they saw two blood-drenched, fur-covered, vicious-sounding beasts standing twenty feet apart from each other. Grobain was standing there with his bearskin dangling off of him like a shredded cape. They could see flesh and bone inside his shoulder as his hair flipped and flopped around him as he moved. The grizzly bear was also looking worse for wear. Both stood there growling, and then dropped to their four legs and charged at each other. Both stood up and smashed into each other. They started bear-hugging, biting, clawing, and maiming. Both Ekorn and Lorne stood there and noticed that the grizzly bear was bigger than Grobain was in every way, and it was winning. The two monsters untangled and separated once more, backed up about fifteen feet, and stood there, staring at each other once more. As they stood there, staring and growling, Ekorn let out three tweets. Grobain quickly looked over towards the trees where Ekorn and Lorne were, and let out a large, quick snap; Lorne swore he had heard him yell "No!"

Ekorn got a frown on his face and cowered down. Lorne looked at Ekorn. "That's it?" Lorne asked. "We're not helping him? What the fuck—he needs help!" Ekorn just knelt down on one knee and watched as the grizz and Grobain charged once more. Lorne looked at Ekorn with a disappointed look on his face. "Maybe this is some tribal thing of yours, but I'm not your tribe, and he needs help." Lorne took off with his stick and knife, but he didn't get as far as he wanted. Ekorn quickly grabbed him by the back of the neck, lifted him off the ground, and put him down beside him. Pissed off once more, Lorne sat there stewing as Ekorn kept his hand on Lorne. Lorne glared at Ekorn as he said, "You are a bunch of odd fuckers, I'll give you that."

Both sat there as Grobain and the grizzly matched blow-for-blow. Three more charges happened until the grizzly ran passed Grobain and sliced through Grobain's stomach with his claws. Grobain turned and dropped to the ground. Lorne watched in rage as the grizzly turned to Grobain and sauntered back to him. The grizzly looked at Grobain for a moment, and then stood straight up and let out a huge roar. Right then Grobain instantly jumped up, and with his one hand he backhanded the grizzly's jaw. As the grizzly bear started to fall back with a shattered jaw, Grobain's second hand came around and swiped the right side of its face off to the bone. The grizzly dropped to the ground like a sack of potatoes and made a loud thump.

Grobain stood there with his arm around his waist, steam rolling off of him and colliding with the mist that hang in the early morning air. Instantly, Ekorn jumped up, leaving Lorne in the trees. In a matter of seconds, Ekorn was at Grobain's side, catching him before he fell. Lorne slowly walked out to see Grobain in Ekorn's arms, looking like a bag of shit. He knew there was no hope for Grobain, so he stood back and left the two alone. He heard the two speaking to each other, but he couldn't make out the words—it wasn't meant for him, anyhow.

Seconds later, he heard a squeak come from Ekorn. Lorne turned around and saw Grobain looking at him, pointing at him to come over. Lorne walked over and knelt beside Grobain, who got a smile on his face when he saw Lorne was covered in blood and his wolf skin. Grobain took his hand and cupped Lorne's whole face. He then said in sasquatch words, *"Ekki stemme, alum stemme. Ekorn lider alum."*

Lorne was not sure what Grobain said, but he knew it wasn't bad the way he said it. Lorne just smiled, took Grobain's hand off his face, shook it, and then replied, "I think I understand what happened here, but I don't have to like it. You're an odd and amazing bunch. Thank you for not killing me and Walter."

Grobain then said something Lorne *did* understand. "Fire Elk... do good." Lorne understood that clearly, as "Fire Elk" was the name they had given him, but he was shocked that Grobain had said it in English. Grobain looked back at Ekorn and put his hand over Ekorn's face, just like he had done to Lorne. Seconds later, Grobain's hand slowly dropped down and fell to his chest. Ekorn sat there not doing anything, while Grobain lay there motionless.

Looking and feeling messed up, Lorne saw the sun start to rise. Cautiously, he tapped Ekorn on the shoulder and pointed towards the day creeping up. Lorne spoke softly. "I'm sorry, but we've got to get you two out of here before anything or anyone sees you."

Ekorn looked around, and then sighed. He got up, slung Grobain over his shoulder, and then looked at Lorne.

"You get him out of here," Lorne said, gesturing to Grobain. "I'll be fine. I just need to catch my breath. I'll be there as soon as I can."

Ekorn pointed north where Lorne saw the top of a glacier. In a gruff and low tone, Ekorn spoke, "Walk... that way... before... sun goes ... down."

Lorne stared at Ekorn in shock. "You knew English all this time?"

"We... know many words... from... many things," replied Ekorn. "Just... don't... like... white man's... words. Too... hard... to learn, and . . . white man . . . need . . . to remember . . . to . . . open mind. Now . . . go home . . . to . . . own tribe."

Lorne stood in silence, sighed with immense relief, and then shook Ekorn's hand, smiling, "I'll miss you guys . . . and thank you."

Ekorn smiled, waved at Lorne, and then turned and jumped into the wilderness, disappearing into the shadows for the last time. Lorne sighed, looked around, and breathed in the fresh, free air. He looked down at the bear carcass and sat using it as a cushion. Lorne soaked up the remaining warmth of the bear's heat. The sun's rays peeked through the trees as Lorne peeled back his wolf skin and watched his own blood seep out of his wounds.

Lorne thought to himself, *I'll just take a rest here for a moment, catch my breath, and then head home.* The sun felt good, really good. Lorne fell in and out of consciousness. At one point he saw Walter. *Huh,* thought Lorne, *Walter looks a lot better right now.*

"Hey, Walter," Lorne said aloud. "Why are you here?"

Walter smiled. "To say good job, and also that you're a pussy."

Lorne looked at Walter confused.

"Did I stutter?" asked Walter. "You heard me. You survived multiple animal attacks, met a whole new species, and hung out with me and kept me company as long as you could." Walter continued, "You have a wicked story to tell. You can't wait to get home. Then when you get the chance, you pussy out and talk to me. Hence, Pussy!"

"I'm just taking a break, I'm hurt here."

"Boo-fucking-hoo. I'm *dead* here. Wrap up those wounds you've got there," Walter ordered. "Use that wicked cool spear-staff as a walking stick and go the fuck home. By the way, that was an awesome spear and knife you had."

"All right, I got this." Lorne rallied. "Thanks. I miss you, bud."

"Right back at you. Now, get moving."

* * * * *

Mike's pencil was still in his hand, but it never touched paper. He looked down at his empty notepad, and then back at Lorne. "Holy shit!" Mike said.

"Well put," James replied.

Lorne took another drink of his whiskey-infused coffee and stared across the table at Mike, Will, and James. "I wish I could tell you what happened to Dan and Lee, but I wasn't there."

Will finally spoke. "I think we can help with that. The story you have just told us actually makes our findings more clear. Knowing that these were not grizzly bears—and with the information and evidence James, Detective Copeland, and I have gathered—we might be able to tell you what happened."

Lorne and Joan's eyes lit up, and they asked Will to proceed.

Will took a sip of his "coffskey" and continued to speak, "When Lee accidentally shot Walter during the altercation with the sasquatch, all hell broke loose."

Chapter XII

Lee saw Walter hit the ground. Any common sense Lee had left went out the window. Lee quickly shouted, "You fuckers are going to die!"

Lee pulled the trigger as fast as possible. Bullets ripped out toward the sasquatches, who ducked and scattered, darting into the bush. One hunched down like a bear and zigzagged into the bush on all fours. Another grabbed Lorne by the ankle and dragged him into the forest, while the other threw Walter over its shoulder like a potato sack and also darted into the bush. They disappeared into the shadows of the wilderness.

Lee unloaded the whole magazine into the bushes after them, and then quickly reloaded and repeated. He reloaded a third time, and then looked around. He saw no sign of the beasts—or of any other animal, for that matter. Lee ran to the truck and got into the driver's seat. He tried to start the engine with no luck. He got out and grabbed one of the packs. He saw Dan's body in the truck bed, bleeding out. Lee bowed his head and then just about shit himself when he heard Dan say, "You know a full round are about ten bucks."

Lee's jaw dropped. "Holy shit, you're alive!"

Dan opened his eyes slowly. "Doesn't feel like it. What's going on?"

"We're getting out of here."

"Where are the others?"

Lee knew Dan wouldn't be able to handle the truth, so he said what needed to be said at the time. "Don't worry about that right now, they both said they'd meet us at the cabin. Let's worry about catching up with them. We have to walk out of here, because the truck is done."

"Well, you best get going without me. It's going to take you forever."

Lee looked at Dan. "It's a lot closer as the crow flies, and this crow is rarin' to go with you."

"I can't feel anything, though."

"Can you still move your arms?" Dan raised his right arm slowly. "You carry the pack, while I carry you."

Dan looked at himself, and then back at Lee. "You're crazy," he said, breathless. "I'm going to die soon. I can see my stomach."

Lee cringed inwardly. "It's not as bad as you think. Also, you're too stubborn to die, and too beat-up to fight me on this."

Lee took his long-sleeved shirt off and tied it around Dan's waist. He jumped out of the box of the truck, slowly pulled Dan to the edge, and then backed up as Dan wrapped his legs around Lee's waist. Dan screamed in pain, but managed to grab the packsack. Lee hauled ass along the road toward the cabin. With Dan on his back and the rifle in his left hand, he kept a steady pace for about twenty minutes, keeping an eye out for stalking monsters.

"Hey, Dan, are you doing all right?"

Dan only moaned in pain.

"As long as I'm hearing something out of you, that means you're good," said Lee. He was slowing down. In another twenty minutes, Lee stopped to lean against a tree while still piggybacking Dan, knowing if he sat down, he wouldn't get back up. Lee leaned the rifle against the tree as well and reached into the packsack, grabbed a bottle of water, downed half of it, and then offered the rest to Dan. Most of the water just drained out of Dan's mouth and onto Lee's shoulder and onto the ground. Lee tried to keep their spirits up and lighten the mood.

"I carry you all this way, wait on you hand and foot, and you just spit it out. When we get back to the cabin, you can get the beers for both of us. You can just toss them to me. You don't have to walk anywhere."

"Just put me on the cooler and wheel me around," groaned Dan. The men chuckled.

Lee let out a sigh of relief and said to Dan, "Good to hear some words from you. So, you already have a plan, that's good. I'm getting thirsty for a couple brewskies just thinking about them."

"Well then, pitter-patter, let's get at 'er." Dan moved his one arm like he was feebly cracking a whip, and whispered, "Hiigghhyyaa . . ."

Lee gripped Dan a little harder and grabbed the rifle. They headed for the cabin again. Lee was starting to make his way from tree to tree using them as leaning posts.

About half an hour went by when he looked up and blessedly saw a rock chimney peeking through the trees. Both were physically and mentally fatigued, but their spirits rose when they saw a fraction of their cabin.

Lee said to Dan, "We're almost there, buddy."

"Good," replied Dan. "I was starting to get tired."

Just then, Lee heard some rustling in the bushes near them. He couldn't see anything, and didn't know what had made the sound, but he didn't wait to find out. Lee gathered all the strength and energy left in him and bolted through the woods to the cabin door. Dan dropped the pack to lighten the load. Lee got to the door, and Dan reached for the door handle. Lee pulled back and the door opened. They burst through and dropped to the ground. Lee kicked the door closed, and then reached up and locked it. He positioned his body in front of it, and then at last took a big breath.

Dan pulled himself up into a sitting position across from Lee. Lee lay on the floor, gasping for air and pondered if he should throw up or not. They both took a few more breaths, resting on the floor for about five minutes, until Lee said to Dan, "Let's have a breather, pack some food and ammo, and then get the fuck out of dodge to the highway."

Dan looked at the blood-soaked shirt wrapped around his waist. He tried to adjust it, but felt his guts shift sideways. Dan looked at Lee and said, "Sounds like a plan. Let's have a beer, and then you pack up some stuff. I'll gather my energy and give you moral support. By the way, we left the packsack outside."

Lee looked around the cabin. "Fuck it. I'll pack our shit in a sheet."

Dan reached over to the cooler sitting on the floor near him. He could feel the fabric tear open his wound even more, but he didn't say anything. He grabbed two beers and tossed one to Lee. They lifted the cans into the air.

"Here's to a weekend that could have been worse," said Dan.

Lee stared at Dan in shock. "How the hell could this weekend have been worse?"

"We could be sitting here on the floor drinking water instead of lukewarm beer."

"Well, I can't argue with that logic."

The men tipped their bottles, and then Lee got up and started putting some bread, water, a blanket and some ammo onto the bed.

He was about to wrap it all up in a sheet when they heard something shake the door handle. Both quickly looked at the door to make sure it was locked. The door shook harder.

"Walter? Lorne?" Dan spoke loud and clear. "Anybody else? Someone better answer, or I'm going to greet you with a shitload of bullets."

The door stopped rattling. They heard footsteps walk around the deck. Dan saw a large figure pass by the window.

"You know that was way too big to be Lorne or Walter," he said.

"I know. I say we just start shooting all over the place through the door and windows. It'll confuse them long enough for me to run out and start the four-wheeler, come grab you, and ride to safety."

"I have a better and more logical idea," Dan said. "These bastards are too big to fit through the windows. You know they'll have to come through the door unless they go through the chimney, or through a two-storey locked window. Prop me up by the stairs facing the door with the rifle and a box of ammo. When they come in, I'll shoot and keep shooting. You go upstairs and sneak out the window and onto the roof. You should be able to jump onto the generator shack and get to the four-wheeler, then haul ass and get the hell out of here."

Lee frowned. "I don't like your idea. Your idea blows. I'm not going to let you stay here and be killed by these things like Walter and Lorne. You're going with me."

"Walter and Lorne are dead?"

Dan bowed his head and said, "I didn't want to tell you that. You had to think about you staying alive."

"Dude, I'm already dead, and you know it. Let's have at least one person make it out of here alive."

Lee was about to argue when he saw Dan's wound pooling on the floor. Dan's eyes slowly closed and his face turned paler.

"I can't win an argument with you," Lee sadly said.

Dan looked up at Lee and replied, "Damn rights. You also have barely enough energy to get yourself out, so get me into position."

Lee sighed, knowing Dan was right. He slowly and carefully dragged Dan over to the stairs facing the door, so if he had to, Dan could fire upstairs, as well. He loaded Dan's rifle and put it into his friend's hand, and then hugged the top of Dan's head with his arm.

"It's been a good ride overall, hasn't it, my friend?" said Lee.

"Wouldn't have missed it for the world, bud, give or take some scenarios."

Lee choked back tears and tried to smile. "I love you man."

"Right back at you, now get out of here, you gay bastard."

Lee let go of Dan reluctantly and then crept up the stairs. Dan sighted up the front door, waiting for one of the creatures to come calling. Lee got to the top of the stairs and went to the window. He noticed it was still locked. He sighed in relief, but heard Dan yell, "Come and get it motherfuckers!" and a large bang followed by what sounded like the front door being ripped off its hinges. Downstairs, Dan watched as two huge arms and paws came through the door. He fired at the entrance as fast as he could. The paws quickly disappeared.

Dan grinned until the cabin door was suddenly flung back through the entrance. It landed on top of Dan. There was total silence.

Lee was shocked by how fast their plan went astray. He peeked down the stairs and saw two sasquatches sneaking into the cabin through the entryway. He rubbed his eyes and swore he was looking at two grizzly bears instead of sasquatches, but he knew what they were, and his escape time was limited. Lee went back to the window and opened it as quietly as possible. He stopped in his tracks, hearing a long, slow growl come from behind him. Lee turned slowly, realizing something had been in the same room with him the whole time. As another sasquatch walked up the stairs, the one that growled at him appeared out of the dark corner in the room. Lee noticed the thing was bleeding.

"I guess you can open and close doors," Lee said. He was suddenly unbelievably tired and frustrated with the whole ordeal. He'd just lost three of his best friends. Lee dropped the homemade pack and gave the sasquatch the middle finger as he said, "I should have killed you and your whole asshole clan when I had the chance."

The bleeding sasquatch pounced on Lee and beat him to a bloody pulp like a rabid gorilla, then sliced his body in half with two quick swipes from its massive claws as the other watched. Downstairs, a third sasquatch sniffed cautiously around Dan. It lifted the door off Dan's body, and satisfied with the amount of blood pooling from the body, tossed the door back outside with a snarl. He looked toward the ceiling, listening to the commotion happening upstairs and started smiling. Then there was a noise at his feet.

"Surprise, asshole!"

Dan, relieved of the door off his body, pulled the trigger of the rifle and hit the sasquatch between the eyes. The bigfoot dropped like a sack of potatoes. The blast startled the sasquatch pair upstairs, who then blasted through the window, one of them with Lee's torso in his mouth. They took the glass and half the window frame with them and then landed on the generator shack, crashing through the roof and disabling the generator. The creatures scrambled over each other and the rubble of the destroyed shed. Within a few strides, they were out of view and into the woods. In one leap, they were up in the trees, swinging from limb-to-limb like two spider monkeys. In a few short minutes, they were two football fields away.

Slowly the two sasquatches began to calm down. They stopped swinging through the trees and landed on the ground. Exhausted and breathing heavily, they each looked at the other's fur, which was matted with twigs, dirt, and blood. One looked to see the other still had part of Lee's torso in his mouth. The sasquatch growled in disgust, grabbed it, and hurled it as far as he could. As both settled down and as the quiet snuck in, one sasquatch tapped the other's shoulder and the two silently turned back and headed back to the cabin to retrieve their fallen comrade.

Ten minutes went by, and then the two stealthy figures were looking at the silent cabin. They crept around to the front door and peeked in to see one of their own dead on the floor. The two looked at Dan, who was also dead. Like a cat, the one crept in through the doorway and knelt to feel the dead sasquatch's leg as the other kept watch. He paused for a few seconds, and then carefully picked his friend up and fireman-carried him out of the cabin and into the bushes. The two let out one more blood-curdling howl and then disappeared back into the darkness.

The Clan

* * * * *

Everyone sat at the kitchen table with full cups of cold coffee and stared at each other. Lorne put out his cigarette and said, "All right. It makes sense to me, if that's what you can call it."

The room went quiet and still for a minute that seemed like ten. Joan leaned over and kissed Lorne, and then put her forehead next to his. James rubbed his hands over his face as Will sat there looking at Mike's reaction to it all.

Mike finally broke up the silence and asked Lorne, "How did you get onto the road where the truck driver found you?"

Lorne shrugged his shoulders and replied, "I really don't know. The last thing I remember was walking around in the bushes, then I felt like I was flying, then I was cold and naked on the road."

"Sounds like you went on a Spirit Walk, my friend," James said. "Chief Gramps would have been proud."

"Well, all I really know now is my eyes and mind are a lot more open than they were before."

Mike responded, "I think all of ours are."

Lorne looked at Mike, "So you believe me, then?"

"I have to, I didn't write anything down, and you're not going to repeat it. I have to put something down though to close this case."

Will mentioned, "Lorne still saw a large grizzly—who *really* knows if there was just one? He also still seems disoriented from his ordeal."

James scratched his face, took a long sip of his "coffee," and then said, "Well . . . it's a shame you can't remember anything after that group of grizzlies attacked you and the others. I think we're going to have to keep the park closed and make it into a grizzly bear sanctuary. Leave those bastards alone."

Mike looked at James and Will, and then cocked an eyebrow. "You're right, James, that's the scary thing about comas, concussions, and whacking your noggin'. No one really knows *what* happens when that happens."

Lorne looked at them both to make sure he had heard them right. He quickly let out a sigh of relief, and everyone saw the load drop off his shoulders. Mike stood up, shoved his three-quarters-full cup toward Lorne, and shook everyone's hand.

"Well, I have a very big day writing up my report, packing up my things, and going home. It was a pleasure meeting all of you and seeing your lovely town."

Lorne got out of his chair and shook Mike's hand once more. "Thank you very much. Me and my family will never forget this."

"At least *that's* something you'll remember," Mike grinned.

James looked at Mike and told him he was welcome back anytime.

Mike excused himself. "Take care, and good day." He shook everyone's hands and then took his leave.

Joan, Lorne, Will, and James sat a little longer, and then James asked Lorne, "So, would you know the way back to the cave if we went back up to the park?"

"No, I'm not sure what side of the river it was on, or even what side of the mountain."

"Sounds like a lot of history could be found there," said James. "Kind of a shame not to know."

Lorne put out his cigarette and scratched his head, "Yes and no." James nodded in agreement. Lorne asked Will, "So what's your next move?"

"I am not quite sure. The fact that you saw a grizzly bear that was still huge makes me want to stay and search. I also do not want to be near your campground ever again. I will have to postpone my findings about your cabin and your friends, but you have a lot of forest here that I can still study."

"Word of advice, if you take a gun, make sure you know what you're shooting, and what to let live . . . it will save your life," Lorne said.

Will happily nodded and James quickly replied, "Good point . . . I'm glad you're home and safe. We should hang out a little more than we did the last couple of years."

"Definitely."

"All right then, I think you should get some rest, so Will and I should get going, also."

All got up from their chairs. Lorne and Joan walked both of them to the door. The men shook hands, and Joan hugged James. Will waved and got into James' truck as Lorne finished talking to James.

"So, what are you going do now, James?" asked Lorne.

"Probably write an appeal to get my job back," James replied hopefully. "Until then, go get a job at the mill—they're always looking for someone. How about you?"

"Take a couple days off, and then go on with life," said Lorne.

"Sounds like a plan," agreed James. "Let's do lunch next week."

"Just call me when you want to go," said Lorne.

James got into his truck, waved, and drove off. Lorne kissed and hugged Joan. He smacked her on the ass as she headed back into the house.

Lorne stood outside for a bit and was looking at the clear blue sky when he heard a thud on the roof above his head. He walked down the porch stairs and saw something on the roof reflecting the sunlight. Lorne walked over to the garage and grabbed his ladder. He put it against the house and cautiously climbed up. Lorne looked around, stopped, and listened. He heard a car horn, people in the distance, squawks from eagles, chirps from sparrows, squeaks from rodents, but of course, he couldn't see anything around.

Lorne smiled. As he reached the package, he found a nicely wrapped fur and an old ancient knife stuck into his roof. He pried the knife out and unwrapped the fur to find out it was the hide of the grizzly bear Grobain had killed. He looked up at the abundant amount of trees in his backyard and said out loud, "Thanks for the gifts, and for everything else you did for me and Walter." Lorne thought to himself, *I'll have to show Will this one day, but now I have to fix a roof with a hole in it.*

The Clan

Printed in Canada